THE KENYA PROJECT

To ALISON
With BEST WISHG

Rame
20/6/.

THE
KENYA PROJECT

BY

RAMESH CHANDRA

such publishing company

Distributed by Gazelle Book Services Limited
Hightown, White Cross Mills, South Rd
Lancaster, England LA1 4XS

British Library Cataloguing in Publication Data
A catalogue record for this book is available from the British
Library.

ISBN 0-9550201-0-7
ISBN 978-0-9550201-0-0

Typeset by Amolibros, Milverton, Somerset
This book production has been managed by Amolibros
Printed and bound by T J International Ltd, Padstow, Cornwall, UK

ONE

ONE

The Discovery was already running by the time Richard jumped in. Lucy was playing a Vivaldi CD and as soon as he slammed the door shut she gave him a stern look and drove away. The clock said seven a.m.

"Plenty of time," Richard said, wiping the sleep from his eyes.

"It's a five-hour drive, don't be bloody silly."

"I'm tired. Late nights don't suit me."

"Well whose idea was that?"

"It's our first wedding anniversary, for God's sake! Can't you turn that music down?"

Lucy lowered the volume, but only two notches. Richard leaned back and tried to go to sleep again, while Lucy stabbed at the accelerator, heading out for the M4 and the West Country. The music still grated, and Richard found it impossible to sleep, so he gave up and tried to *look* as if he was asleep. Personally he'd rather have Radiohead than all this pretentious classical stuff, as he'd told Lucy often before.

She was a good-looking thirty-eight-year-old, and whatever she did she did so for a purpose. Richard was younger – twenty-five – and learning to be a stockbroker.

They'd first met two years ago, when he lived with his parents in Fulham, not far from the flat Lucy was renting. There was a fair bit of overseas travel involved in her job but he wanted her to buy a place.

"Why?" she said. "I'm only home for a couple of months at a time."

It was his idea to get a place together, as without her income he couldn't afford it alone, but this never troubled her – she was happy to subsidise him.

Their first meeting hadn't been auspicious. Lucy was distracted, her father having just passed away – and who wouldn't be distracted, given that he'd left her upwards of £10,000,000. She had no idea what to do with it and was inclined to trust no one.

By their third encounter her attitude had changed and she began to like him, though she knew he was an adventurer – especially when it came to advice on investments. She had a background in finance herself but still went along with his suggestions, trusting him more and more when in a few months her fund had grown by twenty-five per cent. How things had changed in just a few months.

He was dozing less when the Discovery left the M4 to join the M5. It was 9.15. He shuffled across and rested his head on Lucy's shoulder, a gesture she loved. She stroked his hair softly. Richard squeezed her hand in response and rubbed his head against her shoulder.

"Stop it!" she said at last. "Can't concentrate."

He straightened himself in his seat and left her alone. She pulled into a service station.

"I need some coffee," she said.

"Where are we?" He yawned, opened the door and

slowly clambered out. There was a chill in the air, and he put on his coat.

"I don't mind driving if you're tired," he offered.

"Definitely not! I want to get to Akeminster in one piece."

They had breakfast and coffee.

"Anything worrying you?" he asked.

"No."

"Not the new venture? I can take care of it, you know."

"I don't doubt that, Richard."

"You don't sound convinced."

"I don't?"

"Look – I've ditched my career, my job. Sometimes I don't think you really appreciate just what that means."

"We all run risks…"

"You've no regrets investing in the company?"

"That doesn't come into it. It was always my father's dream before he moved to London." The present owner had been a good friend of her father's. Often when picking up his roots he'd spend his entire vacation helping Mr Hawkes.

Hawkes had owned the factory, but due to financial losses he was about to close the place down. Bertram, an old family friend and an Akeminster solicitor, had told Lucy. With not much hesitation she'd decided to use part of her inheritance to buy the factory. She had no intention of running it herself, and suggested to Richard that he should. After a year or so, once it was re-established, he could move back to London. Richard saw it as an opportunity.

Lucy was the only child of John Moore, an accountant, whose wife had left him when Lucy was twelve. John decided not to marry again, but all the same packed Lucy off to boarding school, which she resented – a feeling she hadn't entirely understood until her early thirties. She knew she was cold and detached, and not really capable of love, but that was all because her education and upbringing had been handed over to strangers, or an institution. That institution had taught her that all in life was a political negotiation, and that in order to be successful winning was everything. There was no room for sentiment. This extended into all her intimate relationships, so that Richard was more a possession than a husband, to be dealt with like anything she owned. Richard, having half worked this out himself, saw it as a price worth paying, because he was ambitious himself, and didn't see fidelity to his wife as forming any part of that. One might say their relationship was mutually material.

On graduation she'd found a job with a US merchant bank. Her aim in life was to earn a lot of money, as compensation for the things in her life that were missing. After six months on relocation in New York, her father unexpectedly died of a heart attack – a massive one. Soon after this she got to know Richard, and once, after a party, she took him home to her flat and seduced him. That's really where it all began.

They resumed their journey to Akeminster, and to lighten what had so far been a bad start to the day he asked her if she remembered their first visit to the opera.

"The one you hated, you mean?"

"I didn't exactly hate it. If it's not quite your scene, you never really know what they're singing about."

"Yes – you made that quite clear."

"Is that why you told me it was just a silly love story?"

"It's not easy to deal with the culturally ignorant."

Richard could see he'd get nowhere with this, so he shut up, and instead put his arm round her. She smiled, and kissed him gently on the cheek.

"So you do have a soft spot," he said.

"I do, Richard, I do. It's just that you don't always know where to look for it."

"Boss, I love you."

Richard came closer and hugged her.

"Get lost! I'm driving."

"Truce?"

"Truce."

Some thirty miles out of Akeminster the road was wet and thickly overhung with trees, darkly leaved and slightly depressing. To business, he thought.

"Those factory papers been finalised?" he asked.

"Yes, don't worry. Everything's set up. All you've got to worry about is managing the company."

"We've discussed it a hundred times, I know – but are you *really* prepared to let go?"

"So long as you don't interfere with what *I'm* trying to do, it'll all work out."

Richard hoped so. His mum had warned him not to marry Lucy, but as it was less for love and more for his career it had never occurred to him to take that advice. At the moment he was prepared to compromise everything, because he needed her.

"Sorry to be so snappy," Lucy said.

"I know. You've a lot on your mind."

"I knew you'd understand. I'm here for a week – then you're on your own. For about a year, I guess."

The CD stopped blaring.

"Thank God for that," Richard sighed, and switched off the audio system. He opened up his briefcase and took out the booklet Lucy had given him – "Ashgrow Engineering Limited" – all about the company. He skimmed the accounts page, and told Lucy they should give it no more than three years to succeed.

"I can fund it for five."

"If you allow that sort of timescale there's the danger it will drift."

"Listen – I'm the chairman, you're the MD. I'm prepared to give it five."

"Why can't I be chairman?"

"How would I keep an eye on you?"

The M5 was a long way behind them now, and they were deep into country lanes. Clouds were gathering and the atmosphere was grey. It was 12.30 when they reached the outskirts of Akeminster.

"I expect Bertram's at lunch. Let's book into the hotel and grab a bite to eat. Exciting, isn't it? In just a few hours' time the factory will truly be mine."

Lucy smiled and drove on to the County Hotel, taken by how quiet everywhere was. "Isn't it wonderful here?" she said.

Richard and Lucy had a light meal after checking in and drove to Bertram's office on the High Street, at 2.30 p.m. in time to conclude any remaining matters before the handover the following day.

TWO

After meeting Bertram, they drove back to the hotel, planning to be well rested in preparation for the next day. Unlike Lucy, Richard was restless and only managed to sleep lightly. He was woken at six by the birds. The hotel was situated away from the town in a pleasant rural spot, where you could hear foxes bark and the trundle of farm vehicles. Not much noise came from passing cars, especially at night. He wished he hadn't woken so early, as there was nothing to do. He picked up the notes he'd left on the bedside table and switched on his bedside lamp. The glare of it roused Lucy.

"God, what's the time?"

"Six."

"Bit early, isn't it?"

"Couldn't sleep. Bit apprehensive, I guess."

"Don't worry. Bertram's got everything in hand."

He returned to his notes, but must have dozed off, because when he came to, Lucy was towelling down after her shower. His thoughts immediately turned to sex, but he resisted and made his own way to the shower. When he came out, Lucy was battling to zip up her dress.

"Let me," he said.

She dropped her hands, and her dress falling open exposed her slender back. He spread his hands and very slowly reached the head of the zip to pull it closed. She turned round and very fleetingly had a glimmer of lust in her eye. He kissed her. Slowly, she pulled away.

"Don't tell me – we're going to be late," he said.

Lucy tied a floral scarf to match her dress, which was above the knee and hugged her figure. She did her makeup while Richard threw on his suit.

"How do I look?"

"Stunning as ever," said Richard, his eyes fixed on her face, which still retained its youthful beauty. He put his hands on her shoulders and kissed her cheeks gently, then knotted his tie. He looked at his watch. "Breakfast time!"

Over their grapefruit juice he remarked how fortunate they were that the Foreign Secretary, who was also the local MP, had agreed to perform the opening ceremony down at Ashgrow's. The Rt Hon Alex Millard MP was expected at 10.30.

"What I can't understand," Richard said, "is why Millard's so interested. It's no big deal and it's not as if there are jobs at stake."

"Oh, didn't I say? He knows Hawkes. I mean knows him well."

"And I suppose he's got his local profile to think about."

Lucy had a hat she'd ordered for the occasion. It was black with a pink ribbon. She slanted it meticulously, an operation Richard watched with curiosity. She reapplied her lipstick, then reminded him to ring Bertram's office.

Bertram wasn't at his desk. When, after what seemed an age, he finally came to the phone, Richard told him they were on their way. "See you in twenty minutes." He pocketed his mobile phone, took one final look in the mirror and set off with Lucy for the car. He wanted to drive fast, but the road was wet and he was constantly washing the windscreen. Then of course he had to slow for tractors. Lucy could see his impatience.

"They're having a party after the ceremony," she said. "After that I want our first board meeting."

Richard nodded. They were now stuck behind a milk tanker.

"You'd better get used to this pace of things."

"Doesn't do to be in a rush, does it?"

"You'll adapt."

"Don't think I'll cope with staying in a hotel."

"Rent a cottage. That'll be cheaper anyway."

"Sounds ghastly!"

"It won't be forever."

"Let's hope not. I'm a *very* social animal, and there's not much action round here."

"There's always weekends in London."

They had now reached the town centre, where the *Akeminster Gazette* offices were prominent, which reminded Lucy that one of its reporters was covering the ceremony. She told Richard

"Some scoop!" Richard said.

"Well at least the locals will find out about us."

When they arrived at the factory car park Mr Hawkes was there to greet them. Lucy wound down the window.

"Good morning."

"Lucy!"

"This is Richard."

"Good to meet you, Richard. We're all ready for you." They went inside.

"Your father would have been proud of you."

"We intend to carry on the good work. Richard here's all fired up."

"Glad to hear that, Richard."

"Can't wait to get started," Richard confirmed.

The whole place was neat and newly decorated, especially the boardroom, where Hawkes reminisced on Lucy's childhood in the village, which to Richard seemed all rather pointless. He was glad to get away for a look round the factory. That proved to be not very thrilling either. There was a dank old storeroom, whose huge picture window offered a perfect view below of the whole factory and its manufacturing processes. He could see a handful of workers. The plant was open, with its two doors at each end lifted up. It was black with age, with all the machinery looking antiquated too. Most of the operatives were wearing earplugs. They were working on a partially assembled unit, which had been rolled out on a trolley. They split it into three sections, and once the welders had moved away an electrician started the engine. The plant doors lowered and simultaneously the lower part of the machine closed – this was to extract pressure and immobilise the unit before assembling it. With a big bang, the plant stopped. The engineers checked the alignment of the middle section using a gauge, then, after a hand signal, the electrician restarted the engine. It was all a bit cumbersome, and Richard wondered what he'd let himself in for.

The foreman examined the now fully assembled unit and got involved in an animated discussion with Mr Hawkes, and shortly after that he took one of his boiler-suited men aside and wagged his finger at him angrily. Mr Hawkes then left.

Hawkes in fact had gone off to a small office, from which he emerged with a young woman. She was tall, and had streaky blonde hair, which she wore loose. They returned to the assembly area, where Hawkes wiped down a surface for her to unroll the drawings she'd got. She pointed certain things out, first on paper, then on the newly assembled unit. The foreman compared the work with the drawings. The worker he'd berated picked up a fitting and showed it to the woman, who it seemed had made her point. It looked to Richard that they were puzzling over something new the company had introduced to its manufacturing process.

The woman returned to her office, and Hawkes on removing his overalls returned to his. Richard turned away from the window, wondering how he would cope with the technical side of things, and how to improve productivity.

Valerie, Mr Hawkes's secretary, interrupted him. "Mr Purcell is here," she announced.

"Be with you in a minute."

He strolled to the boardroom, whose large round table was highly polished, having eight chairs, two of which were ornately carved. These, he assumed, were for the Rt Hon Alex Millard, MP, and Mr Hawkes.

"Had a good look round?" Lucy asked him.

"Sorry to keep you all waiting." He pulled up a chair opposite Bertram and looked around. Behind Bertram was a white screen, and in the opposite corner a projector, where there was also a TV and video equipment.

"You two have met?" Bertram asked.

Mr Hawkes nodded.

"Alex is due at eleven, according to his agent. Got some business in London this afternoon, apparently."

"That doesn't give him much time," Lucy said.

"That's life in the fast lane."

"He is at least showing interest in local issues," said Bertram.

Hawkes looked at Richard. "I'll introduce you to key personnel."

"Excellent idea," Richard said.

"Please excuse us." Hawkes rose from his seat and led the way.

The factory occupied 12,000 square feet and was partitioned to make maximum use of it all. The finished units took up roughly half, the production area just over forty per cent, with the remainder as offices and other ancillary space. Away from the offices there were signs of disrepair. Hawkes explained:

"We were due to refurbish this summer." He opened a door marked "Authorised Personnel Only", which led into empty factory space and an inventory room, with a small table and shelves for stock. An employee was busy with paperwork.

"Andrew, please get Roger at once."

Andrew, a mild-looking man around the mid-forties, put his pen down and left. Richard glanced over his entry book, which was of weekly goods movements.

Hawkes opened a metal cupboard and took out some white overalls and safety gear. "Wear this," he said, pulling on his own outfit. Andrew returned with Roger.

"Ah, Roger, this is your new managing director."

"Pleased to meet."

"He'd like to meet everyone. Let's see now – Samantha Bishop, Stewart Hill, Peter Alderman, and Philip Bearish I think – and the computer staff. You might as well include the assembly people. Get them all together, in the workshop say, there's a good chap."

"I'll get all the others, but Samantha's in a meeting."

Much of the stock, Richard saw, was covered in dust, and he wondered whether this was because it was old or surplus to requirements. Either way, it didn't look like good management, and now he had doubts that he could do much better. "I'll either succeed," he thought, "or dust will be *my* monument too."

Out through the window he saw that the employees had congregated in an open space in the assembly area. Roger knocked on the window to draw his and Hawkes's attention.

Hawkes said all the usual things. There were changes, yes, but this was a new beginning. The new boss, Richard Nunn, had everyone's interests at heart. They could all work together. There was a muted round of applause, on the instant of which they were joined by Samantha.

"Guys," she said, "you can surely do better than that!"

Everyone laughed.

"Richard, meet Samantha."

They shook hands.

"Sam heads up the computer department. She's also quality controller."

There was instant chemistry between Richard and Samantha, he with his brooding Italianate looks, she with her classic style – tall, blonde, elegant. She was wearing pink – a dress and a matching scarf.

"Sam's got a degree in computer science. These last couple of years, I don't know what we would have done without her."

"You'd have got through," she said modestly.

"Look after her."

"That goes without saying," Richard said. "After all, we're in the era now when a company's assets *are* its people."

The Rt Hon Alex Millard's car arrived on time, and was greeted by Bertram. Lucy was respectful, though not over-awed. He was fifty-five and had been an MP for twenty years. Uncontroversial, he was regarded as dependable, and had climbed the political ladder on that strength alone. He had no desire to reach the very top.

It was windy and Lucy held her hat as she shook his hand. She was warm and welcoming and thanked him for giving up his time. There were photographers in tow, and among his entourage was his agent, Andrew Green.

Millard took the chairman's seat, and Bertram sat next to him. Lucy sat on his other side. Just as they'd settled down David Tolchard arrived – the reporter from the *Akeminster Gazette*. Val left him in the waiting room.

"I'll let Mr Hawkes know you're here."

Hawkes meanwhile was treating his MP like royalty. "I'm delighted you could come," he said.

"The pleasure's all mine. I'm so glad you're passing on this wonderful firm to such a solid family."

With the news that Tolchard was here Bertram raised his eyebrows.

"That's down to me," said Hawkes. "I asked him to do the story."

Bertram knew David's reporting style and political views, which were usually anti-Alex Millard. Today though belonged to Mr Hawkes, and he had no wish to spoil it.

THREE

Richard was in at the office at eight a.m. On his way he had picked up some business news on the radio concerning massive road-building projects the Indian government was contemplating. He mused that if the company could sell them some of their road-building equipment, it would solve a lot of problems.

Sam was in early too, having coffee with Mr Hill, and reading the paper. He went in search of a telephone list, for the number of the company's agent. He found an index file with cards arranged alphabetically, and flicking through it picked one out and took it to his office, where he dialled for a man called Thomas. There was no reply, so he left a message. He returned the card to the filing system, and when he re-entered his office the *Financial Times* had been placed on his desk. It had a special feature on the Indian economy. This is lucky, thought Richard. He flicked through the other pages for anything useful on road construction, but there was nothing. He had just spotted something interesting in the technology section, however, when the phone rang. It was Mike Thomas.

"Thanks for calling back. I'm Richard Nunn."

"I take it you didn't know," Mike said.

"Didn't know what?"

"I'm sorry, but your tender to supply Ashgrow's macadam-laying units hasn't been accepted."

"Since when, and why?"

"My guys are telling me your units are too expensive. Also they've been offered certain financial inducements by the Korean government, who want them to accept their units. At the moment that's 'unofficial' you understand."

"Is there nothing we can do?"

"To be absolutely honest, Mr Hawkes never manufactured modern units."

"Didn't you ever tell him to modernise?"

"Wasn't interested. Seemed quite happy to keep supplying his three or four existing customers, besides which he never had the capital to invest. Look at it this way, if he'd been successful *you* wouldn't be running the operation."

"Okay. I get the picture. You know anything about this massive road-building project being undertaken by the Indian government?"

"Afraid not. Where did you hear about that?"

"Never mind. You hear anything, you let me know."

"Be happy to. Perhaps we should meet?"

"You can always buy me lunch."

"Be glad to. I'd still advise you to bring out a new product range and work on improving the existing one."

"I'll bear that in mind."

Richard put the receiver down and returned to the *FT*. There was a mention of both a German and a US tooling company as possible manufacturers of the equipment he needed. He wrote down their numbers, then the phone rang again. It was Val, with Lucy on the line.

"Put her on. Darling, what a surprise."

"It's not a courtesy call. Hawkes just rang to give me the news."

"Rang *you*?"

"Well why shouldn't he ring me? He tells me we've lost the contract."

"Contract? It was only a tender! Which wasn't accepted."

"So what do we do?"

"Never mind that. Who gave *him* the news?"

"Is that important? You must know how much he worries about us."

"So someone informed him before I got the message?" The someone was Mike, he guessed. "Maybe Mr Hawkes would have done better to attend to his own affairs rather than other people's."

"Never mind Hawkes. What are you going to do?" Lucy was losing her cool.

"Listen, I heard this news about ten minutes ago, and I've been in charge of the company for under two months. What do you expect me to do?"

"I don't expect you to do *nothing*."

"It takes a long time to introduce a new product range. And remember, you've given me five years to turn this company round."

"That shouldn't stop you acting now."

"What do you take me for? First, I need to build the team—"

"I'd have thought you'd have done that."

"Mr Hawkes and Mike! Wonderful team players they've turned out to be!"

"Unless you get out and meet people nothing's going to happen."

"Are you lecturing me?"

"Richard, we'll talk again." She put down the phone.

He turned and looked through the window at the newly mown lawn, and the phone rang again. He ignored it. A few minutes later, Val knocked on his office door and stepped inside.

"What is it?" he said irritably.

"Sorry, but it's Lucy on the phone."

"Tell her I'm on my way back to London."

Val shut the door, picked up the phone and very politely told her what Richard had said.

A few minutes later she brought him a cup of coffee. "Excuse me, I know it's none of my business what goes on in the upper echelons. What I can say is this: Samantha and I were overjoyed when the Moore family bought the company, with you as MD."

"Let's get Sam in here now." Richard dialled her extension, and asked her in.

"What's the problem?" she said.

"I'll get straight to the point. We've had news today that our tender hasn't been accepted."

"But we knew that before we submitted!"

"How?"

"Mike told us."

"Now wait a minute. You're telling me this was expected?"

"Yes. It's why Hawkes didn't wait before selling out," Samantha explained.

"My God!" said Val, quite shocked.

"And that's why I've been looking at a design to develop a new and more efficient unit. It's looking good. The only thing is we don't have money to invest – or at least that's been the case till now."

"Hawkes said nothing of this."

"Forget about that, Richard – I'm sure we can really make something out of this, but it needs your support."

"That's marvellous, Sam," said Val.

"I can't say for sure that it *will* be a success, but at present I don't think there's anything on the market to rival it."

Richard invited Samantha and Val to sit down on the chairs opposite his desk and then looked at Val.

"Ring Lucy now," said Richard.

Val picked up the receiver and dialled. Richard took the phone and spoke:

"Look, there's been a development. I want you to get down ASAP. I'm bringing the monthly board meeting forward."

"I'll call you back," Lucy said.

In the meantime Richard told Bertram the news, and formally invited him to the upcoming board meeting. Then he turned to Val and Samantha. "From now on we're the new team," he said, "and the purge starts now. Samantha, you need to tell me who to keep and who's expendable."

There were broad smiles on the two women's faces as they set about their tasks.

FOUR

The feature article published by the *Gazette* awaited Richard, with the paper laid out on his desk. He hung his coat and glanced at the headline: "Prominent local family revives ailing company".

The article offered a potted history of the Moore family, with Lucy centre stage, but there was no mention of him. The company's equipment was described in context of the potential for export, and a picture of its ill-reputed product was capped by another heading: "The future of the company". It boldly declared how the company was planning to recover its lost market and restore its fortune.

Richard wondered who in the company had authorised the picture, though Val, when he talked to her about it, didn't seem to share his concern.

"Great story!" she said.

"Um."

"You're not impressed."

"I'd like to know who gave permission for the picture."

"We all thought *you* had."

"Then that was a wrong assumption." He got on the phone, and took it up with Tolchard. "How did you get your material?"

"All the usual channels. Research, other manufacturers – and of course I spoke to Mr Purcell."

"Ah, that explains the focus on the Moores."

"You're a busy man, Mr Nunn. Had we been able to talk, I'd have put you in the article too."

"I'm always available to the press. Frankly I'm surprised local people have that much interest in the company."

"Local people are interested in all sorts of things."

"Perhaps – but you don't interest them in *this* firm without my say so – is that understood?"

"Sorry but there's nothing defamatory…"

"That's not the issue."

"Well what is the issue?"

"You need permission to take photographs."

"You think so?"

"Yes, of course," and with that Richard slammed down the phone and cut Tolchard off.

His next problem was Mcintyre, the bank manager, who rang when *he'd* read the article. "I'm amazed," he said, "you've given the product such an excellent review. You happy with sending out such a message?"

"I'm not happy at all, but I was never consulted. If you want to know, I don't think the management should be associated with this particular product."

"Ah, I see – all media spin then."

"That was my point too. But there's nothing we can do about it." He cradled the phone and consigned the paper to the bin. Then he spoke to Hill, the factory manager, whom he found surrounded by his workers, not only reading the article, but laughing and joking at it.

"Something funny?" Richard asked.

Hill sent his men back to work. "Richard, good morning."

"I'm not so sure about that. The *Gazette* writes a lot about us, does it?"

"Not as far as I'm aware."

"I'm not surprised. What possible interest could the locals have in Ashgrow?"

"I don't know. I suppose a manufacturing company in a small town…"

"You tell me what we're selling locally, eh?"

"I see your point."

"And what if some clever person decided to do a search at Companies House?"

"I don't know – what are you getting at?"

"They'd find the financial information doesn't stack up. Then there'd be a scandal. In future, nothing goes out without my permission."

"But that goes without saying!"

"Oh does it? The *Gazette*'s published this picture when I knew nothing about it."

"Oh! I see. I didn't know that. When the press were here I assumed they'd come through you. It won't happen again."

"Just you make sure it doesn't."

On his way back to his office Richard bumped into Samantha, who was as puzzled about the article as he was. Once in his office the phone rang, and he had to suffer Bertram waxing sentimental about the "wonderful" Moore family, what with all their contribution to the town.

Richard was blunt: "I'm not in any way interested in the Moore family, and I'm not at all pleased to see you quoted by the *Gazette*."

"That's an extraordinary thing to say, Richard."
Bertram was annoyed.

"The company's not a fan club, and it doesn't exist to
the greater glory of one particular family – however rich
and powerful. It's my job to turn this company round and
publicity like this doesn't help."

"There's no harm surely in a little bit of gloss."

"I disagree. Where gloss ends and lies begin is very
treacherous ground."

"If I might say so, you're taking all this just a little too
seriously."

"Business *is* serious. No future statements come out
about the company unless through me."

"And what about Lucy?"

"Lucy's the money, I'm the MD. *I* make the decisions."

"Okay, we'll play it your way."

FIVE

Richard drove to Heathrow Airport to meet Lucy from her US flight. They'd genuinely missed one other and embraced passionately, before bundling the luggage out to the car.

"Tired?"

"Jet lagged."

Once out on the M4 Lucy was asleep. He slowed down, struggling to get his jacket off, and having done so draped it over her. She felt his touch, opened her eyes momentarily and smiled. Then she slept.

On leaving the motorway for the local minor roads it was dark, wet and windy, and generally not good conditions at all. Richard wasn't the most natural of drivers, and he really had to concentrate. He was tired and stiff, and bored. Lucy woke up.

"We nearly there?"

"Not long to go."

She put her head on his shoulder. "God, I just can't wake up."

A sudden torrent of rain sluiced the windscreen.

"Darling, I do have to concentrate."

She pulled away while Richard turned on the

headlights. She closed her eyes and a few minutes later was resting on his shoulder again. Briefly, he kissed her.

"Missed me?" she said.

"You bet."

"Coping?"

"Well, the domestic arrangements are fun. I've got a Mrs Arnold, who comes twice a week to clean. She's marvellous. Does all the ironing." He knew how Lucy hated that chore.

"Age?"

"Not young, if that's what you're thinking."

"Now would I?"

At long last she saw a sign for Akeminster.

"It's just another five miles or so," he said, and soon they were onto the High Street and heading for the country lanes. Then here was the driveway.

"This is it."

A security light came on, illuminating the cottage front. Richard parked up and opened the front door, switching on the lights as he stepped into the hall. He came out again and brought in Lucy's luggage, among which was one of her business suits zipped in a cover. She must have driven straight from the office, he thought.

He activated the car alarm and went inside to find Lucy collapsed on the settee. The TV was on but there was no sound.

"I'll take this gear upstairs."

"Nice place you've found here."

"Bathroom's up there."

"We having dinner?"

"Believe it or not, there are no takeaways. I'll stick something in the microwave, while you're in the shower."

She stretched out fully on the settee with her feet apart. Richard went and checked the freezer. There was some Chinese, and an Indian – and that was it.

"What do you fancy?" he asked.

"Don't mind," she said, "I'm easy."

"Hot curry it is then."

She set off for the bathroom.

"Turn right on the landing," he said. He prepared his sachets for the microwave and laid the dining table. He switched off the TV then went to the garden where he plucked a white rose. He put on a CD and arranged the rose in a vase. It looked enchanting. He'd got some matching white candles, and he lit them. It was all very romantic. He uncorked a red – a 1980, French – knowing Lucy's taste in wine.

Having undertaken all his tasks dutifully he returned to the lounge. Lucy had not come down but the food was still cooking. He put the TV on and killed the sound, then switched to Teletext for the business page.

When Lucy came down she surveyed the scene.

"It's perfect!" she said. They hugged. "And it smells delicious!"

"Sit down, I'll pour the wine." He filled her glass and served the meal.

"It *is* delicious," she said.

"Just something I rustled up," he joked.

"All it lacks is one vital ingredient. Love."

"Well, we can sort that one out, I'm sure." He was happy, because he'd made her happy. But would this be as short-lived as usual, he wondered.

After the meal they took their wine to the lounge, where Lucy rearranged the bathrobe she'd changed into after her shower. She collapsed on the couch and shut her eyes and dozed. Richard sat down beside her and gently touched her forehead.

"That soothing touch," she purred.

"Your glass is empty. I'll pour you another."

She sat up and stretched out for the copy of *The Economist* she could see on the coffee table, then settled back to read, her bathrobe falling open from ankle to thigh. Richard put her glass on the table.

"You mind?" he asked, turning off the TV.

"Go ahead."

He put some music on – soft jazz. He picked up his *FT* and finished off a civil engineering article he'd started earlier. Lucy curved her leg inward to reveal more of herself, to the point that Richard lost his concentration. He lowered his paper and saw that her robe no longer concealed her pubis. She took a sip of wine.

"I've had such a hard few days," she said. "How about one of your massages?"

"I haven't got any oil."

"*I* have – in my toiletry bag." She was now sitting with her legs apart.

He folded his newspaper and went to the bathroom, where he found the bottle of oil. When he got back she was prone on the settee.

"It's my back," she said. "It's been really painful these last few weeks."

"I'll see what I can do."

She shifted position and undid the belt of her robe, and gently Richard exposed her back, then removed her robe altogether. Just then the jazz CD reached a point where the pianist ran his hands up and down the keyboard. For a moment Richard was motionless, transfixed by his wife's slender body. The music willed him on, and he poured a few drops of oil into his palm and began to massage her back. He lifted her down from the settee to the floor. He sprinkled a few drops of oil on her back and began, slowly, to rub it in. A vocalist joined the pianist:

> Oh baby the night is long
> And I need a long night for my dream
> So come near and take me to the dream merchant
> So I can buy a lot of them
> Oh my love oh! My light come
> Don't delay.

The piano rang out, then came a saxophone, then a trumpet too.

"Richard," Lucy moaned, as his whole body began to massage hers. She spread her legs. The vocalist ceased, but the three instruments went on. He probed with his hand, then eased the fullness of his manhood deep into her, pressing harder and faster until, as his grip loosened, they climaxed together. He withdrew himself, but Lucy protested and wanted to go again. She rolled him on his back, and toyed till he was hard again, then beat down on him, wave on ecstatic wave.

It was past one when they finally got to bed, Lucy still hungry for more, but Richard exhausted by then. She stroked his thighs and put her lips to his stomach. She swooped up, putting her lips to his before easing her tongue gently into his mouth. She spread herself, and at last he was ready to go again. She pressed harder and harder against him, Richard motioning her buttocks in his palms, pulling her ever more violently over him. He sucked at her nipples, pressing her breasts to his mouth, then suddenly climaxed again, with Lucy hurrying after.

Exhausted finally, they fell into each other's arms and slept.

Sunlight through the curtains woke him. The alarm hadn't come on, and it was nine o'clock.

"We've overslept!"

He pushed Lucy aside and left her wrapped in the quilt. He shaved, did his teeth, showered. He'd just got in the cubicle when the bathroom door opened and Lucy stepped inside to join him. She did extraordinary things between his legs with the shower gel.

"I can't," he said. "I'm going to be late." He stepped out, towelled down and put on his business suit. He made them coffee, but got impatient at the time she was taking.

"Come on, Luce – time's getting on!"

Finally she came down, still full of dreams.

"Sleepy head," he said.

She glanced up at him, slightly embarrassed.

"Jet lag – and…well, you know."

"Here, coffee. And I've made some toast."

"This what you have every morning?"

"What's wrong with it?"

"Nothing. Nothing at all."

SIX

Richard started the car just as Mrs Arnold arrived.

"Glad I caught you," he said. "Afraid there's a fair bit more for you today."

"No trouble at all, Mr Nunn, no trouble at all."

The house was about five miles from the factory and it would normally take him fifteen minutes or so to get there. He switched on the radio, and as Lucy got in she opened her briefcase and took out some documents.

"Homework, darling?"

"Just a few notes."

"New York beckons."

"Yes. I'm definitely due in Chicago next week though."

"Hope you're appreciated."

"Oh I think I am. It's money that counts, and I'm okay in that department."

"This isn't much of a life together."

"One day you'll appreciate the sacrifice I've made."

"And what about mine? What about the sacrifices I've made?"

"Touchy, Richard."

He went rather sullen and drove with unusual

deliberation. Parking, he said, "Hawkes is here, I see. Bit early for him."

"He *is* a director. And actually it's us who are late."

"Yes – and I'm not sure that's a good idea."

"I'll see you later," she called, and headed straight for the boardroom.

Richard stopped off at Val's office for any messages, but flicking through them none seemed important, so he binned them.

"Remind me to ring Brian," he said.

"Brian, right."

Samantha joined them: "Richard, I rang the Hamburg people to let them know we want to install new plant." She was referring to the state-of-the-art stuff that dried the roads off quickly, speeding the macadam process.

"I haven't made up my mind about that. Anyway we need to discuss training first." He also wanted to talk to Brian about finance. He retreated to his own office, but bumped into Purcell on the way.

"Bertram, you're a bit early – as is Mr Hawkes, I see," he added.

"I'm after Lucy." Purcell was clutching a small bag.

"Try the boardroom."

"Already have."

"She wasn't there?"

"Yes – I've seen her."

By the time Richard made the boardroom Lucy and Hawkes were there, whispering to each other.

"Hope I'm not intruding," he said, sarcastically.

"Just catching up," said Lucy.

"Intimately."

They ignored that comment, Hawkes launching

immediately into the difficulties facing civil engineering.

"You have to wait for Lucy to be around before you tell us this?"

"What do you mean by that?"

"Well, a bit belated, isn't it?"

Richard opened up a report and diagram that Samantha had produced, and began to study it. Hawkes tried to see what it was, but Richard stopped him, folding the paper.

"Am I or am I not Technical Director?" Hawkes rasped, rhetorically.

"We all have our roles. As far as mine is concerned, this is confidential." He tapped the folded paper.

"What on earth are you talking about? Without me there's not a thing you can do." Hawkes looked to Lucy for support.

In came Bertram. "All having fun, I see," he said. "As we're all here we might as well begin."

"Absolutely," said Hawkes.

They all sat down and Bertram called the meeting to order and commenced proceedings. He looked at Lucy, then at Richard.

"You know why this meeting's been called?"

Lucy nodded and looked at Hawkes.

"To sort out the future of the company," Hawkes replied.

This had Richard on his feet. "What future?"

"You'll have to explain that question."

"For God's sake, the new management has only been in place a few months!"

"And lost a big contract to supply twenty-five units to one of our regular customers," Lucy reminded him.

"That's only our second setback in a very short space of time."

"I didn't think we were here to discuss that."

"Well we are. I want everyone's opinion."

"That's all pointless naval-gazing. That order was never in the running. And don't you think it's pointless going over the obvious? Besides, how did *you* find out?"

"Mr Hawkes was good enough to ring me."

"Did you know about this?" Richard looked at Bertram.

"I believe it was mentioned."

"This is all so unacceptable. Why won't you people talk to me?"

"You're fretting too much about protocol, Richard."

"There has to be a level of trust."

"Could *you* have salvaged the deal?"

"That's not the point. Everyone knew the order was doomed."

"But what did you do about that?"

"There was nothing anyone *could* do. We were out of it on price and quality."

"So you just accepted the situation?" Bertram said, looking at Hawkes and Lucy.

"Sometimes you have to. Anyway, I don't like that insinuation. Let me remind you, I wasn't even aware a company bid was in process. Marketing didn't think to tell me. Can somebody please explain what I'm supposed to do in such a situation?"

"Get involved, get real," Lucy told her husband.

Richard went quiet and brooding. Hawkes looked smug and Bertram was taking notes.

"I've a solution," Lucy volunteered.

"No," said Richard. "*I've* a solution."

"Oh?"

"I'm out, I'm resigning – that's what you want." Sometimes his petulance got the better of him.

"Calm down," Bertram said. "No one wants you to go."

"But…"

"Just calm down."

"That's good advice, Richard," Lucy said. "Calm it. We're getting nowhere like this, and all this is time I can't afford to spare."

Richard slammed the door, trudged to his office and sank into his chair. Samantha followed him in.

"What's going on?"

"You'll find out, soon enough. I'm out of here."

"Out of here?"

"Things are going on behind my back. It's not healthy."

"But who's going to run the place?"

"That's not up to me, it seems."

Now Val came in. "Sam," she said, "they want you in the boardroom."

Sam looked stunned.

"You go on," said Richard. "Tell them I've gone for a drive."

It was 11.45 according to the clock in his car, and he decided on an early lunch. En route he stopped at a lay-by and took out his mobile phone and dialled one of his London cronies.

"Hi, Tim, Richard here. How's things?"

Tim gave him the latest gossip from the stock market.

"Fact is I'm after a job. Anything going?"

Tim promised to look into it.

He drove round fields and over a wooded brow, and began to reflect on how completely lost Lucy had seemed when they first met. Now look at her! He'd helped her get on, yet she saw it as all her own doing, and in the work situation treated him like a menial. Then it suddenly occurred to him that the Discovery didn't belong to him and decided to turn round, and headed back to the factory. When he got there, much to his surprise, the meeting was still going on.

"But so what!" he thought. "I'm finished with it." He called in at Val's office.

"I need some paper," he said.

She pulled out a writing pad. She looked on as he wrote, naturally assuming he was penning his resignation. Samantha stuck her head round the door, and told him that Lucy and Purcell wanted him to rejoin them."

"Not possible," he said.

"Oh, come on, Richard, it can't be that bad."

"I said no."

Just then Lucy and Bertram came in, with the news that Hawkes had left the company.

"Not before time," Richard said. "Here's my resignation too."

"We beg you to reconsider."

"Why? You've got all the money – just go and hire someone."

"Take it easy, Richard," Bertram said, putting his hand to Richard's shoulder. "Look, we've given this some thought. We want you to stay."

What Richard didn't know was that Sam had refused to work with Hawkes.

"So why has Hawkes left? He been upsetting people?"

"In a word, yes."

"So only then you decide you need me?"

"That's unfair."

"Let's just forget it." He folded the letter of resignation, gave it to Bertram and said goodbye.

"Please Richard, hold your horses, and come and talk to us again," said Bertram. "For the time being I don't accept your resignation."

"That's your problem."

"I don't suppose you'd consider joining us for lunch?" Richard's reply was a firm no.

Samantha said her piece. "I hope you know that in order to save the company it was me who refused to work with Hawkes. *I* was going to resign."

Richard was shocked. "You did that for me?"

"For you, and for the company."

"That puts a different complexion on it." Bewildering as it was working under Lucy, resignation now didn't seem the right choice. He went to his office and sat there alone for a moment or two. Then he picked up the phone and dialled Val's office, sure that Sam was still there, though she wasn't. She was in her own office, talking to the manager, Mr Hill. Richard stepped in. Hill turned abruptly.

"Forty-five jobs hanging on your decision," he said.

"News travels."

"Stick with us. All the lads want you."

"That's the nicest thing I've heard all day."

"We like your ideas. I shouldn't say this, but we didn't feel the same about Hawkes."

"Go on, Richard, hang on in there," Sam said.

"Okay, you win. However, there is just something I need to sort out." That something was his terms, which he explained to Lucy. "If you want me," he said, "I'm chairman as well as MD."

"That's a big step," she told him.

"It's fine by me," Bertram said.

"I want you on the board as a non-executive, and Sam's to be made a director, forthwith."

"You drive a hard bargain."

"You deserve it. But that's not all. From now on I call the meetings. There's to be no, I repeat, no interference – from anyone. You've got to give me five years, then you can judge my performance."

"You're forcing my hand," Lucy grumbled.

"Yes or no?"

"If I say no, do I lose a husband too?"

"That's the gamble."

"Okay, round one to you, Richard. But I want to see some action."

"Excellent!" Bertram interjected. "I'll draw up the relevant papers."

"You do that. I'm heading back to the Big Apple – as soon as possible."

SEVEN

It had been nearly two years since Joe Bishop's death, a double blow for his wife Dorothy. She'd needed all his care, as she suffered from multiple sclerosis. He'd done everything for her, and now she was left without him. Before the disease, Dorothy had been a secondary-school teacher, teaching English and Latin. Joe had taken early retirement from the civil service once she was wheelchair-bound.

She'd been sure she'd pre-decease him, but that wasn't the case. Her nearest family now was Samantha, their daughter, who did everything she could in her spare time. Dorothy and Joe had always been regular churchgoers, and had been well known at St Matthew's, where they always went to mass. Joe had also been a keen fundraiser, his last aim being for the £10,000 to renew the glasswork inside the church and out. The roof too needed attention, but Joe had died before that work began.

Dorothy was heartbroken, but Samantha realised that her mother's best outlet *was* fundraising.

"Carry on Dad's dream," she said.

How could she? On her own, Dorothy was incapable of doing anything, so Samantha helped, pushing her everywhere in her wheelchair, or if *she* couldn't, getting her aunt, Dorothy's younger sister, Barbara, to help.

Dorothy took part in church fêtes. She was fond of cooking and was greatly helped by Barbara. After some while the *Gazette* noticed what she was doing – or at least David Tolchard did. He decided to do a report, and called on Sam.

"I'm interested in your mother," he said.

Immediately David was attracted to Samantha. He liked her round honest face, and in all her mannerisms she seemed so gentle.

"This man's a reporter," Sam said to her mother.

"What does he want?"

"To do a story about you."

"Me?"

"I've been struck by how you've refused to give in." David sounded enthusiastic.

"Well, I do a little fundraising like."

"That's what will interest people."

"Well, I've no objection," Dorothy smiled.

David pulled up a chair and began to take notes. He learned how she'd raised a paltry £300 in two years, and so still had a long way to go.

"We'll help," he said. "With the *Gazette*, you'll get the exposure."

"Yes, I suppose that's true," replied Dorothy.

It was arranged. The Friday edition carried a front-page story, under the headline "Brave fund raising effort by Dorothy". It showed her picture.

When Richard came to read the story he soon worked out it was Samantha's mother. He was moved by Dorothy's dedication, and he was touched that Samantha had never brought her situation up in conversation. He knew how hard it must be for her.

"What do you think," he asked Bertram, "about the company donating £500? There could be a raffle or something."

"Sounds a good idea."

They told Samantha.

"Your mother's an amazing woman."

"We don't ever think of it like that. We just do what we have to do." She was less happy than Richard to associate Ashgrow with Dorothy's affairs. She felt uncomfortable about all the sudden publicity.

Richard got in touch with Dorothy, who told him that all the admin was in David Tolchard's hands, so Richard got on to him – or rather left a message with his voice mail. He didn't ring back. A week later he called Dorothy again.

"I don't know what's gone wrong," she said. "I'll get him to ring you."

That afternoon, he rang.

"Thanks for your interest," he said, "but you really should talk to me, not Mrs Bishop."

"I left you a message. You didn't get back."

"Oh. Can't think how that happened."

"Never mind. Point is, Ashgrow would like to sponsor a raffle in support of her fundraising, and that's what I wanted to discuss."

"We're also working on a raffle. I'll have to talk to the committee. I'll get back to you."

Richard had a feeling there *was* no committee, a suspicion that seemed to have substance when Tolchard did get back – not to him though, but to Bertram.

"We'd like to accept Ashgrow's generous offer – and thanks."

"Who's going to be guest of honour?"

"Not yet decided. I was hoping the Bishop of Bristol."

Bertram didn't think much of that suggestion, and cited Alex Millard as an alternative. "I'll approach him myself, if you like."

"Thanks a lot – though I *would* like to consult the others. I'll get back to you."

Richard wasn't too pleased with the way Tolchard had handled this, and was determined Millard *would* be the guest of honour. He told Dorothy, who was compliant, so in the end Tolchard had to abandon his own preference.

For the four weeks leading into the event the *Gazette* carried a regular article building it up. David made a point of calling in each morning at Dorothy's house, which also gave him the opportunity of meeting Samantha. It was something Dorothy didn't approve of.

"It isn't that much to put up with," Samantha said, "and after all, he is helping with the fundraising."

The raffle captured the whole town's imagination, with David in charge of ticket sales, which boosted *Gazette* circulation threefold in only two weeks. Graham (David's editor) was happy, so long as the whole thing turned out a success.

The original estimate of fifty looked a little light, and now that Alex had given his support it looked as though three times that many would join in the event. The vicar was very enthusiastic.

"It's a wonderful thing our local press has done – God bless you, David."

Half of the third week's issue covered the event: "Enter

our raffle draw," it boldly invited, when 3,000 tickets had already been sold. It was clear that David had hijacked the event for his own publicity.

Dorothy didn't wish to be photographed, as she loathed being in her wheelchair. Samantha continued to refuse publicity on her behalf. Richard, Lucy and Bertram's contribution in selling over half the tickets wasn't acknowledged either, with David determined to take all the credit for himself.

When the day of the draw arrived, a Saturday, the church hall was decorated with blue and white bunting and balloons, and was lit from the outside. Inside, the local choir was in its final rehearsal, with the vicar in the porch ready to receive his guests. David and his army of photographers were waiting to take pictures.

After the Bishop finished his sermon, Alex's speech commended the efforts of Dorothy and of the whole town.

"We're deeply admiring of people like Dorothy. On behalf of the town, I salute you."

Samantha gazed proudly at her mother, who was overcome by emotion and had to wipe her eyes. Alex ended his speech by thanking Ashgrow for its magnificent support, and also gave credit to the *Gazette,* though he didn't mention David. Lucy had flown over from New York to draw the raffle.

In the end the event raised well over £5,000, where it had only needed £3,000, the rest coming from the Church and the Community Fund.

"We've a surplus of £2,000," David said to Dorothy. "How would you like to dispose of it?"

"I've no idea."

"Perhaps I can help. I know of a charity that cares for

the elderly, which at the moment is trying to acquire a TV, DVD player and new audio system for its daytime visitors. What do you think?"

"Sounds an excellent idea."

David arranged the purchase and got himself into the newspaper again, together with the coordinator of the charity. He was immensely pleased.

After all the excitement of fundraising, David needed another story. He'd long ago shelved his ambitions to be an investigative reporter for a national tabloid or the TV, but every now and then he hankered after the scoop that would project his career into that stratosphere. It was on such occasions that his objectivity suffered badly, with the story he was after less a matter of concrete fact and more the floss of his stunted imagination. He was a typical small-town newsman, some might say, where had it not been for his uncle (who owned the paper) he would have found some other occupation long ago. He turned his attention to the vicar, an enlightened man apparently, now in his fifties, who liked to be known by his first name. Despite his age he was well preserved, and threw much of his energy into fêtes, flower shows and choir competitions.

His sermons were far from traditional, and he didn't shy away from social issues. He visited the sick when hospitalised, and he helped with the local playgroup. He greatly encouraged the Dramatic Society, whom he was keen to see nurture local talent. He was also a governor at the local primary school. His church hall was often used for charitable events, and in these he would participate joyously. Above all he had popularity and charm.

"Call me Charles," he would say to people.

But Charles, thought David, is just too good to be true. "I think I'll have a closer look at him."

Then some ministering angel called him on the phone and told him yes, he ought to take a long hard look at Charles Shepherd. Abruptly the caller, a woman, rang off.

"Hello! Hello!"

No response, and the number had been withheld. He plodded into Graham's office.

"What have you got on our vicar?"

"Why do you ask?"

"I just had a call – anonymous. Someone thinks I should look into him."

"That's likely to be a hoax, David. We get them all the time."

"I don't know – she sounded pretty upset."

"I can't imagine anything in Charles's closet."

"Well, I've got nothing better to do. I'm going to give it a look."

"Not another of your wild goose-chases I hope."

"Only time will tell."

A first obvious inquiry was into any former female employee who might bear him a grudge. He visited the council offices for information about the church, and en route stopped at the church itself to look around, which didn't yield much. All he learned at the council office and library was the age of the church – it was nearly 700 year old – and the fact that it was one of few that remained in full working order.

The following day he called at the vicarage. A woman in her early seventies answered the bell.

"I'm from the *Gazette*. Is the vicar at home? He and I worked on the church fundraising."

"Yes, I know who you are. But sorry, he's not at home. Can I get him to ring you?"

"No, that's okay. I'll pop back."

"He shouldn't be long."

He drove off in his rusty Fiat and parked a few streets away, and returned to the vicarage a short while later.

"Afraid he's not back yet."

"Oh. Well anyway, do you mind if I come in? The *Gazette* wants to run a story on the church, and I thought I'd get the ball rolling."

He stepped inside.

"When was Charles appointed?" he quizzed.

"When the last vicar retired, ten years ago."

"Lives alone?"

"His wife's in Birmingham. She's a teacher. When he came, it was on a temporary basis, but he stayed." There was the sound of an engine. "That's his car."

When Charles came in, David was waiting.

"David, what a pleasant surprise!"

David explained his mission.

"This is Grace, my housekeeper. *She's* the one you want to speak to. You see she's been here for the last three decades."

"Wow! That's quite some time."

"I'll leave you two to it."

That evening David decided to go back to the church and take a look around, his curiosity very much aroused. He was dreaming again of a scoop.

The place was in darkness and all shut up, but then suddenly a young girl appeared, as if from nowhere.

"You waiting for Charles?" she asked.

"I'm taking a stroll."

"Oh, I see. It's my turn to practise the piano. Charles lets me use it."

"He does such a lot for the community."

"He's the best! All the women say so."

"His reputation precedes him."

David, not wanting to be recognised, left in a hurry, the thought crossing his mind that the vicar's relationship with all these women who adored him might be worth investigating.

"Be ironic, wouldn't it," he thought, "if the vicar, whiter than white, was up to something...?"

The next day he had the chance to question Grace again.

"What about Charles's timetable?" he asked.

Grace gave him the catalogue: "Prayers for school assembly, the drop-in centre for mums and kids, the work he does for vulnerable young women, daily visits to the hospital."

David took notes.

"After lunch there are prayers – then he takes a nap. Come early evening there's his after-school club."

"He's involved in everything," David remarked.

"He's tireless. Some evenings there's his bible class, and that's not to mention christenings, weddings and funerals. He's active with the Dramatic Society, and the Boy Scouts, and the Guides as well."

Later, when he discussed it all with Graham, he couldn't help but point out how much contact the vicar had with boys and girls.

"What are you suggesting?" Graham quizzed.

"That there's a lot of that stuff in the Church just now – and Charles doesn't live with his wife, after all."

"Just you be careful."

"I will." He rang the council education department, to find out if all these peripheral duties run by the church had to be registered, and if so what were the rules.

"Anyone working with children is subject to police checks," he was told.

"And what about the premises, and other adults there?"

"The same."

David felt he'd made progress, and now wanted to know if the appropriate checks *had* been made.

"What a surprise!" Charles greeted David cordially.

David waded straight in about the police checks.

"How could you think such a thing!" said Grace.

"I'm sure it's just routine," said the vicar. "As it happens, David, I don't run these classes – it's all done by the mothers. But you have a good point. I'll speak to all involved."

"I thought you'd want to. You wouldn't want any surprises just as we're going to press."

That, Grace agreed, was one way of looking at it.

Yet all this wasn't enough for David, and he decided – rather melodramatically – to keep a closer eye on the vicar, by hiring a van and parking it near the church, from which he spent several days spying.

Nothing much turned up, and the only time Grace didn't accompany the vicar was with the Dramatic Society and the youngsters at their piano practice. He decided to approach some of these children, three girls and a boy, ostensibly for copy. Their parents couldn't praise Charles enough, and the children themselves were eager and buoyant. "Nothing here," he thought, but nevertheless decided to stick with the van for one more day.

A red XJ6 rolled up, and out stepped a man in an overcoat and fedora. David took several pictures in quick succession as the man turned and walked to the vicar's front door. Charles answered himself, shook hands firmly and led the man inside.

"How very unusual," thought David. About forty minutes later the door opened and the man came out, to be whisked away in his XJ6. Nothing more happened over the following hour, so he drove back to the office, where he arranged to have his film developed.

The man in the XJ6 turned out to be a Mr Reed, who ran a catering firm. Reed had a reputation for extravagant living. Was he clutching at straws, or might it be worth looking into this as a possible gay relationship? Graham didn't think so, but was prepared to talk about it. "See if this Reed calls again tomorrow," he suggested.

David was bolder this time. He took the street next to the vicarage, and in a few days' time saw Reed visit again. Graham in the meantime carried out a search on Reed's company and found it had just gone into liquidation, with massive debts, and so clearly this was a time of financial distress for Reed, who may only be seeking spiritual guidance.

"He might also in the days of his plush have helped the church financially, so this could be pay-back time."

"You could be right," David agreed, but wasn't about to give up. He turned to Grace and asked about the vicar's former life. Although Grace didn't divulge much, David knew the vicar had spent time in a diocese in Birmingham, and that was what he looked at next. When Charles was next due to visit Birmingham, he followed him, taking the same train. It was going to be difficult to follow him without being spotted, so he decided to come right out into the open.

"What a coincidence! You in Birmingham too! And such a busy station! I'm visiting my sister. How about you?"

"This is my city," Charles said. "I'm attending a service."

"I wouldn't mind coming to that."

Charles wrote down an address in Edgbaston, then was picked up by a woman driving a red Mini. That same car was parked outside when David arrived at the service. He was early, and was greeted by an elderly man.

"I'm looking for Charles Shepherd. My name's David. That I believe is his wife's car parked over there."

"No – actually it isn't."

David wondered who the woman was, his thoughts racing at yet further possibilities for scandal.

The service began at nine a.m., but Charles wasn't there. David collected a prayer book but took the old man aside.

"Can we talk?"

"Depends what about."

"I'm a reporter from where Charles lives. I'm doing a story on him, but I'm finding it hard to get to know anything about him."

"I'm not surprised. He'd quite a reputation when he was here. You'd never see him with his wife at church, but he'd got a young girlfriend. That's why he left."

"That surprises me. Where he is now, he's a pillar of the community."

"Well, that's as much as I know."

Wondering how he could ever corroborate the story,

he headed back for the train home. In the morning he told his boss what he'd found out.

"You sure about this?" Graham asked.

"I followed him to Birmingham. One of his former parishioners told me all."

"How do you know it wasn't someone with a grievance?"

"I saw him with a woman, and it wasn't his wife."

"His wife!"

"Yes. He's left her in Birmingham."

"I see. Could be something in that, I suppose. But with the Reed thing there definitely isn't. He went to see Charles because of a donation he'd promised, which because of the liquidation he can't now stump up."

"Lucky I looked at this other lead then."

On Wednesday his phone rang. It was Grace, to let him know that Charles's wife was staying for a few days, in case he wanted to photograph them together. That finally flummoxed him, and when Graham heard of it he called him off the story altogether, and it was back to square one in his pursuit of journalistic stardom.

EIGHT

Richard arrived early, to find Samantha already at work. She was busy with computer designs.

"Come on in. I went to see the purchasing director of Adam Civil Engineering. I've got him interested in this new product. We'd have to find the machinery to produce it."

"There's the Munich trade show – we're bound to find a supplier there."

"Very likely. There are a few suppliers in Germany and Switzerland. And the one in Sweden looks promising." She made an adjustment to her design. "That'll make it faster, but I'm not sure it'll carry enough earth. But let's take this to Munich anyway."

"Yes – and in the meantime get everything else we need to make the equipment viable."

"And hopefully at least one firm order."

"Right! Only then can we really get cracking. That's a few months off I reckon."

Mr Hill tracked him down. "Richard, we have a problem. I've only two weeks' work for the production team, and unless something happens I'll have to lay some of them off."

"Leave it with me, I'll let you know after I've have consulted the others about it."

For a few days Richard avoided meeting Stewart about the staff lay-off. Eventually Stewart went to see him on the day of Richard's and Samantha's trip to the Munich trade exhibition. "Richard what are you going to about the lay-off issue? Things are getting desperate—you need to do something." Stewart was straight to the point.

"I'm aware of it and as soon as I am back from Munich we'll have a meeting. Now I've got to dash. I'm due at the airport for 11.30."

"Have a good trip."

"Thanks."

Richard carried the luggage out to the car, and started the engine. Sam joined him, carrying the case with her laptop and printer.

"How will your mum cope with you away?"

"My aunt's going to be there for the next few days."

"Good move."

At Munich their transfer was waiting to take them off to the Hilton International. It was Samantha's first trip abroad, and to her it was all so exciting. After checking in, they were directed to room numbers 545 and 546. Richard arranged for a taxi to the fair so that they could check out the Swedish Tool and Heavy Engineering Company, Deutsche Metal NV, and the Swiss company they knew about.

"You try and pin down your people, and I'll look around" Richard suggested.

Sam went her way, while Richard talked to some Far East delegates. He then introduced himself to a Mr Mwanga, Permanent Secretary to the Ministry of Planning and Development for the government of Kenya. There were five people in Mwanga's delegation – three men, two women – with the men all wearing navy blue suits. Mr Mwanga had a deep voice and a loud laugh. He took out a cigarette, and immediately one in his group, called Musa, was ready with a lighter.

"What sort of flight did you have?" Richard asked.

"Very good. We've all had a day's rest at the embassy."

"What's your hotel like?" Richard wanted to keep the conversation going.

"We're not at a hotel. We're staying at the ambassador's residence."

Richard got chatting, and having told them he was MD of a manufacturer of road-building plant and equipment, he went on to say he was looking for customers. "We're also looking to buy machinery to manufacture better equipment."

"That's interesting," Mwanga said. "Perhaps we'll see you later." He and his delegation went off to look at the stands." He had an air of authority that the others all seemed to obey. As they left, Musa looked back at Richard as if he were trying to communicate something, which indeed he was.

Musa then broke away from the delegation and made his way to Richard.

"I'll come straight to the point," he said. "If you want a meeting with Mr Mwanga, which may prove beneficial to your company, I can arrange it – for a fee. How about it? Why not give me your hotel phone number?"

"That's a bit abrupt. I'm really not sure."

"It's a once-in-a-lifetime opportunity. You want to do a deal or not?"

"Deal? What deal?"

"Any deal – anything at all. There's nothing he can't do. You interested or not?"

Richard wrote down his number, and grabbing the notepaper Musa hurried off.

Richard, slightly taken aback, ordered himself a coffee and hoped he hadn't exposed himself to danger. He looked at his watch and realised he had left Samantha alone for a long time, and so he caught up with her.

"How are you getting on?" he asked.

"Very well. I've had my designs faxed to the factory in Sweden. How have you got on?"

"Difficult to say. I've had a brush with the Kenyans."

"They buying?"

"Who knows! Look, I'm starving. Let's grab a late lunch."

"I won't say no to that."

Next morning Richard was just getting ready when the phone rang and the receptionist told him that there was someone asking to speak with him.

"Okay, put him on."

"Musa here. I'm calling as arranged. Really we need to meet."

"I can see you at the fair."

"That wouldn't be too convenient. It's easier to talk in the hotel."

"That's awkward. I'm with someone and we're about to leave."

"That won't do. We must meet alone."

"Why all the secrecy?"

"What I have to say must be between the three of us."

"Three?"

"I'll explain when we meet."

"I'm inclined to say I don't like this already."

"Without knowing what it is?"

"I don't like mysteries."

"You'll understand when I show you the deal. I just need five minutes of your time."

"All right. When?"

"Thirty minutes."

On the pretext that something urgent had come up, Richard suggested that Samantha went on her own and that he would meet her later at the fair. She wondered why, but didn't question it. After she'd gone, there was a knock at his door. It was Musa.

"Hello again," said Richard. They shook hands.

"I take it there's no one around," said Musa, suspiciously.

"I'm alone, as you can see."

Musa walked to the window and looked down to the street where there was a black Mercedes. Richard was curious, and came to look.

"Keep away from the window," whispered Musa.

Richard held back. "Am I being targeted by a drugs gang?" he wondered. He sat on the bed while Musa made a call on his mobile, telling the other person to join them. "You've got the all clear," he said.

Richard thought about phoning reception, but then came a knock at the door.

It was a man in a black hat, clothes streaked with rain. He removed his hat, followed by his glasses, which he wiped. It was Mwanga.

"How are you? Can I get you something from the restaurant – tea, coffee?"

"No, thank you – we don't intend to be long," Musa interjected.

"I'll tell you why we're here," said Mwanga "We have a proposal that we think you'll find interesting."

"Go on," Richard said.

"We want you to set up a manufacturing plant for some of your equipment in our country."

"Is that it?" Richard laughed. "I was expecting something dangerous."

"It won't do for us to be seen together by my government's agents. They tend to give us trouble."

"But why? What do they – or you for that matter – know about me or my company? And why should that trouble anyone?"

"We know what your company manufactures and we're confident of doing some big business together."

"We're not part of a big group – I hope you understand that."

"A small company is just what we're after."

"I can't make any judgement until I know more."

"There's a demand for the equipment you make all over Africa, and we'd like to partner you in mopping up the market."

"That could be very interesting. Why isn't it something your government's thought about?"

"They won't get funding. Secondly there's the question of the transfer of technology."

"How would the deal work?" asked Richard.

"My government will give you the assistance you need, I'll see to that."

"I see. Your job is to deflect any political problems?"

"Well, something like that."

"You'll have to let me think about it."

"All right – we'll get back to you. In the meantime, we'll ask our Finance Ministry to draw up a plan, for subsidy and so on."

"Isn't that premature?"

"We don't think so. There's a great deal of money in this for you – but we must be discreet."

"I see."

"There's one favour we need from you first."

"Go on."

"To oil the wheels, we'll need $2,500 – in cash. Today."

"That's not possible, I'm afraid."

"Think about it – the work's underway. Either you want a slice of the action or you don't. We can just as easily find someone else. After all, everyone's here at the fair."

"Five hundred's the most I can raise, at short notice."

"Make it a thousand, and you're in."

Richard hesitated. "Okay, leave that with me. I'll see you at the coffee bar, back at the fair. If I give you a white envelope, it's $500. If brown, it's a thousand."

"If it's less than a thousand, keep it – the deal's off."

"I'll see what I can do."

"Good. We'll keep in touch."

Musa looked out of the window again and told Mr Mwanga it was safe to leave. Mwanga put on his overcoat and hat and hurriedly left the room.

"We'll make you plenty of money," Musa said to Richard. Then he too left.

Richard breathed a sigh of relief and collapsed in a chair,

wondering if he'd been utterly stupid or if this was his golden opportunity to cement his position at Ashgrow. He feared the former, but being so very vulnerable he devoutly hoped for the latter. He thought of a plan to get the $1,000, and arranged to draw the amount on the company credit card, then called for a taxi and went into town.

After picking up the cash he returned to the fair, where he met up with Samantha. They did further business, distributing their cards and brochures wherever they could. He was quiet and Samantha sensed there was something not quite right. He slipped away to find Musa – though unbeknown to him she kept a watch on him. She saw him and Musa warmly shaking hands, and was surprised and puzzled at this, for they hardly knew each other. Musa pointed the way and Richard started walking. She followed them to the coffee bar, and concealed herself in a corner behind a newspaper.

Two cups of coffee were served, then Richard put his hand inside his coat and took out a brown envelope, which he bent down and dropped between his feet. Musa squatted down too, pretending to tie his shoelaces, and picked up the envelope. He said something – but she was too far away to hear. Then Musa left in a hurry. Richard also disappeared.

Sam returned to one of her Swedish representatives, as she now favoured their machinery. Half an hour later Richard joined her. It was two p.m. and neither had had lunch. She was subdued, and Richard assumed it was tiredness.

"How have you got on today?" she said.

"Still just probing."

"You see a fit for us here?"

"I've a few ideas. What would be great is if we could introduce a new product. You think we could do that?"

"If the prototype runs to my specification, yes – there's a market. Adam was very receptive. If we could sell say two dozen units to *his* company, others would come in."

"When will we get the prototype?"

"Engineer's ringing me at the end of next week. We're looking at a timescale of two to three weeks for the partially completed unit. Fingers crossed."

They decided on some sightseeing, though not before Sam's final briefing of her Swedish engineers. A taxi took them all round the city, and just as they were climbing into it she caught sight of Musa, who glanced at her meaningfully and brusquely turned away.

NINE

When Richard got back to his office lots of messages awaited him, mostly to tell him that Lucy had called.

"How was your trip?" Val asked.

"Very successful. Bertram in today?"

"I'll get him on the phone."

Richard started sifting through his post, then took the phone. "Bertram, how are you? Something urgent's come up." Just then Sam walked into his office. "Not something I can discuss on the phone. I'll see you at 2.30, your office." He cradled the phone. Meanwhile Val stood in the corner listening to the conversation.

Sam said: "Richard, here's a quote from the Swedish tool company. We need $3.5 million plus the cost of installation."

"What about training?"

"We'd need to go there. Should take about two to three days. All being well, we're in business."

"Anything else?"

"I need to discuss the modifications with Stewart. Then I can send Adam the drawings."

"I'll catch you later this afternoon."

Sam and Val left together.

"You any idea why Richard's meeting Purcell?" Sam asked.

"Haven't a clue."

"You think there's a problem with Lucy?"

"It wouldn't surprise me."

Later Sam received a fax from the Swedish tool company, with their own results from testing the prototype, which were better than hers. She referred all this excitedly to Mr Hill, who shared her delight.

"Wow! Amazing! This has got to be the most advanced macadam-breaking machinery ever."

She snatched the fax printout Hill was clutching and went to give Richard the news, but he'd gone to see Bertram.

Samantha cooled, as without Richard's backing she was unable to progress. "Better not get carried away," she thought, and, disappointed, left the room.

The phone rang and it was Lucy. "He's back, yes," said Val, "but I'm afraid he's out visiting Bertram. I'll tell him you called." Val put the phone down. "She's not happy," she thought.

Meanwhile Richard had arrived at Purcell's office, and was warmly greeted by his secretary.

"I'll tell him you're here."

A few minutes later Bertram appeared and they walked upstairs to his office.

"So, Richard, what's so urgent?"

"I'd like you to arrange a meeting with Alex Millard."

"May I ask why?"

"It's a bit of foreign trade, but it's all bound up with government red tape. I don't want to tread on anyone's toes."

Bertram, knowing Millard's soft spot for Ashgrow, got him on the phone.

Richard took the receiver. "Richard Nunn here, MD, Ashgrow. Good of you to talk. I've got some business, and I think our embassy in Nairobi can help." He soon got down to business.

"I'm down for my surgery in a week or so," Millard replied. "I'll talk to you then."

"That's excellent," Richard replied and handed back the receiver to Bertram with a broad smile.

"Well done," Bertram said.

"Well, let's hope so. I was approached in Munich by the Kenyan Ministry of Planning and Development people. They want Ashgrow to build plant to produce our equipment for sale all over Africa."

"But why you? Ashgrow's tiny!"

"It's because we can offer more than just an assembly plant."

"Can't they do it themselves?"

"Who knows their reasoning! But this is just the lucky break we need."

"But very risky, right!" Bertram warned.

"Let's see what Millard says."

"Well, good luck."

"Thanks. And thanks for your time. Appreciated."

As Richard was about to leave, the phone rang. It was Lucy. He frowned. "Okay, I'll take it," he said. "Lucy, yes, I'm back. Feet haven't touched the ground." There was a pause while he listened. "Okay, sounds good. See you in ten days' time." He put down the receiver, and left. Bertram was slightly uneasy.

TEN

It was Saturday morning and Richard had been for an early morning walk around the fields. Lucy had arrived a few days earlier, but he had yet to tell her about his plans to expand into Africa. He collected together his weekend newspapers and on his way back home dialled Bertram on his mobile.

"Bertram, I don't want to go too deeply into this, but for one reason or another I haven't told Lucy why we're meeting Alex. She thinks it's a social call, and for the moment I want to keep it that way."

"Won't that be difficult?"

"Just let me handle it. See you 12.30, King's Head. Thanks."

He found a bench near a scrub of land and opened first his *FT*, then his *Telegraph,* reading with interest of government commitment to manufacturing.

When he got back home Lucy was still asleep. He fried two eggs and buttered some toast, and poured himself coffee. He settled down with his *FT* again. There was an article that featured infrastructure projects in the Indian subcontinent and in southern Africa. He carefully noted details of civil engineering companies in those regions, intending to contact them later.

Sleepily, Lucy joined him, wearing a silk see-through nightie and an open dressing gown.

"Sleep well?"

"Like a log."

She poured herself an orange juice, but found no food in the fridge. "We need to shop."

"I'll give Val a list. She gets me groceries when she does her own."

"Why can't you do it?"

"You know me and supermarkets."

"Slob!"

"And good morning to you!"

"Don't take it personally."

"I'll try not to. You want breakfast?"

"Just coffee."

"It's made. Don't be too long in the shower. We're meeting Alex Millard, 12.30 – remember?"

"I hadn't forgotten." The phone rang, and Lucy answered. "Val," she said. "Expect you're after the shopping list. Not to worry, I'll sort it."

Richard put on cotton cream-coloured trousers and a pale brown shirt. He decided against a casual jacket, preferring a grey check with small leather patches to the elbows. Lucy selected tight-fitting blue jeans with a white blouse and a light blue scarf. She brushed her hair and, poised at the mirror, put on lipstick.

"You're stunning," Richard said.

"As ever. It's how you win friends and influence people."

Richard took her by the shoulders and planted a lingering kiss. She opened her mouth and the kiss became more intense. Then the phone rang again, and this time Richard answered. It was Bertram. Lucy ran her tongue around Richard's mouth while he was trying to talk.

"We'll meet you there," he managed to say.

"Okay, but don't be late. Alex will be with his agent, and I don't think will be able to spare more than an hour."

"No problem – 12.30." He put down the phone and pulled Lucy closer to him, kissing her again, but she protested.

"Now we don't want to be late."

She tore herself away and rearranged her hair, then put on her jacket and picked up her purse.

"You win," Richard said.

When they got to the pub Bertram was already there. He bought a round of drinks, Richard opting for mineral water, Lucy a Cinzano with lemon and ice. A murmur among the staff signalled Millard's arrival.

"Bertram, good to see you again!"

"The pleasure's ours."

"May I introduce Andrew, he accompanied me to the opening ceremony, if you remember. Let's get a table."

They found one tucked away in a corner, with a modicum of privacy.

"I have to confess,' said Richard, "I've been here for a few months now but this is the first time I've set foot in this pub."

"Should hope so," said Lucy. "You're far too busy to socialise."

They ordered food, and another round of drinks.

"Good health," said Alex. He turned to Richard. "Now tell me all about your exploits."

"Yes. Every problem's an opportunity. Mine is, I need to get assembly plant into Nairobi, but can't help thinking I shall need the embassy to help."

This was all news to Lucy.

"What is it you want the embassy to do?" Alex asked.

"I'd like to see it making representations to the Kenyan government on our behalf."

"That's a commercial matter, which is of course of economic interest, but we can't be seen to promote your company."

"I realise that."

"The best and the honourable thing is if I put you in touch with the Department of Trade."

"But surely your people place value on foreign investment."

"Better to blow your own trumpet," Lucy interjected.

"It's all a matter of protocol. You might consider financial help from the Department of International Development."

"I've met one high-ranking delegate from the Planning and Development Department of the government of Kenya, who's willing to help. Couldn't the embassy make a link there, or with the Finance Ministry?"

Alex smiled at Richard's suggestion. "I'll give you a contact at the World Bank."

Their meal arrived.

"I'm very grateful," Richard said.

"Well, perhaps we can rely on your company for a party donation?" Andrew asked.

"I had in mind the figure of £10,000," Richard said, without hesitation. He looked at Lucy, who took a bite of her sandwich and didn't look too pleased.

"That's very generous. It has to be said that what Alex is doing he would do for *any* UK businessman. It's just that he takes a little more interest in his constituents. The donation has nothing to do with it.

"Indeed."

Lucy, supremely bored, began to file her nails, then added to that her lipstick and makeup mirror – not entirely appropriate as far as Richard was concerned. He shot her a look, which she ignored.

Andrew suddenly got up, having spotted David Tolchard from the *Gazette* making his way to their table.

As David knew Alex, after the usual preliminary niceties he said, "Now don't forget you promised me an interview."

"I hadn't forgotten. Not today, I'm afraid."

"We'll call you," Andrew said. He took yet another of Tolchard's business cards.

Tolchard turned to Richard. "How's the factory?"

"On the up, naturally."

"Very glad to hear it. This town needs its successes. I'd join you in a drink, but I'm due to cover the football."

"That is a shame."

They said goodbye and Tolchard left, and that was the sign for all of them to leave. Richard thanked Alex for his time.

"A pleasure. Just get in touch with Andrew if I can be of further help. Richard, Lucy, lovely to meet you. Bertram, I'll catch you again."

The party broke up, and it was a gloomy drive home for Richard and Lucy.

"Was it really necessary, at such an important meeting," Richard asked, "to do your beautifying routine?"

"That, Richard, was a very boring meeting. All Alex Millard wants is people like you to fill his party coffers. He saw you coming."

"You want to get things done, you've got to play the game."

"You didn't have to be so naïve."

"I resent that."

"Do you? And what about me? Don't you think I should have some say when it comes to donating *my* money?"

"You'll get it back – several times over."

"How can you be so sure?"

"I know these things, but you have no idea how businesses work."

"Shut it."

"I won't be insulted."

"I won't have you throw away my money."

"This gets us nowhere. As things stand, the company has nothing to offer any of its existing customers. Investment's the only answer. I've found an investment and you should back me. I can't put it plainer than that."

"Stop the car, Richard. Drop me right here. I don't know when I'll be home."

He didn't argue, and without further words dropped her at the corner of the High Street. Coolly, he set off for the office to check his mail, and when he finally got home Val was stocking his fridge.

"Sorry," she said, "I didn't get the list, so I guessed."

"Val, you're too good. I think though Lucy intended to shop."

"Where is she?"

"We, er, have had a slight disagreement. She'll get over it."

"Oh, sorry. Bad timing."
"No problem. See you on Monday, hey?"

ELEVEN

On Monday Richard drove to work alone, Lucy's airline having arranged for a limousine to collect her for her flight. He couldn't help but be embittered at the low opinion she had of him where business was concerned. He thought everything had been settled when he'd almost resigned, and yet Lucy still didn't see him as fully in charge of the company.

He spent some moments in his office browsing through the newspaper, until Val – his PA by default – showed him his diary.

"Thanks for reminding me."

"You're welcome. Lucy's back in the US, I take it?"

"You guessed it."

She left him to his thoughts. His next visitor was the company accountant, John Brimell, concerned about one of his entries.

"It's this one for $1,000," he said. "Unusually, not supported by any receipts."

"Oh, that. Put it down to client hospitality."

"Really? The amount drawn is a round sum."

There was a knock, and Sam stepped in, though was immediately ushered back out. "I'll see you in a minute," Richard said.

She hung about outside, a bit put out, and John followed her shortly.

"High finance," she said.

Rather defensively, John replied: "Far from it. Just a few credit card statements."

Richard was about to ask her back in when his telephone rang. It was Andrew, Millard's agent.

"Just wanted to let you know that Alex has put in a word at the World Bank."

"That's very nice to know."

"The person you need to talk to there is called Waterton – that's Mr Waterton. He's based at the London office. I'll give you his number."

Richard wrote it all down. "Thanks. I'll make sure you get the donation at the end of the month."

"No great hurry."

"Give my regards to Alex."

Richard put the phone down. "Result!" he said to himself.

Samantha was hovering, and came back in.

"I've got the prototype report from Adams," she said.

"And?"

"They're very impressed. He's making a case for fifteen units, with an option on a further twenty-five in twelve months' time. The Swedes will sell us the plant and the tooling – but at a cost of $3.5 million. From where I'm standing, that's a lot of money."

"How soon can they deliver?"

"No idea. Why – can we afford it?"

"I'll come to that later."

"You do know we'd have to go to Gothenburg for training?"

"Speak to John and get the total cost. I'll talk to Brian at the bank. Now, please, I've a call to make."

She left, and he immediately called Mr Waterton. "Richard Nunn here. Alex Millard said I should call."

"Ah, Mr Nunn, yes. Now how's this date for your diary…?"

Richard wrote it down – next Friday. Wary of prying eyes, he scored through the whole of Friday 16th August in his desk planner, and pencilled in something spurious about an office reunion. He started to draw up a business plan, and collected manufacturing details from the workshop. He then ordered a copy of each international magazine covering civil engineering and micro projects on the African landmass.

The next morning Richard went to work late, phoning Nairobi from home.

"Musa," he said, "I'm carrying out a feasibility study. You'll need to give me an idea of the type of units for export."

"Is that so? Let me put you right. This is the office of the Ministry of Planning and Development."

Richard saw his mistake. "I'm carrying out research regarding road-building potential there in Africa. It's to raise funding for my investment in Kenya. I need information as to what countries might be involved."

Musa still wouldn't talk, so Richard gave him his email address, hoping that would do the trick. As it was already past ten, he left for the office. He had five days to collect his data and prepare the report. It had to work.

In his office, Val had spotted the factory manuals and processing notes stacked on his desk.

"You want to become an engineer?" she joked.

"Couldn't wear the clothes," he quipped. "I want to see if we can cut out irrelevant processing time and save on costs."

She made herself scarce when Samantha arrived, who was asked to create a plan of action on the basis that the new machinery had been bought and the company was able to introduce new products. "Sit down with John and prepare some cash flow projections."

"Aren't we jumping ahead?"

"Not really. First we want to see if the project is sustainable, so obviously we need to incorporate an estimate of revenue." He looked at her and then picked up a file to put away in his drawer.

"What's that doing here?" she said, taking the file from him.

"It's only the new plant. Take it."

"Do you really think we can pull this off, Richard?"

"Let's have some serious figures before we decide. By next Monday we must have your plan and if necessary you can see our external accountants. If the project looks viable I want to go ahead – agreed?"

Samantha found this somewhat arrogant, but put it all down to a second round with his overbearing wife, which he'd obviously won.

Alone again, he thought about Musa. He'd prefer to establish contact before his visit to the World Bank, and had a very distracted day working through his reports. Finally, at about five o'clock, he couldn't wait any longer and decided to go home. He shuffled his papers into his briefcase, and left, saying goodnight to Val as he went. She couldn't help mentioning this to Sam.

"Bit early, isn't it? Wonder what's going on?"

"I don't think all in the marriage nest is as it should be."

"That explains a lot."

"Best not to get involved."

"Wouldn't dream of it."

Both of them knew that wasn't strictly true – for either of them.

The first thing Richard did on getting home was check his email. There was one from Kenya:

> Would like to visit you in London. Mr Mwanga and I are leading a London delegation, one month's time.

The email address was Musa's, and Musa was on-line at that moment. Richard replied:

> Intended London visit noted. How much revenue can we achieve?

And the reply:

> Am not an accountant, or a businessman. Can't advise. Surely you have this information. Try talking to the Commerce and Finance Department here. Will let you know our itinerary in due course.

Relieved to have made contact, Richard threw himself on the settee, springing up again to play back his phone messages. Then he got back to writing his reports. When he'd done all he could it was well past midnight. Details of projected sales were still missing, so he couldn't call it complete, though he still had four days to go. He hoped to God Musa would send the details he'd asked for. He went to bed. As fragile as their relationship was, he wished Lucy were here. He couldn't sleep. He got up and opened a bottle of Scotch, but that didn't help. Bizarrely, he phoned up Val. Sleepily, she picked up her phone.

"Val. It's me, Richard."

"Have you any idea what time it is?"

Richard looked at the wall clock. "God, it's past one. I'm sorry, I shouldn't have called."

"You sure you're all right?"

"Well – actually – not too good. I just need someone to talk to."

"I'm hardly awake."

"I'm sorry, I know. Do you mind coming for a drive?"

"A drive?"

"I'll pick you up."

She found herself coerced.

Richard jumped back into the clothes he'd worn that day, and drove off in a hurry. He parked the Discovery behind Val's Honda and flashed his headlights, rather than ring her bell. He could see her moving behind her bedroom curtains, then a minute or two later she appeared at her front door in a grey tracksuit and jogging shoes.

"Good of you to do this," he said.

"Well, never mind – good to be of some assistance."

He promised they wouldn't go far, and somehow that meant going back to his cottage. "Come inside. I'll make you some coffee," he said.

He followed her in to the lounge, then, spontaneously, took her in his arms. She didn't resist.

"Been on your own long?" he asked.

"Too long."

He gently kissed her lips. She shut her eyes and allowed him to slide his tongue into her mouth. Her back was against the wall as he drew closer. She cradled his neck. He ran his fingers through her hair, then slipped his hands up her back and unhooked her bra. She unzipped his trousers, massaging his hardness. Then she lowered her jogging bottoms, and pulled him on top of her onto the settee.

Val, the PA, was in her late forties. Her husband had left her five or six years before, so she saw herself as free. Besides, she felt sorry for Richard, and she didn't approve of Lucy – he could easily have married someone better.

"This is our little secret," he said.

"Our little secret. Now take me home."

TWELVE

It was awkward the following morning back at work, Richard hardly wishing to engage in conversation with Val. She greeted him nevertheless.

"Hi," he said, careful to avoid eye contact.

"Umm – if it's about last night, I know how you feel. I shan't say a thing."

"That might be for the best. You know I'm out on Friday, don't you?"

Samantha interrupted them.

"Ah, Sam – what news from Gothenburg?"

"All in hand. What are we going to do with the old plant?"

"Ask them if they'll take it in part exchange."

"They won't – I know they're not interested."

"Shame. I'll talk to Brian. In the meantime get a quotation. I'm out all day on Thursday, by the way."

"I thought you were out on Friday."

"I'll be working from home. Too many distractions here."

He indicated that the conversation was over by taking out his laptop and starting to key in figures for the financial report he was working on, which ran to nearly forty pages.

He produced two copies on his printer and put them in his briefcase. After that he called his mother.

"How are you?" she said.

"Couldn't be better. I'm coming up for a couple of nights. I'm hoping you can put me up."

"You don't have to ask."

"It'll be till Sunday."

"And Lucy?"

"She's in the US. Give my love to Dad."

At four he was grilling Samantha.

"Get me a concrete proposal by Monday. Speak to Adam. Tell him we're about to invest heavily in new plant. We need to know how many units he wants."

"You're sure about this?"

"Absolutely. We've talked the talk – now it's time for action."

He avoided Val on his way out.

At home he checked his email, but there was nothing. The phone rang, and it was Lucy.

"Pleasant surprise!"

"I rang the office. You weren't there."

"Sometimes I get more done here."

"I hear you're off to London for a few days. You'll be staying at the flat?"

"No, with my parents. I'm back Monday."

"Oh well, happy reunion."

"It'll be a bore, frankly, but these things have to be done."

She hung up.

He woke at the normal time despite his best intentions to leave for London early. He'd put the finishing touches to his report and rolled into bed late. It was all in his briefcase ready to go, but he got it out and checked it over one last time. He didn't want any slip-ups. After a quick shower he packed his suit and headed off for London. The appointment was for 2.30 that afternoon. It was now 8.30 and altogether it took him four and a half hours to reach London. The M4 was at a usual grinding halt, so he phoned his mum.

"I'll be about another half-hour. Traffic's terrible."

When he got there he couldn't find a parking space nearby. He drove around for a good fifteen minutes in frustration before finding one, and just managed to squeeze his Discovery into a slot not too far from his parents' home. His mum was waiting with a pot of tea. He sat down drinking the tea thirstily.

"You've lost weight, how do you fancy a lovely sirloin steak for dinner tonight?" she asked.

"Sounds terrific, Mum."

He trotted upstairs and changed into his suit. He downed a second cup of tea, then dashed off with his briefcase. He flagged down a cab, which stuttered through a logjam of traffic to his appointment. He couldn't help but reflect how he had once really enjoyed the hustle and bustle, but now after his quieter life in the country he couldn't imagine why. However, he put those thoughts aside. What was imperative now was the future of Ashgrow, and if he failed there was the very real prospect that Lucy would have him removed. Were that to happen, he'd lose Lucy as well. A lot depended on this afternoon's meeting.

He allowed himself a few seconds outside at the entrance to smarten himself up, then strode into reception. A girl in her mid-twenties took his details.

"The name's Nunn, Richard Nunn. To see Mr Waterton."

Waterton's secretary, who said her name was Anne, came to collect him. "Please follow me." She took him up in the lift and ushered him in to her boss's office.

"Pleased to meet you," Waterton said, and shook his hand. He was a tall man with small, wire-framed glasses, mid-fifties, slightly balding. He wore a blue shirt with white stripes, with a light blue tie, no jacket. "Mr Nunn, how can I help?"

Richard sat down. "My company, Ashgrow, wants to invest in Kenya."

"Manufacturing?"

"Yes. Road-building equipment: a motorised unit that lays macadam once the road's been dug up."

"Do you have support from the relevant Kenyan authority?"

"I believe so. The Ministry of Planning and Development says it wants Ashgrow to install the facility in Kenya. Idea then is to export to other African countries."

"And this would involve the transfer of technology?"

"Yes, we'd be selling the entire plant, with the first six months say overseen by one of our seniors."

"And this is a joint venture with the Kenyan government?"

"That depends on what they're offering. Our objective

is twofold: to create jobs in Kenya, and to establish an export base in Nairobi for our machinery. But Ashgrow is small, with limited resources. We have a plant that's fast becoming redundant, and we're keen to produce a new range of equipment."

"And finance?"

"We need initial funding to acquire the plant and start the production stage. In all, $3.5 million."

"And the Kenyan authority's prepared to fund it?"

"That's yet to be resolved. I'd hope they'd give us tax breaks, fund the local employment element, and provide us with a loan for the working capital – interest-free and unguaranteed."

"What's the export potential?"

"We're waiting for firm projection figures, but initially the local contractors are expected to buy every unit we make – that's for the first two years to meet their own needs. According to the Kenyan Foreign and Finance Ministries, they'll also support us in our export aim."

"You've done your homework."

"It's all in this report." He placed it on the desk.

"The FO's helping, I suppose?"

"I wouldn't know. What do you think our chances are with the World Bank?"

"I can't give you any answers at this stage. The best you can expect from this organisation is what's known as IFC-backed assistance. IFC funds private investment and the World Bank assists government projects and programmes."

"To me the World Bank and the IFC are the same thing – and by the way, is it worth you talking to the Ministry of Planning and Development, two of whose representatives are visiting the UK? I could try and set up the meeting with you."

"I'll be quite happy to talk. But since they're not authorised by government – their government – I can't do so in any official capacity."

The meeting wound up, with Waterton asking how Richard had found himself running such an unusual company.

"My wife invested her inheritance in Ashgrow Engineering. Her father was a good friend of the previous owner, who sold his stake to Lucy my wife. I'm now running it as MD."

They shook hands and Richard left. When he got home his father was there.

"How did it go, son?"

"Hard to say. I'll have to wait and see."

"I'm sure it'll all work out," said his mum.

"When's Lucy back, son?"

"That's another imponderable."

"Everything okay between you?"

"Don't worry, Dad – everything's fine."

After supper Richard rang his old workmates and arranged to meet in a West End pub, and felt pleased at least that his reunion story wasn't a complete fabrication. His pals were Duncan, Patricia, Lauren, Vicky and Philip. Sadly Vicky was terribly maudlin after her latest failed affair, and with Lucy away she more or less threw herself at him.

"Careful, Vicks," said Duncan. "His wife will eat you up."

She didn't take the hint, got herself outrageously drunk, and tried to inveigle him into a taxi back to her place, where she'd just taken delivery of all kinds of sexual toys, which she couldn't wait to try out.

"Another time," Richard said, fighting off temptation.

"Oh come off it! Who's going to know?"

"My wife has spies everywhere."

"So what! Live dangerously!"

"I'm flattered, Vicks – but I'm really not up for it." He went home feeling wretched, opening the door quietly so as not to wake his folks. He lay awake for a long time, thinking. In the end he convinced himself that funding from the IFC *would* be forthcoming, and he more or less decided things would move ahead. When he headed back home his mood was lighter, and he looked forward to getting in touch with Musa.

Back at the cottage, he found that Val as usual had filled up the freezer. He tidied up the post he'd collected, then fired up his computer before emailing Musa, with whom he'd established a code by now (it demanded certain wording in the reply before any conversation took place). The email he sent didn't get a reply, after several hours of checking.

"Odd," he thought.

He'd still heard nothing when he returned to work, exceedingly early on Monday.

The entrance to the production area was locked and the only other person who had a key was Mr Hill. Richard unlocked the front grille and lifted it half way to open the main door. He switched off the alarm system. He found the hall very cold, but rather than start the central heating system he took an electric heater to his office.

There were a few messages on his desk that he ignored. He took out the manual for the plant and equipment they were proposing to buy. He studied the manufacturing process very intently, and made notes. Then eerily he heard a noise from the front door, as if someone were trying to get in. He looked into the car park but saw only his Discovery, and started to feel worried. He went to the reception lobby, and there stood in a dark corner as he watched the door being opened, fingers curling round its panels.

"Who's there!" he shouted.

Val tumbled in, and fell straight in his arms.

"God, it's you! What are you doing here?"

"You scared me."

"What an earth are you doing?"

"Couldn't sleep. Decided to come in early. I've missed you."

"Don't be ridiculous."

She looked at him forlornly, so he raised her up and kissed her on her lips. She devoured him back. He unbuttoned her blouse, and whipping it off brutally massaged her breasts. She groped for his fly, and pulling out his cock petted it and took it in her mouth. He pulled her up, then rolled her onto the hard cold floor, where he fumbled to get the rest of her things off.

"I'll do anything," she moaned.

He straddled her, then she straddled him, then suddenly he shrieked. "God, the CCTV!"

They pulled their clothes back on, then frantically searched for keys to the security room, where, finally, they spent an anxious hour wiping the all-incriminating tape.

"That was close."

"Damn right. Let's have some coffee."

"Not for me. I've got work to do."

He returned to his office, where Val rejoined him, mug in hand.

"You want me to come over this evening?" she asked.

"No," he said gruffly.

"What's wrong?"

"You know what's wrong. It's all this pressure."

"Take your mind off it."

"Not tonight, thanks."

She left, none too enthralled. Richard returned to his booklets, telling himself that he would need to know how to operate the new plant.

That evening he put a packet of chicken curry and rice in the microwave, and drank several cans of beer. Before he went to bed he left another email for Musa to ring him at the office. He'd decided to go ahead with the initial plan, and was only waiting on feedback from Mr Waterton. He wanted to ring up Lucy, but desisted. He watched too much TV – all of it mindless – and tired but not really sleepy took himself off to bed.

In the morning he checked his email, finding plenty of spam but nothing from Musa. On his way out Mrs Arnold – the cleaner – stepped in.

"You're here very early."

"Got a lift, that's why. Not inconvenient, I hope."

"Not at all. Left you a lot of washing up, I'm afraid."

"That's all right, Mr Nunn. That's what I'm here for."

Their chat held him up and he arrived at the office after Samantha, whose car was first in. Val's, he saw, wasn't in yet. Hill was the first to see him, and he acknowledged him grumpily. It was not an auspicious start to the day.

Sam followed him into his office.

"What's up?" she said.

"What's up?"

"Hill says you're in a foul mood."

"A bit fatigued, perhaps – but I'm fine."

"Well this'll cheer you up. There's been a security scare."

"A security scare?"

"Someone wiped a CCTV tape – but there are no signs of forced entry, and nothing seems to be missing. Security only found out today, they reckoned it happened yesterday."

"Oh, that must have been me."

"Oh?"

"Got in ultra-early yesterday – had a lot to do. I noticed a coffee mug sitting on my desk, which was odd, I thought. The cleaners don't usually miss things like that."

"What's that got to do with the CCTV?"

"Thought I'd check the tape. Must have wiped it inadvertently in doing so."

It was an explanation he'd already rehearsed, and it seemed to satisfy Sam.

There was a gentle tap at the door and Val came in. "Here's your mail." She plonked it down and left, as did Sam. The phone rang.

"Richard, Musa here."

"At last! I'll call you back from my mobile." Then, from his cell phone: "I don't want people here to know what's going on."

"That's your affair. Mr Mwanga and I are coming to London next week. We can meet."

"It's a must."

"I'll email the details." Musa rang off.

"Thank God for that!" Richard thought. At last his plans were falling into place. He called John to his office.

"I want you to make a cheque out for the party donation – £10,000, but leave it blank for now."

John was astonished. "I don't think it's right that you overrule our system by issuing a blank cheque," he said.

"What is right and wrong is my problem. Just do it."

"Okay! I'll do it this one time only."

"Good. Off you go."

Richard then rang Andrew and arranged to meet at the local party office. In the meantime, Sam discovered what was going on, and knew about the cheque when he called her in. He was on the phone when she strolled in and sat down. He put the phone down.

"I'm optimistic," he said. "I think we're in a position to get the new plant. Perhaps we'll even get a good price for the old stuff."

"How?"

"It's one of my hunches."

"Richard. I have my duty as a director. I'm not necessarily against hunches, but I need a little bit more to go on than that."

"You'll have to trust me on this one, Sam. You, or John, or both, must now find the best deal for the old plant. I also want you to be available for a trip to Gothenburg in the next ten days. We need some basic training."

"They won't just give it. There's no guarantee we'll buy the plant."

"We'll offer a small deposit."

"How small?"

"You know the people – you find out."

THIRTEEN

Richard spread the whole lot of documents on the meeting table in the boardroom, and continued to make notes. He referred to his IFC report, and then phoned Hill.

"What's the remaining working life of the plant?"

"Eight, nine, possibly ten years."

"As much as that?"

"Yes, but with heavy commitment to maintenance."

Richard's enthusiasm evaporated. "What's the best we can make of all this plant?"

Hill switched on the speakerphone and called in one of the techies: "We've looked into that. We'll have to replace bearings and diaphragms. That only increases the working life – it doesn't make the operation more efficient."

"Can all that be done here?"

"Yes, but the company's engineers will have to supervise and approve the work."

"Good – and thanks. Please find out how soon we can get the parts, and when their engineers can come."

Hill intervened: "I think that'd be a waste of money."

"I know your views. Please get me the answers I want – this afternoon."

"We'll try."

"You do that."

Later Samantha joined Richard in the conference, discussing the fate of old machinery. She informed him that she had a gut filling that it would take over a week for refitting at a cost of around £250,000. She considered they would save £30,000 if dismantled and used as parts

Richard was jotting down these amounts when Sam raised questions about patents. "Richard, why do you concern yourself with this revamping matter? This is mine and Stewart's job."

"I'm totting up the value of revamped plant, should we decide to do it."

"But I can do that."

"You can, but there isn't any need. My worry is Hill. I've asked him to speak to the service company, but I bet he hasn't done a thing about it."

"You *can* trust him, Richard."

"Let's hope so."

"Okay, let's find out now. I'll call him." She did, and found Richard's suspicions confirmed. She was obviously embarrassed and rang the service company herself and got the details.

"You see!" Richard said. "People here want me to fail."

"Nonsense! What you have to ask yourself is who'd want to buy this old junk."

"Someone always will."

"Now, what about these patents?"

"Another time," Richard said, waving her away. He keyed figures into his computer and produced a printout, the results of which delighted him. Revamped, it seemed, their machinery was worth about £1,000,000.

"You're joking!"

"New it costs £2.5 million – and that includes some significant advances."

He began to wrap up his exercise and put away his documents. Samantha had already left his office, bewildered.

Richard got home late, and considered his next move. He had to be in London early next week, and to some this might be too soon after the first trip. Just as he pondered that one, his mother rang. She was worried about him being on his own

"No, I'm not suffering," he assured her.

"When's Lucy coming home?" she wanted to know.

"Soon."

"I worry. Living apart is not the best foundation for marriage."

He bit his tongue, wanting to say that being under the same roof didn't work that well either.

"It was never like this in our day."

"Things change, Mum. Society moves on."

"Well, I just hope you know what you're doing."

"Don't worry. How's Dad?"

"Chipper as ever."

"Retirement suits him."

"You take care of yourself."

He opened a bottle of wine and sat down to another TV dinner. After that he listened to jazz, which sent him drifting in and out of sleep. This went on for a couple of hours until he phoned Lucy.

"Oh, you're there. I was about to put the phone down."

"I'm running late. How are things?"

"Not bad. Missing you."

"And I miss you."

"I don't suppose you've got a break in your busy schedule for a trip to Kenya. I'm about to finalise the deal. We could go on safari."

"That sounds tempting. When?"

"I'll know by the end of next week."

"I'll wait for your call. How is business?"

"It's fingers crossed, but I'm confident. The next week's crucial."

The following morning he got in very early. The foreman was the only other one about. Richard went through the records of units currently in stock and also studied the testing and performance results. Roger, the foreman, offered to help.

"Have you really got a buyer for this stuff?" he asked.

"That's beside the point. It makes good sense to keep at least two or three in good working order."

"But there are so many better alternatives on the market."

"Roger, are you working for us, or not?"

"I'm in, of course."

"Good. I make the decisions."

"Sorry, boss."

Hill showed up. "I've got those details you asked for," he said.

"Too late – all done."

"Done?"

"I sorted it, with Sam's help."

"But…"

"Next time, when I ask you to do something, do it!"

Val was filing documents in his office, when he returned.

"Richard, how are you?"

"Ripping. How are you?"

"I called you last night."

"I must have been asleep. It's that sort of week. Look, if you don't mind, I'm busy. I've got to go to London again."

"Why?"

"Business."

She got on with her filing. Richard picked up the phone and tried to draw cash – £5,000 – on his credit card.

"I'm sorry, Mr Nunn, you only have £150 available."

Richard hung up, but the figure of £5,000 stuck in Val's mind. Why should he want such a sum? When she left him, Richard asked John to come in.

"Look, John, I've got a very important sales trip and I need some cash, for expenses."

"How much?"

"Five thousand."

"May I ask what for?"

"Client hospitality."

"What client – the cabinet?"

"Don't joke. Look, if you can't handle this…"

"No – no problem. I'll draw up an IOU. I'll need a proper account in due course."

"There's a good fellow."

FOURTEEN

His appointment was at the Park Lane Hotel, and he arrived early. He wore a navy blue suit and a red and white tie, and had his best leather briefcase. Reception buzzed the appropriate room.

"Thanks," he said. A girl answered and Richard asked for Mr Mwanga.

"Bwana, it's for you," he heard her say.

The next voice was Mwanga's. "Richard, you made it."

"Not too early, I hope."

"Come up. You'll find us on the seventh floor, room seven-one-o."

Richard took the lift and knocked at the door. A young woman opened it, shadowed by Mr Mwanga. They shook hands firmly. Richard stepped into the room, where the young woman was introduced as his secretary, a Miss Kyombe. Musa was there too. They nodded. Mwanga pointed to a chair, Richard sat down.

"Been in London long?" Richard asked, politely.

"Since yesterday," said Mwanga.

"Still getting used to conditions," Musa added.

"Jet lag. It takes a while. How many of you?"

"Us four, from the Ministry of Development, and the minister is staying with the ambassador."

The two women were sifting papers. Miss Kyombe particularly had a professional look. She was early thirties, with cornrow hair and a bangle. Her glasses tipped her nose. Her legs were long, and she wore high-heels, a shiny black. Her colleague was older and wasn't so attractive. She had a white top with black trousers, and a very large rear. Miss Kyombe appeared to be the junior. She took orders, and served coffee.

"Black – no, white!" Richard said. He turned to Musa and asked for projected sales figures. Musa called for his briefcase, producing a bundle of documents.

Mwanga intervened. "Don't rush ahead. What about wrapping up negotiations first… . What have you got for us?"

Richard questioned the women's presence.

"Don't worry about them. They're part of the team." Mwanga asked Miss Kyombe in Swahili "Kooja hapa?", patting his thighs.

She sat down on his lap and stroked his crotch. He fondled her breasts.

"Sorry, I'd rather talk to you two privately," Richard insisted.

The two women were waved away. Richard took out a brown envelope and gave it to Musa.

"There it is – £1,000. You'll get the rest when I know what's in it for Ashgrow."

Musa handed over the envelope to Mr Mwanga, who opened it and pocketed the notes.

"We'd be able to help you set up operation in Nairobi, but the initial investment will have to come from you.

The Kenyan government will not be making any investment."

"When you say help, what kind of help?"

"Two kinds. Firstly, the Ministry can buy equipment from your company. We can also ask the Ministry of Finance and Foreign Affairs to help with the export. Ostensibly made in Kenya, this makes it easy to market over Africa."

"You have a projection for this?"

"What figure did you have in mind?" Musa countered.

"I've no idea and was hoping that you'd come up with figures."

"I'm sure the Ministry of Finance will come up with a subsidy," said Mwanga.

"Glad to hear it."

"Get anything else you need from our two women."

"I'll bear that in mind."

The women now rejoined them.

"When can we have the balance – the £4,000?" Musa asked.

"Shortly." Richard turned Mwanga. "I'd like your presence when I meet Mr Waterton at the IFC."

"Sorry – no way! I don't want myself or our government to be seen to be associated with your investment."

"Well then, what about introducing me to the Ministry of Finance?"

Mwanga asked Miss Kyombe for some papers, which he gave to Richard saying, "What you need is all there," and handed over the file.

"Thanks. How about we all have lunch?" said Richard, flicking through the file.

Miss Kyombe declined.

"Nonsense! Everyone's invited. I've booked the most famous restaurant in London."

"Sorry. *We're* having lunch downstairs."

He suggested dinner, and that they agreed to.

Richard booked a table at the Carlton Club for eight p.m. The minister was unable to come, which was a disappointment. He'd hired a dinner jacket and had just gone upstairs to change when his mother called him down with Lucy on the phone. She wanted to confirm holiday arrangements in Kenya. He briefed her about his plans for that evening.

"Things are moving," he said.

"I'm sure. But you've got to watch these Kenyans. Don't let them bamboozle you."

"Don't worry. Now, I'd better hurry up. Time's getting on."

"Goodbye," she said, somewhat icily, and she hung up.

"Why is she constantly ringing you?" his mother asked.

""She doesn't trust me. She thinks I'm after her millions."

"Money – always a problem, whether you've got it or not."

"Sad, isn't it?"

"We had nothing like this in our day."

"Times are always changing. I'd better get going." He put the rest of the cash in an envelope and left to pick up his guests, hailing a taxi first. At the Park Lane Hotel, Musa was seated in reception.

"You waiting for me?"

"Yes. But first Mr Mwanga wants to collect the money. Got it?"

"Taken care of. Follow me into the lift, I'll give it you there."

Inside, the doors closed, and Musa took the envelope and pocketed it. They were met by Miss Kyombe, who was wearing a knee-length dress, tight on her breasts and drawn at the waist with a belt. She'd discarded her glasses. She was ready to go, except for a coat.

"Can I offer you a drink, Bwana?"

"No, thank you."

Mwanga and Musa were wearing black business suits, and were engaged in animated conversation.

"Ready to go?"

"Just about."

They left as a group, Miss Kyombe wrapping herself in a shawl. In the taxi, she sat next to Mwanga, while the other woman – her name was Mrs Mongo – sat on his other side. Both ran their hands up his trouser legs. Richard and Musa sat facing the threesome. Mwanga spread his arms and fondled the women's breasts. Miss Kyombe stooped down and administered a blowjob. The two other men effected not to notice, even as Mwanga's deep contented voice rang out.

At the club, they were led to their table, though by now Richard had lost his appetite. The others ordered their starters as if nothing exceptional had happened. Richard went through the motions, ordering a bottle of champagne and two bottles of wine. Then, to his astonishment, Alex Millard and the group of people he was with were ushered to a table. Richard stood up and shook hands, and introduced him to Mr Mwanga.

"Our UK Foreign Secretary," he said.

Mwanga shook hands vigorously.

"Tell me, Richard," Alex asked, "how are you getting on with all my friends at the World Bank?"

"It's promising, but a lot depends on Mr Mwanga here."

"You've no need to worry about that," Mwanga said.

"I can see you're in good hands, Richard."

Richard thought about the taxi ride earlier on and wasn't so sure.

"We'll talk again."

Mr Mwanga couldn't help but be impressed, and was now a little more forthcoming. He told him it was his government's aim to create jobs and improve living conditions, with infrastructure and road-building a principal target. "What we have to do is attract overseas investment from people like you, who are vital for sustaining development in Kenya."

This was the first positive statement Richard had heard. "I am," he said, "very committed. A pity your minister couldn't make it tonight."

"He *will* meet you, don't worry."

Starters were served.

"How do you think your minister would like to visit my factory?"

"He'd be delighted, I'm sure. I'll talk to him. But I'm going to ask a return favour."

"Go on."

"You must introduce my minister to Alex Millard."

"I'll see what I can do."

Finally coffee was ordered to round the evening off. The two women had had, it seemed, a little too much to drink, and were giggling. Richard, sober and aware, looked around for Millard, though another group now had his table. He called for the bill. Mwanga invited him back to their hotel.

"I'm asking our minister to join us," he said.

Richard was tired but didn't want to miss an opportunity.

Musa left the table and organised a cab, which once they had all piled in meant much the same routine – another orgasmic bout for Mwanga. Richard, initially baffled, decided this must be normal behaviour for them, and tried to look detached. Perhaps it was all a condition of Miss Kyombe's job.

It was 10.30 and Mwanga instructed Musa to ring the minister, whose name was Mr Mwingi. Musa got through on his cell phone. The minister answered straightaway, and agreed to meet.

"Thursday all right for a visit to Akeminster?" Musa asked Mr Mwingi and also looked at Richard for his confirmation.

"It's fine by me," Richard said.

"Thursday it is."

Back at the hotel they ordered whisky for the men, Martini and lemonade for the women.

"You secure your investment in Kenya," Mwanga said, "and we'll buy up some units. As soon as you're ready, come on down to Nairobi. There we'll settle everything. I can't be fairer than that."

At that moment their guest was announced, and Musa went down to collect him. Like Mr Mwanga, the minister had a very deep voice, and laughter that boomed around the room. Mwanga introduced Richard to him as a "friend of Kenya", and the two men shook hands.

"So you're the man investing in our country."

"Yes. I'm so glad you're coming down to Akeminster this Thursday."

"Wouldn't have missed it. You're a friend, I hear, of the Foreign Secretary."

"Our paths tend to cross."

"That's just wonderful."

The next morning, his mother woke him.

"Thought you'd appreciate an early call," she said.

"That time already, huh?"

"Lucy rang last night – twice."

"Any message?"

"No."

"Can't have been important then."

"Why not ring her?"

"I will – later."

"What do you fancy for breakfast?"

"What is there?"

"I could do scrambled eggs, toast."

"Sounds marvellous. I just need to ring the factory."

She scurried off to the kitchen while Richard called the factory on his mobile. It was Val who answered.

"Richard, hello. Lucy's been calling."

"She's called here too. Put me on to Sam, would you..."

"Sam here. Richard, hello."

"Get ready, Sam, for the big one. We've got some very important guests on Thursday."

"You had a good meeting then."

"Excellent. Keep the guys busy. Keep three units fully operational for demos."

"Who's coming?"

"Only the Minister of Development for the government of Kenya – plus four support staff. They're not expecting to stay overnight, so it's a flying visit – but you will need to organise a buffet. Call the *Gazette*, get some coverage."

"Wow, it's all happening!"

"I'll explain more when I get back. Also, can you find out about Gothenburg? I'd like to get the initial training over next week, and the proper operating instructions after the plant has been delivered."

"You think, then, we'll be able to buy new plant?"

"I'm ninety-nine per cent certain. Listen, I've got to go. I need to see someone today and if I can conclude that meeting by three you'll see me later."

"Okay, good luck."

While breakfast was cooking he phoned Mr Waterton.

"Richard Nunn here. I'd like to brief you re my meeting with Mr Mwingi, the Minister of Development in Kenya. Extremely useful session. I think they're planning to buy our units as soon as the factory's operational. They've also agreed to help on the export side."

"Pat yourself on the back. What I suggest you do now is get further details concerning the finance they're offering. And you'll need some ballpark revenue figures. If you could let me have the revised schedule incorporating new figures, it would be extremely useful. Then I can forward your application."

"I can sort all that out early next week. I need a firm indication of the likely outcome and an idea when approval might be granted."

"I'll do my utmost and, bearing in mind the size of the funding, it shouldn't take long. I think we're probably looking at about a month for an offer in principle."

FIFTEEN

On Thursday, Richard picked up the Kenyan delegation from the Akeminster station, knowing the Discovery was roomy enough to accommodate them all – Mwanga, Musa, the minister, and the two women. There was a welcoming party back at the factory, including Val and Samantha. With the preliminaries over, they took a tour of the factory, Mr Purcell having joined them.

In the inventory room they put on overalls. The workshop was humming with activity, even with plant they'd ceased to manufacture. Everyone was busy, in a businesslike atmosphere, which Richard assumed must have been Samantha's doing.

"Well done," he whispered to her.

"Joint effort," she said. "Val did most of it."

"She's a pearl."

"You think it's done the trick?"

"Deal's in the bag, it's got to be. Mind, we'll have to move fast on the new plant."

"Aren't you going to wait till the contract's signed?"

"Too cautious! I'm for heading out to Gothenburg as soon as I can."

"You're the boss…"

By now all the employees had lined up for handshakes, supervised by Purcell. Richard took over.

"Hope Mr Purcell has been looking after you," he said to Mwingi.

"He has indeed. Mr Purcell has filled us in on Ashgrow's illustrious history."

"We're impressed," Mwanga added.

"May I?" Samantha asked. "There are a few things more to see."

"Lead on."

The group set off, and in conversation with Mr Mwanga Richard discovered he'd got a degree in civil engineering, and that Musa was a quantity surveyor.

Samantha briefly explained the working of some of the units, and even organised an impromptu demonstration. The unit had massive tyres, designed to carry a heavy load. There was a crane mounted on its structure as lifting gear, and a small attachment so that it could also be used as a digger. It was fuelled by diesel. Mr Mwingi seemed particularly enthusiastic about this unit, and saw it as ideal for use in Kenya. He asked Samantha if he could drive it, and once given the go-ahead he climbed up for a test drive. He turned the key and started the engine, and with enormous confidence drove through the factory door, to the applause of all the staff. After a few circuits of the yard he brought it to a stop and insisted that Mr Mwanga should have a go.

"I can think of several uses for such a machine," he said. "Not to mention the export opportunities. We should put in a tentative order for six now – the rest can be made under licence."

Miss Kyombe asked a question: "What's the working

life of one of these units?"

"It depends on the maintenance regime, and usage," Samantha replied.

"They require regular servicing then?"

"Naturally. A complete overhaul once every three years is about average."

Samantha continued the tour. At a small mechanical digger, Mr Mwanga stopped to look at it. He tried to kick-start it, but gave up.

"Battery looks flat on this one," he said. Then he muttered something incomprehensible, before adding: "You got any more of these?"

"I'm afraid not. It's not in demand. We only make them to order."

Mr Mwanga next took a great deal of interest in a soil carrier. "This looks ideal for our small roads."

"Let's get to the point," Mwingi added. "What we're looking at here is a deal in technology transfer."

Richard could hardly disguise his excitement.

"I'm happy to recommend we proceed," the minister concluded. "Send us your proposal, ASAP. I'll make sure it gets to the Finance Ministry."

They took lunch in the boardroom, a light buffet, no alcohol. Bertram got into small talk with Mr Mwingi, who asked him if he also knew the Foreign Secretary.

"Personally," Bertram said. "Been my MP for years."

"He's approachable?"

"Very. And a very good listener."

"I'd like to meet him."

"I'm sure that could be arranged."

At this point Tolchard from the *Gazette* was announced.

"Send him in," Richard said. "You don't mind a few words with him?" he asked, turning to Mwingi.

"Back home I have no problem with press people. Here I understand they print whatever they like."

"That's the price of liberal democracy."

They all laughed at the joke.

Val ushered the journalist in, and found a place for the interview. He seemed very keen on the two women and started to talk to them first. Mwanga kept a close eye on that, to ensure they weren't being coaxed into saying something detrimental. He introduced himself, and very adroitly manoeuvred Tolchard away. The interview commenced.

Samantha dealt with the two women. Richard was relaxed, and talking to Bertram.

"Deal's as good as done," he said.

"Not in my book."

"What's the problem?"

"I don't say there is one. I think as a general rule it's politic to take things slowly."

"Ye of little faith!"

"Anyway all this requires a full meeting of the board."

"I wasn't intending to bypass *that* stage."

"I'm sure you weren't, Richard."

"I suppose you're thinking about Lucy."

"That had crossed my mind."

"Don't worry. I'll call her tomorrow. I was bound to do that anyway before Sam and I zoom off to Gothenburg."

"I think you should hold back on that."

"I don't question your judgement, Bertram, but I would have to say I disagree with you there."

"Oh well. We shall see what we shall see."

So absorbed had they been in conversation that Tolchard had slipped away, having completed his interview, without the debrief that Richard had intended. "Damn it!" he said.

SIXTEEN

The report when it came out highlighted the proposed deal the company was about to enter into, which would mean transferring the manufacturing process to Kenya, with all the benefits that would bring to both parties. It placed great emphasis on the Kenyan government's approval of Ashgrow, and was generally much too positive in tone. Richard was not impressed.

"I take it you've read this report," he said to Bertram.

"Yes. Surprising, isn't it? Seems to suggest the deal is done and dusted."

"When nothing's been finalised. Why have they done this?"

"I've no idea. Tolchard said he'd be in touch before going to press."

"What do we do?"

"You tell me."

"We ought to demand a correction."

"Is that really a good idea?"

"Perhaps not. I'll ring Mwanga. Ask for an explanation."

"That's not the only person you should call. I faxed the report to Lucy."

"You did what!"

"Sorry. I felt she needed to know."

"Thanks for nothing. Keep your powder dry, that's my advice, Bertram."

Val, on the other hand, was impressed with the article. "Clever you," she said to Richard.

"Well, thanks – send Sam in, will you…"

"What is it?" Sam asked.

"It's this article."

"Oh, that. Mr Purcell did sound upset."

"What did he say?"

"That Lucy hit the roof."

"That's all I need."

"Talk to her. Tell her what happened."

The phone rang, and Val answered. She turned and said, "And you'd better tell Brian Mcintyre what happened."

"What's *he* want?" Richard took the phone.

"You've kept me completely in the dark," Brian raged. "How on earth have you raised the funds?"

"Don't believe all you read in the papers, Brian."

"The story's wrong?"

"Just a bit. But don't worry – I'll sort it." He immediately called Mwanga. "That reporter," he said. "You were right. Gone and printed whatever took his fancy. He has emailed me his report"

"That's your English press for you."

"Somehow he seems to think the transfer of technology is already in place, and that a site's already been chosen in Nairobi. Where did he get that from?"

"Beats me. Mr Mwingi's mistake perhaps was to tell him to put the story in its best possible light."

Next, Richard phoned up Tolchard, who said, "I wondered when you'd call."

"You did, did you? I don't suppose it ever occurs to you to try and report the facts?"

"There are facts, and there are opinions. It's my job to report both."

"It's not your job to peddle harmful propaganda."

"Sorry, but I'd have thought that article does nothing but good for Ashgrow."

"We're not media celebrities! We're running a business!"

"I'm well aware of that, Mr Nunn."

"You haven't heard the last of this."

At this point Lucy was waiting on the other line. She was furious. "What the hell is going on?"

"Lucy, please…"

"What you've done is put assets at risk without shareholder approval."

"Lucy, I'm not selling anything."

"You're selling your soul, Richard – and all on the back of my father's money…"

That did it. Richard slammed down the phone. Already, his second letter of resignation was forming in his mind. He put on his jacket, and was heading for his car when John came in.

"What do *you* want?"

"A receipt, for the £5,000 you withdrew."

"I haven't got it. Just show the cash as Kenyan project expenses."

"I'm sure you know our policy."

"Stuff your policy. I'll sign an IOU."

"That doesn't set a good example for the rest of senior management."

"What on earth are you on about?"

"I don't approve of cash going out without the proper supporting documents."

"Watch my lips. I'll sign an IOU."

"Are you saying this is a personal loan?"

"It's not a loan at all. Just do what I tell you."

"It's too large an amount for an IOU."

"Who do you think you're talking to?"

"A system is a system. If you breach it again, I'll be forced to make a report to the board."

"Look, John, if you want me to fire you, just keep doing what you're doing. Or would you prefer to resign? Now out of my way. I'm out of here."

He went back home, and having munched half-heartedly on a sandwich poured himself a whisky, then another, then another. He slumped on the settee and dozed a drunken doze, which was shattered by the phone ringing. In no fit state to answer it, he let the answer machine cut in. It was Lucy. When he woke again it was four in the afternoon. He stumbled into the kitchen, where he splashed his face and made coffee. He dialled for a taxi. While he waited for it to arrive he played back Lucy's message, together with four others – three from Val, one from Sam. He ignored them.

The taxi arrived and took him back to the office. Val watched him, rather dishevelled, getting out. He struggled for change, and tottered to the foyer.

"God," she said, "what happened?"

"Don't get excited."

"Lucy's after you. She called half a dozen times."

"*She* would. What about some coffee?"

"There's some already made." She bustled away and cornered Sam. "He's been drinking," she told her.

"That's all we need."

Val poured a coffee, and was skimpy on the milk. "Drink this," she said, bursting into Richard's office.

"Thanks."

"Richard, I'm off early tonight. I'll phone you at home."

"Don't be so hideously grave."

"As I said, I'll call you."

"Goodbye."

She left, and Samantha came in. "Feeling better?"

He smiled, embarrassed.

The phone rang and Sam intercepted, saying no, he wasn't here. It was Lucy.

"Why tell her I'm not here?"

"Look at the state you're in."

"Yes, you're right, of course." He was touched by her concern.

She looked away, overcome by her shyness. "There's a report you should look at," she said, "on one of the new machines."

"I'll read it tomorrow. Would you mind driving me home a little later?"

"Of course, I'll drop you."

An hour later they were ensconced in her red GTI, a car she was particularly proud of – alloy wheels, cream leather seats, all immaculately clean. Her perfume transfused its whole atmospheric interior, and Richard, sober now, could already feel a new priapic twitch. It was a beautiful drive, with the last of the afternoon light fading, and the trees silhouetted on the hillsides.

"So wonderfully rural here," he said.

"You hardly notice, when you're born here."

"You don't know what you've got." He was ogling her tight black skirt, riding up her thighs.

They drew up to his house, and he went inside, somehow having failed to find the pretext on which he could ask her in. He was horny and lonely and sick of his marriage. He switched on the TV and then went into the kitchen. He took out a clean glass and poured more whisky, this time adding ice cubes. The phone rang, and it was, not surprisingly, Lucy,

"Where have you been?" she shrieked.

"Sorry, love – I've had meetings all day."

"Well now that I've pinned you down, what about this article?"

"Between them the *Gazette* and your Mr Bertram screwed up."

"Bertram?"

"I can see no other explanation."

"That's not how he sees it."

"You're not upset with *me*?"

"I worry, Richard, about the money."

"I worry about that too. But you don't get money in the first place if you're not prepared to gamble – that's what your daddy always said."

"He also knew how to consolidate."

"And don't you think that's what I'm trying to do?"

"I don't doubt the intentions. It's the method I find hair-raising."

"You're a hard woman."

"Here in the States they think I'm an honorary man."

"What's that do for your feminist hackles?"

"We'll talk tomorrow. Meanwhile get this *Gazette* thing sorted."

"You can depend on me."

He put the phone down and swigged his whisky, then refilled his glass and sat in the lounge. He watched but didn't take in what was on TV, his mind wandering up Samantha's skirt. In his haze he couldn't be sure exactly what he felt – was it lust only? – but wished she was with him now. Finally his head slumped forward, and he slept, snoring loudly.

The phone woke him again, and it was Val. "You all right?" she said.

"Everything's just great," he said sarcastically.

"I'm coming over."

"What's the time?"

"Eight-thirty-ish."

"There's really no need."

"I'm coming." She hung up and in twenty minutes was knocking at his door.

"Look at the state of you," she said.

Richard eased off on the whisky and agreed to eat something – anything, a sandwich would do. Then he fell asleep in her lap when they'd settled down to watch TV.

She shook him gently. "Come on, I'll help you to your room."

She put him in his pyjamas and tucked him into bed.

"Wimp!" she thought, as she left, "but I can't help mothering the guy."

SEVENTEEN

He arrived early at the office the following morning, just as the foreman had opened the factory, and before his office staff. The telephone sprang into action immediately, and it was Lucy, still up at three in the morning Stateside, it seemed.

"Listen," she said, "I've tried to smooth this thing over with Bertram, but he's not happy."

"*He's* not happy? *I'm* not happy!"

"Try to be objective. I know you feel you have to prove yourself."

"That's a cheap shot."

"We've all got to try to work together on this. How about if I come over next weekend?"

"Well it would be nice to see you once in a while."

"You *know* what I mean," she said sincerely.

"Okay, I'll be there. Well maybe not this weekend actually. I'm planning this trip to Gothenburg."

"All right then, after you return from Gothenberg."

"Yes, we'll try for that. Though I am expecting to hear from the IFC, and we won't really be able to delay shipping the plant to Kenya."

"We'll touch base. Love you."

"Love you too, Lucy."

"What's she after?" he thought when he put the phone down. Whatever it was, he wasn't going to postpone his trip to Gothenburg. Just then Val arrived.

"Must say you're looking a lot better today," she said.

He made a motion towards her but she pushed him gently away. Other office folk were streaming into the building.

According to reports from Gothenburg, the Swedish company was willing to honour its quote on the price of the machinery despite Ashgrow's failure to place an order. What was really needed was confirmation of the IFC's backing, he thought, as he angled his chair to the window. He picked up the phone and called Nairobi.

"Bwana," Mwanga greeted him.

"How are we progressing?"

"This is an austere time economically, to be honest. When are you coming over?"

"Do I need to come over?" Richard asked.

"Yes – to look for a factory!"

"You have some ideas for premises?"

"I'll get Miss Kyombe to pull something together."

"Good. My wife and I are hoping to get over – in two to three weeks, say."

"We look forward to that."

Richard mulled it over. The only thing missing was backing from the IFC. He put in a call to Waterton.

"Richard, good to hear from you. I expect you're wondering about your application."

"Yes. You know how it is. People everywhere are

pressing for decisions. Long and the short of it is, if we don't get the IFC's approval our only option is to upgrade existing machinery rather than buy new."

"Personally I think your application stands a very good chance. But the final decision of course is politics not commerce."

"How soon will I know?"

"Let me make some calls. I'll get back to you."

His heart leapt. It sounded as if it was all just a mere formality. He searched his drawers for his copy of the application he'd submitted, and was still looking when Samantha walked in.

"Lost something?"

"Our copy of that application for funding for the Kenya project."

"Oh, that – I gave it to Val to file."

"Thank God. Thought I'd lost it."

"Richard, I need to talk to you."

"I'm listening."

"You've fired John."

"That isn't quite correct. What I've asked him to do is resign."

"But why? He's easily the longest serving member here, and he's certainly one of the most loyal."

"He was undermining my authority."

"He was doing his job."

"Look, I just don't need this, Samantha."

"But you just can't make decisions of that magnitude and expect us all to agree."

"You'd better be careful what you say, Sam."

"What's the point of my being a director if I'm not ever consulted about anything?"

"I don't need your opinion for every little thing."

"This is *not* a little thing!"

"Sam, when I need you I'll call you. Now, if you don't mind, I'm busy."

His face was ashen when she left, but he immediately dialled her extension.

"I forgot to ask in all that excitement," he said, "but you *have* got the Gothenburg thing sorted – yes?"

"All booked! Anything else I can do for you?"

"No need to jump down my throat!" He put down the phone, vaguely worried that hers would be the next resignation. He didn't want to lose her. As he was pondering this, Val had important news.

"Faxes from Kenya," she said.

"Good, let me have a look."

He started to browse through them, making a note of cost and location, and the kind of facility on offer. By one o'clock lunchtime he'd covered so much ground he decided to mull it over with one of his surveyor friends, Tim Bridgewater, who, it seemed, couldn't see anything untoward. Then, with John much on his conscience, he phoned Lucy.

"What is it?" she asked. "I'm in a meeting."

"It's about John."

"What about him?"

"I've fired him."

"You've fired the accountant?"

"I believe that's what I said."

There was a pause while Lucy weighed what he said. "Actually, Richard, I don't blame you. I've come close to firing him myself."

"You've had run-ins too…"

"Yes. Plenty. How's he taking it?"

"Better than Samantha is."

"She's a cow. Ignore her."

"Lucy, what's come over you?"

"I have only the company's interests at heart – and of course yours."

"When am I going to see you?"

"Not sure. I'll ring."

"God!" he said to himself, putting the phone down, flabbergasted. He called Samantha back in, who was pert with him still.

"Will you please calm down and listen! I wanted to tell you John won't be with us and that's a majority decision."

"What do you mean, majority decision?"

"Lucy backs me on this."

Sam was flummoxed.

"Look, Sam, I'm sorry. Sometimes these difficult decisions have to be made – by the person who can make them."

"It's all so Machiavellian."

"Don't take it too much to heart. Look – *you* can appoint his replacement. I won't interfere in any way at all."

A large tear formed in her eye, but she didn't let it tumble down her cheek. Richard was such a bastard.

EIGHTEEN

On Wednesday, Richard and Samantha were finally off to Gothenburg. There was a glow at Richard's inner core, which was all to do with the fulfilment of his dreams and how he was now beginning to establish credentials as a successful businessman. Just in case his reconciliation with Samantha wasn't going to work, he'd decided to be especially friendly with Lucy. But the deal had to be on *his* terms, and to achieve that he was prepared to do anything, no matter who got hurt. He was, at this point, still dependent on Lucy's wealth, so appeasing her was his first priority. He would have liked a tender relationship with Sam, but that he was prepared to surrender to attain his goal. With all these calculations in mind, he rang Lucy. It was three a.m. New York time.

"Sorry to call at such an eccentric hour."

"It's okay – I'm still up, just."

"Guessed you would be. That city never sleeps. Look, I'm planning to get over there."

"That's wonderful. When?"

"Next week. I'm in Sweden for three days, then I'm free."

"Can't wait."

"Love you."

"Love you too. Oh, good news, by the way. Guess what my latest bonus is."

"Half a mill?"

"*Two* million. Isn't that wonderful?"

"Simply fantastic – and ironic, really. I want support for a mere five and they can't make up their minds."

"Let me know how you get on. You can always liquidate stock."

"I'm trying to avoid that eventuality."

"Very heroic, darling. Take care. I'll see you next week."

"Ciao."

He reflected how he worked hard for a salary of £70,000, while Lucy was given a bonus of $2,000,000. Crazy world.

Samantha rolled up in a taxi and dragged her things out of the boot. He went out to help, transferring her luggage to the Discovery.

The post had just arrived, and there was no one in the factory. He made coffee for them both. Sam got busy with files on her computer.

"Give me a ring when you're ready," he said.

Some of the staff including Val now began to arrive, and to kill time Richard took a stroll round the workshop. The machines were being prepared for a production run, and Stewart, Samantha's subordinate, was dishing out instructions. Val was delivering post.

"Can I see you?" Richard said. He went back to his office and awaited her.

"Yes?" she said.

"I'm expecting a message from Mr Waterton's office, and one from Mr Mwanga. Please ensure you fax them on to me."

"But you're only away for three days."

"A lot can happen, and things move fast."

"Okay – leave it with me. That be all?"

"Yes, that's all. We're leaving soon." He checked the time on his watch, then without warning embraced and kissed her.

"What are you doing?"

"Just wanted to say farewell."

"Why couldn't *I* go with you, instead of Samantha?"

"It's Samantha's skills I need."

She knew the logic of this. "Then let's get together when you get back."

"I can't wait."

They were met at Gothenburg Airport by a Swedish representative and driven to the Hilton International.

"If only the traffic were this light in London," Richard remarked.

The buildings were as in any modern city, but the roads were clean and the people relaxed. Samantha studied their itinerary, and the technical brief, the schedule being short and opportunities few. When they reached the hotel and had checked in, she suggested visiting the factory immediately – half a day had already gone.

"Don't you want to eat first?" Richard said.

"Time presses, Richard."

"You're right, of course. I'll tell the manager to arrange for a taxi in ten minutes."

Their transport was waiting for them when they came down and the taxi drove them to the factory unit, located outside the centre of town. It was on a plot filled with small to medium sized firms, with just a few cars parked. It seemed affluent. They were met by the managing director, Mr Gabrielson.

"Welcome to Sweden. We're very pleased to see you."

"Our pleasure," Richard smiled.

"Trust you had a good trip?"

"Very good indeed," Samantha replied.

Mr Gabrielson took them inside and introduced them to the production manager, then to an IT controller.

"These will be your immediate contacts. Any queries, talk to our quality controller. Failing that, the finance officer."

They got on with business, with the promise of a table booked for seven that evening, Samantha getting on with her training session with the IT personnel, while Richard spoke with the quality controller.

Richard looked at the production unit he intended to acquire. It had two large bearings at each end, with various manufacturing operations performing in the middle leading to the assembly of each part to a semi-completed unit. The unit was then transferred via a platform that was driven by an air-film transporter, without causing any friction. The platform was attached to a semi-permanent structure, so that when the two rostrums were connected it transformed into a production area, shifting the components made earlier into a larger unit. Finally, the unit was fitted with wheels and painted.

Richard was impressed, and slightly anxious that the firm shouldn't sell to rivals in the UK.

"No problem there. It isn't our aim to make the facility commonly available. We'll have to apply to the Ministry of Trade for permission to export, though."

Richard saw why permission was required when he spotted the mark of the Swedish Army on the equipment. He was relieved because he wanted *his* factory alone to use the production facility. After seeing it in action he rejoined Samantha in the IT lab. She was being trained in how to set measurements and calculate modifications. She was scribbling notes and looking at her manual.

The IT consultant switched on a computer for Richard, which was networked to the one that Samantha was working on. He paid particular attention to the codes she was inputting, and compared them to the working of the plant he'd just examined.

"I feel we can train our guys to handle the process without any problem." He looked at Samantha.

"Now you take over the technical training and let me see if you can do it," she suggested. She pushed away her keyboard, having saved her work. She was sure Richard wouldn't be able to handle the codes.

"What are you going to do?"

"Modify their formula and then test run the result to see what happens."

"Don't rush."

When the consultant moved away from his desk to change the disk, he asked her not to modify it in his presence as he'd thought of some additional function he didn't want the Swedish company to know about. Sam showed her displeasure at this.

It was six when the first part of their training was over, and Gabrielson suggested they finish for the day, and under shadow of nightfall they repaired to the Hilton.

Sunset was in its final afterglow and the streetlights were bright against the darkening night.

"Why didn't you let me amend their computer codes?" asked Samantha. "I really wanted to see how my formula worked."

"I think we can put this plant to more than one use and I didn't want to give away our secrets."

"What secrets?"

"Tell you later."

"They'll have access to our processor as part of the maintenance arrangement, so I don't see how you can keep any secrets."

"I'll tell you everything when we're alone."

Since when did he know about computers, she wondered.

Richard, sensing her annoyance, helped himself to a newspaper from the pocket at the rear of the driver's seat. It was in English, and he pretended to read. All passed quietly thereafter, and when they got to the hotel desk, to his disappointment, there were no messages.

The driver waited outside, as they had only twenty minutes to be ready for dinner. Richard fished a telephone number from his pocket diary, and dialled Val from his room phone.

"Val, it's Richard."

"What a surprise. Missing me already?"

"Of course, pet. How are things at the factory?"

"We're all cracking on."

"Has Lucy phoned?"

"No."

"Any other calls?"

"Only the bloke from the IFC."

126

"What do you mean, 'only'?"

"Just my little joke, Richard. There was no message. Bloke said he'd ring you next week."

"That all?"

"He said you'd be pleased."

"If they contact you again, ask them to fax you, in case it's urgent – and let me know immediately."

He showered and dressed for dinner.

Samantha, having rung her mother as usual, was ready before him. Hers was a black, knee-length dress with a crossover at the top, set off with a necklace of black and red beads. While she waited she watched some TV, surprised she could tune to Super Sky and the BBC.

Richard, still oblivious to the fact that she felt he'd interfered – precious as she was over her area of expertise (a typical computer boff) – tapped on her door with a lightness in his tread.

"Our taxi is here. You look enchanting," he told her.

She ignored his compliments.

The car threaded its way through a network of streets interspersed with canals. Tram tracks ran parallel to all the routes they took.

"First visit to Gothenburg?" Gustav, the driver, asked.

"First ever visit to Sweden," Richard said. "What's that tower on the left?"

"The Guldhedens Vattentorn – the water tower. Something of a landmark." Gustav brought the Volvo to a halt outside the Bistro Mannerstrom and ushered them out.

"Thank you, Gustav." Sam smoothed down her jacket and fussed with her hair.

Gabrielson, Bergman, and their respective wives –

Christina and Selma – were waiting. Champagne was served, with a toast to success. The meal was breast of wild Swedish duck with a confit of bacon purée, and potatoes served in a cabbage shell – which they enjoyed.

Samantha softened as the evening wore on, though she was still a little short with Richard. He ignored her little asides, and carried on as normal. That infuriated her, a feeling compensated for by being the star attraction because of her computer expertise.

"Richard also has computer knowledge," she said, rather sarcastically.

"You're a man with wide experience for one so young," Gabrielson complimented.

"These days you've got to keep abreast, or you sink," Richard explained. "I'm never afraid of the new."

All four strolled after dinner in the Avenyn, a short distance away, and famous for its huge bronze fountain. When Richard and Sam found themselves alone, he ticked her off.

"You're not giving out the best signal," he said. "You didn't come here to show off your computer skills. May I remind you I'm your MD. If I choose not to insert your code into their program, there's a reason. Understand?"

"No, I don't. What reason?"

"It's like this. I reckon with only a slight modification, we can manufacture a small carrier that the military can use to transport equipment over difficult terrain. Just imagine the potential in that!" He took out a diagram. "Look."

She was amazed. "Why can't they see this themselves?"

"High moral purpose, I should think."

Samantha pointed to a part of the diagram. "This is the bit we change?"

"I would imagine so. It's up to you and the team."

"Richard, it's brilliant!"

"Not just a pretty face, eh?"

Their hands were gently touching as they walked.

"Friends again?" Richard asked.

They stopped, looked at each other, then softly she kissed him.

They returned to the bronze fountain, where they'd arranged to meet Gustav, who drove them back to the hotel.

"You think we ought to write the new code now?"

"It's only eleven," he said. "I don't see why not."

"Your room or mine?"

"Mine."

"Okay. Let me slip into something more comfortable."

After changing, she knocked on his door, wearing jogging bottom and shirt. His eyes fell on the necklace she wore hanging gracefully around her neck with the triangular shaped pendant resting gently between her breasts, visible as the shirt top button was undone. She'd got her laptop, which she switched on immediately once he'd asked her in.

"Have you rung your mother?" he asked her.

"Several times today, yes. Thanks for asking."

They pulled up two chairs to his correspondence table and got down to work. Almost effortlessly, their modification worked with the original program, and both were staggered.

"God, that's easy," she said.

Richard got up and filled two glasses with cognac, and as they began sipping their drinks, somehow they found themselves sitting down together on the edge of his bed.

Richard lifted her necklace and said, "This thing suits you perfectly, I haven't seen you wearing it before."

"I only wear this at night, I feel at ease when I put it on."

Richard smiled and let his fingers skim her breasts. Samantha smiled coyly and didn't protest as he went to undo the second button, exposing her bra. He came closer and very gently kissed her lips. She sat motionless.

He looked at her, full of lust, and bent down to kiss her breasts.

"Not happy with Lucy, huh!" she giggled, and pushed him on the bed kissing him furiously.

Samantha undid all her shirt buttons and untied her bra, which at that instant came off.

He lunged at her nipples, which were hard and empurpled, and sucked. He unbuckled his belt, removed her jogging bottom and put his hand down her panties just as his proudly crowing cock popped out. She resisted, turning that member aside. She got up, half pulling on her underwear, which, gently and caressing, he removed a second time. Slowly he massaged her breasts, then raised her ankles up on his shoulders, easing his throbbing phallus into the velvet his fingers had already probed and made moist.

"There," he said, and they went at it several times that night.

NINETEEN

The Sweden trip had been altogether a glowing success, with Samantha particularly showing a gleam in her eye. Negotiations to acquire the plant had been finalised, and the draft contract had been drawn up. Richard's only problem now was the resumption of the professional relationship he'd formerly had with Sam, which to her could never be the same. She wasn't predatory like him, and their night of passion wasn't something she'd easily forget.

It was late on Friday afternoon when they arrived at Heathrow Airport. Richard collected the car from the parking bay and struck out for the M4 before the worst of the weekend traffic. Sam was tired, and luxuriated in the passenger seat, as a result of having had very little sleep for the previous two nights. Richard tuned the radio for jazz. The evening sun made lengthening shadows around them.

With about twenty minutes left on their drive she suddenly woke up. "Kiss me," she said.

Richard bent his head and kissed her lips, keeping his eyes on the road. She embraced him.

"Steady, Sam – I've got to concentrate."

She loosened her grip. "Shall we meet tonight?"

"I thought you'd want to spend time with your mother."

"She'll understand."

"I'll see what messages there are. I'll call you."

"But I guess we mustn't be seen."

"That's okay. You can come to the cottage. Anyway, what's all this! You're normally so reserved."

"I had a stunted teenage. Got to come out some time!"

When he reached the town he drove to the factory. "Better just check everything's okay. Want me to take you home first?"

"You going to be long?"

"Hopefully not."

"That's okay. I'll wait."

"On the other hand, I might be. Think I will take you home. Meet you later."

He dropped her off en route to the factory, where there was a big surprise in store. A note among the paperwork on his desk told him Lucy was back.

"Shit!" he said. "Bitch should have warned me!" He rang Sam and told her the news.

"Typical!" she said.

"Never mind. Catch you on Monday."

He took a brief look around the factory and locked the front door, and then drove home. This wasn't in his plans: instead of making love to Val or Samantha he'd now have to entertain Lucy, who'd probably screwed like a rabbit herself in the plush apartments of New York. He parked up by the picket fence and dragged his luggage to the porch. Just as he'd found his key, Lucy flung open the door."

"Surprise!"

"Darling, you're home." He embraced her fondly.

"Big hugs!"

"You should have let me know."

"I've got a few days unexpectedly free."

"That's wonderful – and you look fantastic!" Inside, he crashed down on the settee. "Long day," he sighed.

"My darling needs some sleep," she said, stroking his forehead.

"I'll survive. Though I don't fancy cooking. Let's eat out."

"Exactly my thoughts. I'll book somewhere."

He took a nap while she phoned, booking a place at the Moonlight, which was a steak house in one of the neighbouring villages, where the Moore family had long been known. Over supper, they talked about Gothenburg.

"Everything's in place. I'm just waiting on the loan application. Wish they'd hurry up. It's not as if it's a vast amount I'm asking for."

"Don't worry, I'm sure it'll all go through."

"Don't quite know what I'll do if it *isn't* approved." Behind this comment lay the thought that he'd rather scrap the whole scheme than ask Lucy for financial assistance. Then suddenly he was overwhelmed with fatigue and longed for his bed.

"And you must be jetlagged," he said.

"Me – I've had two days to recover working in London."

"You returned when?" he quizzed.

"Wednesday."

"Wednesday? But when I rang you that day you were in New York." He felt confused.

"It's only a seven-hour flight, remember?"

"Bloody crafty woman," he thought.

They settled the bill, and after a polite brief chat with

the restaurateur drove back to the cottage, Richard dozing all the way.

"Sleepy head," she said, turning off the engine.

"Where are we?"

"Home, sweet home."

He dragged himself upstairs and fell into bed, where through the fog of his tiredness he could faintly hear Lucy in the bedroom. He peered out from under the duvet and saw she was already in only her bra and knickers, all of which she took off before climbing into bed. He touched the top of her thigh and thought it felt moist. Then, spontaneously, she was over him and caressing his balls. That perked him up and she took his hardness in her mouth, her tongue and her lips expertly coaxing him on to the threshold she craved. He palpated her breasts. He rolled her over, and now on top of her spread her legs and thrust down hard and deep.

Exhausted, he slept, to be woken again when she'd got one her sex aids probing round his rectum. His cock stood up again, and on her haunches now she slipped it between her legs. He was sore, but kept on going, Lucy insatiable tonight. They went a third and a fourth time, with a dildo and vibrator, and finally they slept.

"What time is it?"

"Come on, Richard. It's after half past eleven."

"God, I should be at the office, checking the mail!" He tore out of bed and put on his gown.

"You're not going in today, surely?"

"Got to. You not coming?"

"Count me out. Can't it wait till Monday?"

"No! I'm anxious for the reply to my loan application – they rang whilst I was in Gothenberg."

"Well you can't do much today, even if there is something."

"Perhaps I'll get Val to drop it in, when she brings the shopping."

"She isn't coming. I rang her."

"You rang her? Why?"

"Because I know what's going on. She as good as me in bed, Rich?"

"I don't know what you're talking about."

"Don't worry. Go ahead, admit it. Don't think I'll allow these little adventures of yours to jeopardise the business."

"You're paranoid."

"I'll still stump up the five million, if I have to – even if you *are* screwing the office tart."

"She's not a tart. And I won't take a penny from you!"

She let him go, but he spent an age in the bathroom. She knocked on the door. "Come on – I'm hungry. I thought we'd hit the County Hotel for brunch."

He was astonished, and it only made him think of the sexual adventures *she* must be having. Moreover it was with an amazing sense of calm that they drove to the hotel, which for the time of day wasn't that busy. They'd just settled down to a cappuccino followed by scrambled egg and salmon when Alex and Andrew arrived.

"Won't you join us?" Richard asked.

"Be delighted."

Inevitably, they talked about Kenya.

"Let me say everyone's so impressed with Richard's determination."

"Richard has many qualities," Lucy averred.

"Let me know when you're heading off for Kenya and I'll notify the embassy. *They'll* look after you."

"That's going to be a great help, I'm sure, Alex. Thanks."

"Not at all. Now, got to rush, I'm afraid. Can't miss my surgery." As he was leaving, Richard pulled him to one side and told him about his extra-mural plans regarding the military, and asked for help getting in touch with the procurement office.

"I'll see what I can do. Let us know when you've manufactured it."

"Thanks. You'd better get going. David Tolchard's seen you."

"Thanks for the warning."

They left through a back door, an escape that didn't go unnoticed by the reporter.

"God, he's seen us all together *again*," gasped Lucy.

"So what?"

"He's a journalist. If I remember correctly this is the third time he's seen us with Alex in the past three months – and you know he's after a story."

"That's his problem."

"Too often it's *our* problem."

"Don't worry, I'll take care of him."

"Once and for all, I hope." She changed the subject. "I'm planning to ask Bertram and his wife out for supper – tomorrow."

"Best bib and tucker."

"You could say that – at the Moonlight."

"Where else is there?" he smiled.

Richard found it hard to sleep that night, unable to banish thoughts of his mail on the mat at work, and news from the IFC. He was anxious.

Sunday was a lazy day, with not much excitement until the evening, and the dinner engagement at the Moonlight. He drank too much, trying to blot out his anxiety, and also to accelerate himself into the following day – Monday!

They returned home at 1.30. Lucy fell asleep in no time, but Richard lay tossing and turning. What would happen if the IFC refused to back his project? He'd have to leave the company, and he didn't much fancy managing an operation that wasn't his own.

He racked his brains for alternative projects within the company, but couldn't come up with even one. Nor did he much relish living in this little town for longer than absolutely necessary. With no exciting challenge, that would be unbearable.

He decided that were he unsuccessful in securing funds, he'd tender his resignation, and, having reached this decision, he felt more at peace with himself. He resolved also not to end up living as Lucy's mere sex slave.

He was wide awake, and long before the alarm. Outside the birds were singing. The clock said 5.30 – half an hour to go. Daylight filled the curtains. He could hear work on the farms, distantly.

He pulled himself very slowly away from Lucy so as not to disturb her. Her arm was round his hip. He tried to remove it, but she resisted, and he gave in for a while. He tried again, but she wouldn't let him go. The more he tried, the more she latched on to him.

"Lucy, move over. I want to get up."

She disentangled herself and moved away. He went to the bathroom, shaved, showered, had an early breakfast of coffee and toast. He wanted to be at the office as Val arrived – had she talked to Lucy? He hung around, listening to the radio. Then he went upstairs.

"Lucy, I'm off now. I've called a taxi, left you the car."

She grunted.

"I'm off. See you later." He bent down and kissed her on the cheek, then hurried off to work.

At the office, the car park was empty.

"Blast! Val isn't here yet."

He wandered into the factory and saw Mr Hill at his desk, reading the newspaper.

"Ah, Richard, good morning. Pleasant trip?"

"Very satisfactory. How's Adam's contract?"

"Just waiting on the welding."

He went to his desk and sifted his pile of post yet again. Disappointingly, he didn't find what he was looking for, so he watched the window for Val. She was along shortly."

"Val, you're here."

"Lucy not with you?"

"No. Heavy night. She's sleeping it off. I was expecting something from the World Bank. It's not in my post."

"There was a brown envelope, I'm sure – FAO you, so I didn't open it."

"Where d'you put it?"

"On your desk."

"It's not there now."

"I'll help you look."

They couldn't find it.

"Could it be on *your* desk by mistake?"

"I'll have a look." No luck there either. "Do you suppose someone's walked off with it?" she asked.

"Bloody well hope not."

"Lucy! I'll bet she's got it."

"But she'd have told me – or maybe she wouldn't."

"Why ever not?"

"She suspects *us*."

"She can't do. How?"

"Don't ask me!"

Hugely disquieted, Richard pulled up a chair and sat down.

"You'd better phone her."

"God, I hate this!" He felt paralysed, and didn't know what to do.

Samantha arrived, and went straight to her office, where she began to empty her briefcase. Richard followed her in.

"You won't believe this," he said.

"What's happened?"

"I've lost a very important letter."

"What letter?"

"Val can remember seeing it. She thinks it's a reply to my loan application. But now it's disappeared."

"Can't help, I'm afraid. What do you think of this?"

"What is it?"

"I tried to refine my earlier code, and I think with this new instruction the thing'll work even better." She handed him a paper.

"You worked on this over the weekend?"

"It was nothing."

"I'm afraid I've been busy with Lucy."

"I know. I drove past the factory two or three times, hoping you might be in…"

"Sorry," he said apologetically. His eyes brightened. "How's your mother?"

"She's well, considering. My aunt went back yesterday. How long is Lucy staying?"

"Your guess is as good as mine." He returned to his office and put in a call to Waterton.

"I'm afraid he's away all week. Can anyone else help?"

"No, thanks – I'll call next week."

He was incredibly frustrated now, and at a complete loss. He leaned back in his chair with his hands folded at the back of his head, crossing, uncrossing his legs, repeatedly.

"Lucy rang," Val announced, bursting in. "She's on her way."

He picked up last week's production report but was unable to concentrate on it and so started pacing aimlessly. Presently Lucy drew up in the Discovery, and headed straight for his office.

"Forgot to tell you," she said. "I picked up this letter on Friday. Thought it must be important so I nearly opened it." She handed it over.

Richard hastily ripped it open. "My God, it's here! What I've been waiting for. Why didn't you tell me?"

"Slipped my mind."

He scanned the letter hastily, none too sure that Lucy hadn't opened it before him, though he gave her a look only, saying nothing.

"What's it say?" she asked.

"Application's been approved – subject that is to certain action on the part of the bank in Nairobi."

She didn't show any particular enthusiasm.

"I can see you're overjoyed," he said, sardonically.

"If you're happy, I'm happy. Remember, I did offer you a loan – $5,000,000."

"That hasn't been forgotten, dearest."

"Don't be so prickly. What I'm trying to demonstrate is this: I've no intention at all of holding you back. It's good to see you getting on."

"Don't you think that sounds a little bit patronising?"

"It wasn't meant to be patronising."

"Okay, truce. Are you still on for this Nairobi trip?"

"That depends when it is."

"Next two to three weeks, I suspect. You *could* help me look for a factory."

"Can't you take Sam for that?"

"I could, but I'd like to spend some time with you."

"Firm up on a date, and get back to me."

"Sure. Look at my hand – it's trembling."

"Exciting times, Rich. Let me warn you: the more successful you are, the more enemies you have."

"Well I'm not aware of any at the moment."

"That will change, I assure you."

"Not me! I'm going so fast I'll be on the other side before anyone knows what's hit them."

"Now that you're engrossed in the Kenya project, I think you must relinquish the chairmanship in favour of Bertram," Lucy said.

"If that makes you happy, I don't want to rock my plan. Okay then, I'm resigning as chairman with immediate effect."

"That's best for all concerned."

Val stumbled in with two cups of coffee.

"Do you know, Val," Lucy said, "I haven't had breakfast and everyone here's too busy to take me anywhere."

"I'm sure Samantha wouldn't mind joining you."

"Samantha has a code to write for the new software," Richard cut in.

"Richard – you game?"

"Half an hour. That's your lot. Booked anywhere?"

"Not necessary."

"Give me a moment while I just ring Kenya."

"It's their lunchtime now," said Val.

"I'm not driving," he said to Lucy.

She motored them out to the County Hotel, and in passing reminded him that she was off to Bristol in the afternoon for a meeting with one of her old acquaintances – a banker. They made it just in time for the last of the breakfast menu, where they had rolls and gallons of coffee.

"Sorry about that letter," she said again.

"Don't worry. Turned out right in the end."

"Well – good luck anyway."

"When are you back from Bristol?"

"Not sure. Nigel and I have a project on, but the fool refuses to relocate Stateside. It means I *could* be quite some time."

"And when are you jetting back to NY?"

"Why do you ask?"

"Only that *it could* have an impact on my arrangements."

"I'll ring my office tomorrow – get them to check the diary." She felt relaxed, secure in the knowledge that her subterfuge with the loan letter hadn't caused him suspicions.

She dropped him at the factory, and then headed out to Bristol. The first thing he did on stepping in to his office was put in his call to Nairobi.

142

"Musa, it looks like it's go. The loan application's gone through. We'd like to pay a visit. How about the twenty-eighth?"

"How long are you staying?"

"It's looking like three weeks at this moment."

"That may not be sufficient. I'll email you current property details from all the industrial parks. That'll save you time."

"What about your business?"

"Talk to Mr Kitole, at the Ministry of Finance. I'll let him know you're calling." He gave Richard the number.

"Give my regards to Mr Mwingi."

"I will. Goodbye."

Val and Samantha descended on his office.

"Has she gone?" Val asked.

"To Bristol. Back tonight."

"What happened about the letter?" Sam asked.

"Nothing really. She forgot to tell me."

"It's my opinion that envelope she gave you had already been opened."

"How do you work that out?"

"I could tell by the seal. It had been broken, and glued back not very expertly."

"Well I'll be—!"

"That must mean she knew what the letter said but deliberately kept you in the dark."

"She hates your success," Sam added.

"Can't think why. After all, our turnover is as much as her bonus."

"Can't you see? She wants this hold over you!"

"Val, if you don't mind my saying, isn't that a bit melodramatic?"

Samantha looked absolutely astonished.

"And let's not forget – she does own the factory."

"Yes, sorry."

"Don't worry. Now, could you book two seats to Nairobi for the twenty-eighth, provisional, returning in three weeks time?"

"Yes, I'll do that." Val scuttled off to her office.

"While we're away, Sam, could you please test run the production process on the new plant – ideally before we disconnect the old one for export."

"I don't know if it will have been delivered by then."

"Pressure them – it will. The bridging loan will be in place, so why not send them a deposit?"

"I'll contact them tomorrow, but I'm really not happy doing the modification until you're back."

"I'm sure you can manage. Just key in the new codes in a temporary file, until we're happy."

Sam agreed and returned to her office to get on with it. Richard prepared an email for Musa, incorporating a fund flowchart. Having had a difficult day so far he moved very slowly, and even began to feel tired. That feeling stayed with him all day, but somehow he kept awake till it was time to go home. However he looked at things, Lucy's shadow seemed to loom large.

Val drove him to the cottage and clearly wished to come inside. He said he couldn't be sure when Lucy would be back, and as she seemed to know all about their liaison it probably wasn't a good idea. Alone, he collapsed on the settee and soon was fast asleep.

When he woke, the room was completely dark. He got up and peeped outside. It was almost nine, and as yet he hadn't eaten. He couldn't be bothered to cook so he microwaved something from the freezer, which he merely picked at before he went to bed.

Lucy roused him very much later.

"God, what time is it?"

"It's three, darling."

"Uh?"

"Go back to sleep."

"You had a good day?"

"Night, darling."

Richard woke up at his usual hour and quietly got ready for work, but, on looking for the car keys, couldn't find them anywhere. Nor was the Discovery outside on the drive.

"Lucy," he said, gently rousing her from slumbers, "the car's gone."

"Uh?"

"The car – it's gone. You did lock it up properly?"

She opened her eyes. "What on earth…?"

"The car!"

"Relax. I left it with Nigel. I was over the limit, so he dropped me off. He's going to have the car sent on."

Richard phoned Val and asked her to pick him up, slightly annoyed that, having set himself a new policy regarding punctuality, he was going to be late.

"Your car broken down?" Val asked.

"Not exactly. Lucy's left it with a friend."

"Heavy night?"

"Something like that."

At work, Richard focused on the trip to Kenya. He was trawling his email, looking for news from Musa, when Samantha entered his office.

"Well done," she said. "Looks as though your adaptation *will* work."

"Excellent. Have you thought about how your mother's going to cope when you're abroad?"

"It depends how long I'm away."

"If it's a lengthy period I'm sure the firm will pay for an attendant."

"That's very generous."

"Not a problem."

"Oh, look – someone's just driven your Discovery into the car park."

"Ah – that'll be one of Lucy's friends."

"A man. He's getting out."

"That'll be Nigel. Don't worry, he's married."

"Well it's none of my business, of course."

"I expect he'll want someone to drive him to the station. Could you please ask Val to deal with it?"

Samantha edged to the door, looking first curious, then suspicious.

"It's no big deal," Richard said. "And listen, once I return from Kenya you'll have about four weeks to prepare for the relocation, so keep me in touch regarding your mother."

Samantha, who for the first time dared to think her boss's marriage was on the rocks, opened the door. "Okay. I'll get Val to sort out Nigel. He's already at the door."

When Lucy phoned the office it was past midday.

"I'll ask Samantha to pick you up," Richard told her over the telephone. "Why did Nigel bring the car here, and not drop it off with you?"

"I don't know, darling. He must have assumed I'd be at the office."

"Sam'll be on her way shortly."

Sam drove her Golf GTI to pick up Lucy from the cottage and couldn't stop herself finding out more about Nigel.

"According to Val, Nigel is a nice chap," Samantha told Lucy.

"He's a sweetie," Lucy replied.

"So nice of him to drop your car back."

"He's got the time for people now, now that he's booted out his wife."

"So many marriages end that way."

"Shocking, isn't it? To be honest, Sam, I'm not at all sure what happened last night – only don't let on to Richard," knowing full well that Richard would get all the goss. "Not as if we were late or anything – half past eleven – mind you I was pretty pissed. Poor man insisted on driving me home, though I'd just settled down and was ready to crash at his place."

"*Must* be a good friend."

"We're thick as thieves."

Sam had a spring in her step once they were back at the office. As for Lucy, her supposed hangover didn't seem to exist as, with her usual ruthless authority, she threw herself in to an afternoon's work. More or less certain their marriage wouldn't last, Sam got on with things with similar gusto, mildly aware that possibly a door was open to her.

TWENTY

Lucy flew back to New York, with a return planned for three weeks' time, when she and Richard would take their trip to Nairobi. She was against the whole business undertaking Richard had engineered, and wanted to stop him, yet worried at the same time about the likelihood of losing her possession of him, and with that her jealous control. She was, too, feeling a vague sort of guilt about having slept with Nigel, but managed to convince herself that through the haze of drunkenness her memory wasn't that clear, and perhaps she *hadn't* slept with him after all (though that wouldn't explain how she remembered peering with cross-eyed curiosity at Nigel's throbbing circumcision).

If Lucy was against the Nairobi project, Bertram was very supportive of it, believing that without it the company would shrink. That didn't matter to Lucy. Her prime intent in agreeing to the trip was to keep an eye on Richard, and when the opportunity arose scupper the project. However, in the US there was nothing she could do, and Richard advanced his plans.

One warm and pleasant afternoon Sam and Richard were going through the computer test reports, and steadily, by whatever subterfuge she could, she broached the subject of his marriage.

"Everything's fine," he insisted.

She didn't look convinced.

"You think my wife is having a little adventure with Nigel, don't you?"

"That's not for me to say, Richard."

"Well what is it you *are* trying to say?"

"I can't help thinking of you and me."

"Don't think too much. That was a beautiful evening we had, but it ends there."

"I sensed you'd say that. But don't you ever worry about Lucy alone in New York?"

"She's all grown up and can take care of herself. Besides, for one reason or another, I need her as much as she needs me. We have that understanding."

"Where does that leave me?"

"I've told you."

"Is it just not possible, a future together?"

"It's not impossible, but this is just bad timing."

"That at least gives me hope."

"You have some very fine qualities, Sam. What you ought to be asking is do you really want to throw them away on me?"

"I don't see it like that."

"Give it time. Think it through. Besides, you've got your mother."

"She's not going to be around forever."

"Come on in," Richard said, as Val ushered Bertram into his office. "Val, what can we get Mr Purcell, please?"

"I'll organise some coffee."

Richard produced a white envelope. "Your six-monthly fee."

Bertram acknowledged the envelope and put it in his jacket.

"Really I want to quiz you both as a lawyer and as our chairman."

"Oh?"

"You know Lucy and I are flying out to Nairobi in a few weeks…'

"Yes – to look at factory premises."

"You know me – convinced the project is going to succeed…"

"But?"

"That's perceptive, Bertram. The 'but' *is* that the price of success is a kick-back to the people on the ground in Nairobi."

"When has business ever been done in any other way?"

"We are, Bertram, men of the world."

"So – what's the bribe?"

"Let's not put it quite like that. We are after all dealing with high-ranking government people. It's in both our interests that these little ex gratia payments are on the right side of UK law."

"As long as they can produce an invoice, there's no problem. You may have to talk to the auditor. Does Lucy know about this?"

"I'll brief her in Nairobi. I suppose the company will be able, legally, to make such a payment?"

"Be clear about the terms of contract," Bertram offered, slightly cynically, knowing that such payments were normally made outside of contracts anyway.

"I'll do that, Bertram."

"I'll look it over before you sign."

"Thanks, Bertram."

This was his game plan. By having this meeting with Bertram, Richard could tell Lucy that Bertram was aware of the transaction and had cleared it, which obviated any move she might make.

The day before Richard and Lucy were due to fly to Nairobi, he left work early in order to do his packing, the flight being from Heathrow and requiring an early start. Lucy had returned from New York and was spending a few nights at the London flat. Richard was going to drive up and leave the car there.

Samantha wished him loads of luck.

"Thanks. Take care of your mother. I'll be in touch."

"I wish I was going with you."

"Next time maybe."

"Instead of Lucy, I mean."

"We've had that conversation." All that was on his mind was the trip to Nairobi, and the deals that had to be made. But as he walked to the door, he flung his arms round her. "You have to understand, leaving Lucy is the last thing on my mind."

Samantha was shocked at herself for the strength of her feeling and the things it was driving her to do – but she couldn't deny herself. "I have faith," she said. "We *will* work something out."

"We'll see." True, Richard couldn't really imagine being with Lucy forever, but Sam wasn't necessarily a part of his plans either – she was sweet and innocent and a novelty in bed. Lucy was tough by comparison, and more than his equal, and if life with her was hard he couldn't be sure he no longer loved her. Above all, it was her ambition he admired. He wasn't sure if Samantha had that strength of character, a necessity for him in any prospective partner. Reflecting thus, he managed to leave having kept the lid on her emotions. He drove home, and hadn't been there long when Val appeared.

"I'm just on my way to the post. Thought you'd like a lift to the station."

"Sweet of you to think of me – but actually I'm driving up."

"When, now?"

"As soon as I've packed."

"I'll take your milk then. You don't want it to go off." She marched into the kitchen, but instead of opening the fridge she lifted her skirt to show him she had no knickers on. "One last fuck before you go," she said. He unzipped immediately, and took her right there on the kitchen table.

"I'll miss you," he said.

It was about nine when Richard arrived at the flat in Fulham.

"You've had a long day," Lucy said. "I've arranged to eat out." She poured them both a glass of wine. "Don't worry, darling. There'll be a cab at the door."

He sat in front of the TV and watched hideous game shows before they headed off for the local French restaurant, the one he once hated but since had developed a taste for. From the window he gazed at the hustle and bustle, which he was also beginning to miss.

Just before flying out, Richard smoothed over all that remained outstanding with the IFC. He was given a contact name and telephone number – of the commercial attaché at the embassy in Nairobi. Checking-in time at the airport was eight p.m. – finally the deal was happening. Success, he felt, was imminent.

They flew first class, Lucy being accustomed to that. The flight arrived at nine a.m. local time, with the temperature at Kenyatta Airport uncomfortably high, under a pure blue sky.

They filled out their immigration cards, and on stepping outside the aircraft were taken aback by the hot dry wind pounding on their faces.

Richard felt suddenly fatigued (it had been an eight-hour flight), but Lucy, a seasoned traveller, showed no adverse reaction.

"I suppose you're getting used to these long flights," Richard remarked.

"You'd better get used to them yourself."

They queued at immigration, where the officer quizzed him as to the purpose of his visit.

"Business and pleasure," he explained.

"Enjoy your stay."

They collected their baggage, and heard the announcement for Mr and Mrs Nunn: "Please report to the information desk." They weren't expecting to be met. Curious, they went to find out what it was all about, and were met by a tall black gentleman wearing a business suit, who showed them a letter signed by Musa.

"My name's Dogo Simba. Pleased to meet you. Musa has asked me to receive you. Did you have a good flight?"

"Very pleasant, thank you. That was nice of Musa."

"I've been asked to look after you."

Dogo drove them in his car.

"Mr Simba…"

"Please call me Dogo."

"Dogo," Richard corrected himself, "please could you drop us off at our hotel?"

"Let me check that with my uncle, Mr Mwingi."

"Mr Mwingi's your uncle?"

"On my mother's side. I'll find out what the instructions are."

The car was a black Mercedes 300, immaculately polished and beautifully appointed inside. Although the roads weren't that busy, Dogo had a hand permanently to the horn, warning people to keep out of his way. The roads were narrow and dusty, and in need of a really good sweep, the markings being barely visible. Such people as they saw were all brightly dressed in colourful clothes.

"Dangerous highway," Richard commented.

"You get used to it."

"It's a big country, eh?"

"We number 10,000,000."

The Mercedes zigzagged its way, through thin if chaotic traffic, and it took some time to reach the hotel.

"I can see it – the Hotel Kenyatta," Richard exclaimed, pointing.

"Named after our first president, Jomo Kenyatta – a freedom fighter." The car pulled up and any number of hotel porters descended on them instantly, all in search of a few shillings. Dogo picked one of them out, who helped with the luggage.

"You command their respect, Dogo."

"They have no choice. Unemployment's very high."

Lucy felt some sympathy, and adjusted her sunglasses.

"Sir and Madam, you take some rest and I'll work out your routine for the day."

Richard, on the point of saying don't bother, watched Dogo drive away.

"I have a feeling your Dogo's going to be hard to shake off. I think you need to talk to Musa."

They checked in at the reception desk, from where the porter took their luggage to their room.

"I'm exhausted," Lucy declared, letting herself fall into an armchair. "It's so bloody hot." She fanned herself.

"I'll order some drinks."

"Cold lemonade would go down well. Then I'm taking a nap."

She shut her eyes. Richard ordered the two glasses of lemonade and looked at the daily paper, *The Nation*. He ignored the local politics and turned to the property section. Disappointingly, there were no factory units either for sale or to let. The business section wasn't any more inspiring, dealing with news about commodities and crops. He folded the paper and dumped it on the bed. He went out and stood on the balcony, which overlooked the swimming pool. He was tempted to go for a swim.

"Hey, Luce, how about a splash!"

"Not now. Too sleepy. You go."

Their bell rang and it was an attendant with their drinks. His uniform consisted of a white shirt and extremely tight-fitting black trousers – completely out of the question back in England, Richard thought. He drained his glass quickly and crunched the ice. Then he changed into his swimming trunks and set off for the pool.

The water was clean and blue and dappled in the

sunshine. He lifted his face up to the sun and smiled. He sat at the poolside dipping his legs and swirling them around. There was an older man swimming lengths, who stopped to have a chat.

"Nice to meet a fellow-countryman!"

"My wife and I arrived an hour ago. Nunn, Richard Nunn."

"Hello, Richard. Cockrell, James Cockrell." James's company had sent him in from Yorkshire, which they did twice a year. "You here on business?" he asked.

"Yes. I'm MD of a firm called Ashgrow."

"You've got to watch the scallywags here, I'll tell you that for free. I trust *no one*." He returned to the other end of the pool, doing backstroke.

"Richard, meet my wife, Lily."

Richard waved, then he jumped in the pool. Lily swam towards him.

"You here alone?" she asked.

"No. Lucy's sleeping. Long flight. Just arrived."

"Shame. Jim's tied his business up and now we're off on safari – in a couple of days."

"Sounds wonderful. We were thinking of doing the same."

"Perhaps you could join us."

"That *would* be fun."

Richard hauled himself out of the pool, and now saw that Lucy was in her swimwear coming to join him. She still looked fabulous for her age, which he couldn't help but drool over.

"There was a phone call from Mr Mwingi's office. Apparently we're dining out with him and his team."

"Where?"

"I can't remember. I've written it down."

"You know Mr Mwingi?" James asked. "The minister?"

"Yes."

"Lucky you. We're trying desperately to get his department interested in *our* company."

"I'll put in a good word."

"Thanks, but be warned. He's a reputation for taking backhanders."

Lucy's eyes widened when she heard this.

"James, this is Lucy, my wife."

"Very pleased to meet. Let me introduce you to Lily."

Lucy smiled, and turned to James: "So what do you know about this guy?"

"There's a lot of corruption here, and Mwingi's not above it, I'm told. Because we won't play ball, it's cost my firm. Kenyans are fine people on the whole, but the likes of him are not."

Lucy found herself a lounger and settled down to soak up the sun. After another dip Richard joined her.

"I hope *you* haven't offered bribes for favours?" she asked, hardly lifting her sunhat.

"Good heavens no!"

"Come on, Richard, how much?"

"You don't believe me?"

"You might as well tell the truth – I'm going to find out sooner or later."

"Don't be daft! How could you think such a thing? I'm shocked."

She gave him the benefit of the doubt – for now.

"Thanks for the vote of confidence," he said. "Do try to bear in mind that I'm your MD."

"That, Richard, you constantly remind me of."

"I'm going on up to the room. It's too hot out here. I'll fry."

Undoubtedly he'd got a problem. Mwingi was going to expect favours, and the deal depended on that, but now with Lucy in tow – and fearless as she was – the truth would out, if he didn't take care. "I'd better prime him," he thought – and that went for Mwanga and Musa too. He looked out from his balcony, and saw Lucy and James in animated discussion by the poolside, while Lily cut an elegant breaststroke. His phone rang.

"Dogo here. I'm instructed by Musa to pick you up at seven. You're to dine with His Excellency the Minister of Public Projects and Development, at his club."

"Thank you, Dogo – we'll be ready."

He had the benefit of the hotel's air conditioning, but ordered a local beer nevertheless – it was called Tusker – and then opened the book he'd brought with him, all about Kenya. He fell asleep with the book open and the beer at his elbow, to be woken by Lucy, who returned at roughly four. He told her about their plans for the evening.

"Why's he being so generous?"

"We're his guests."

"But he's ignoring James."

"We've got something his country wants, where James perhaps hasn't."

"Why would James come all this way with nothing to sell?"

"I couldn't tell you. I've known James for precisely one afternoon. Let's not screw things up, huh?"

She took a shower, and soon found that Richard had followed her into the cubicle

"It's the heat," he said. "It really makes you randy."

He slid of his underpants and was immediately standing proud.

"Oh Richard!" she gasped. "It's enormous!"

"Want some of that, my love?"

In reply she smothered it in shower gel.

At last Lucy was relaxed and happy. "Let's join James and Lily on safari," she said.

"Why not! They seem like good company."

"What do we wear tonight? Should I ask Lily?"

"Why not your white dress and matching shoes?"

"Could do. I'd like a second opinion all the same." She dialled reception and asked to be connected to the Cockrells' room. Lily answered. Lucy explained her problem.

"Come on over. I'll see what I can do."

Lucy trotted off to their room, returning to find Richard all ready for dinner. He had on a business suit and bow tie, and Lucy decided on her pink dress with a white belt.

"Let's wait in the bar," he suggested.

He ordered Scotch with ice and for Lucy a Bacardi and orange. Briefly, James and Lily joined them, to a background of lively traditional music. The concierge interrupted their flow when Richard's transport arrived. Dogo was waiting in the lounge, and having led them to the car drove straight to the club, which was exclusive and buzzing with socialites. The parking lot was a swamp of black limousines, one of which was the British High Commissioner's, and another the American Ambassador's. The place was full of influential people.

Musa met them, shaking hands firmly. "Mr Mwingi

and the others are waiting. Come. Unfortunately Mr Mwanga has another engagement."

At the table, Mr Mwingi stood up. He greeted them and introduced his wife, who was in traditional dress. "Perfect timing. It's the end of the open golf championship and now it's the annual dinner dance. You can meet all the golfers – international stars every one. You play golf?"

"Not really. Not much time, I'm afraid."

He obviously assumed Lucy didn't play, as he didn't direct the question at her.

Richard was dazzled by the event. Lucy, however, was not. She had met some extremely wealthy and influential people in the course of her work, so to her it was all a commonplace.

The British and US envoys shook hands with Mr Mwingi, and he in turn introduced them to Richard and Lucy.

"Richard, they're just trying to impress you," Lucy whispered.

"You're such a cynic."

"I don't think so. Why do we need all this razzmatazz?"

"They're just being hospitable."

"Well you just let me do the negotiating."

"You want to spoil my chances?"

"Of course not, Richard. At the very least you must square anything with me, before you agree to it."

"That I thought was well understood."

"As long as it is."

When the crab and avocado were served, Mr Mwingi turned to Richard. "Trust you've sorted out your itinerary."

"As I see it, what needs to happen next is on the property front, then we need to consider the next stage of development."

"We think we might be able to help you with a factory unit."

"Thank you, Mr Mwingi, but we were planning to take a look around the building ourselves."

"Just as you wish."

"We do appreciate your help," Lucy added. She was concerned at the power Mr Mwingi might exert over Ashgrow's affairs if not checked.

"Obviously Richard is very much aware that what is good for us is also good for you."

"That's absolutely it," Musa concurred.

"Except that," Lucy said, "our objectives are different. In that sense the project will have to satisfy both of us."

"You're not getting cold feet, I hope."

"Not at all," Richard assured. "As you'd expect, we do have our brief, and we do try to stick to it."

"And of course there are other directors to satisfy – Mr Purcell, for example." Mwingi had done his homework.

"Why don't we leave the issue of property aside. What's *your* business plan? Let's see where *you* think we'll be in five years' time," said Richard.

"Let us first talk about the running of the factory and we'll worry about the five-year plan later," Musa said.

"That's all very well, Musa, but don't you have to inform your Treasury about that?" Richard asked.

"The Treasury accepts whatever we give them."

"That all might sit well with government, but we're a small firm and have to be fastidious."

"We'll make sure your company doesn't suffer," said Mwingi. He turned to Lucy. "You'd go along with that?"

"As Richard said, we're a small company. We can't afford not to think for ourselves. You might not remain in charge of the department, and then where would we be?"

Mwingi laughed heartily: "If I might say so, you can have no idea as to the workings of our government."

"That I would concede. But I'm sorry, sir, we need to plan for all eventualities."

"You're not afraid of us, I hope. I've got any number of other companies waiting to do business. Why should I choose you?"

"I hope because you can see we have integrity."

"The food is so good, don't you think?" Richard dropped in, trying to change the subject.

"It's excellent."

The band had stopped playing for a moment and the Club President invited the Vice President of Kenya and his wife onto the floor to lead the after-dinner dance. The other guests followed and Mr Mwingi asked Lucy if she would dance. She obliged. This left Richard with Mrs Mwingi, who had the grace of a hippo, and trod on his corns several times. Nevertheless, he felt privileged to be among such influential people, and having extricated himself from his dance partner managed to introduce himself to the UK Ambassador. Then he found Musa, on his own, sipping wine.

"Great party!"

"It's *the* annual event in Kenya."

"I feel so lucky to be here. What I'd like to know, as a matter of interest, is on what basis *you* select the property."

"We're the partners…"

"Hang on a shilling. Are you telling me your government's an investor in the project?"

"That's not what I meant, no. Mr Mwingi, Mr Mwanga and I have an interest in the project, so what is good for us is also good for you."

Richard, astonished, did not reply to that.

By now Mwingi and Lucy had returned to their seats, having left the dance floor.

After the party, Mr Mwingi said to Richard that his new manager would be pleased to take them back to their hotel.

"New manager? Do you mean *my* new manager?"

"Yes, Dogo."

"Oh! I beg your pardon."

Lucy whispered in his ear: "Tell Mr Mwingi we're not hiring him."

"Are you joking! This is one influential guy. I'm not going to end up in jail."

"Richard, you need to get a grip on all this. He'll end up dominating the whole project. It's my company, don't forget."

"It's our company."

"All right then, *our* company. But please just try to see what's really happening here."

TWENTY-ONE

The phone alarm rang at ten, with Richard and Lucy in no hurry to get up. Lucy had her hand across Richard's tanned chest, the sheets having long been cast off overnight.

"We'll miss breakfast," she yawned.

"We can go into town. And actually we could ask James and Lily to join us. In fact James has already offered to take us round the business district in search of property."

"Two birds with one stone."

"You ring them. The sooner we get this sorted, the sooner we can go on safari."

"*You* ring."

"All right, after my shower." He kissed her and got up.

Lucy sat flicking through the newspaper, bored at the local news. There were few international items. She turned to the entertainments page for the cinema listings, and was surprised to find that relatively new films were on release in Kenya. She would have expected to see them six to nine months behind the UK, but this was obviously not the case. Further than this, there was a lot of coverage on crime, from armed robbery to murder, and she wondered how safe it was to be out on the streets. She even rang the British Embassy, to ask for advice.

"After dark," she was told, "it's not a good idea to be out. Always travel by car, and always be vigilant. With sensible precautions, you'll be absolutely fine."

"Thanks. I'll bear that in mind." Next she dialled James and Lily's room. It was James who answered.

"How was the party?" he asked.

"Really quite something. You doing much today?"

"What have you got in mind?"

"Richard wants to see some factories."

"I thought Mr Mwingi was looking after you."

"No – we've bypassed him. Why don't we meet up for breakfast, or brunch – depending on when you last ate."

"That sounds good. We'll come on over."

"I'll tell Richard to get out of the shower."

Lucy wandered into the bathroom with only a sheet wrapped round her. "Richard! Why on earth do you want a factory here?"

"Why, what's happened?" he asked, towelling down.

"The High Commissioner's Office has just painted a very disturbing picture – the place rife with criminality. It's hardly encouraging."

"Well they would do that. They're just protecting themselves."

"I'm not sure about that, Richard. Anyway, hurry up. James and Lily are on their way."

Lily arrived in khaki shorts and a pale orange blouse. Richard placed her in her late forties, in very good repair considering.

"Where's James?"

"Buying a newspaper – essential when you want to find a factory."

Presently James arrived, clutching his newspaper. "*The Nation* – about as good as it gets. There do appear to be some properties."

"Breakfast first," Lily said.

"One thing I don't understand is why you need to do this when the government's supporting your project," James commented.

"It's sort of semi-government backing. Mwingi might have agreed to assist, but his government as such isn't directly involved."

"Richard, be very careful. That man's a snake in the grass."

"Thanks for the warning."

Downstairs, where they tried to order a taxi, Lucy saw Dogo and the black Mercedes. James advised diplomacy. "Tell him you're out with friends – you'll ring him later."

"Good idea," Richard agreed. He knocked on the driver's window. Dogo wound it down.

"Jambo, bwana," he greeted him.

"We're tied up this morning. I'll call you when I need you."

"But bwana, Mr Mwingi sent me."

"Thanks, but it isn't necessary."

Lucy came across to find out what was happening. James and Lily, who had decided not to get involved, were getting into a taxi. In the mirror they saw Dogo shaking his head furiously and speaking on his mobile phone. It didn't look too healthy. Eventually Dogo muttered something to Richard and Lucy, who then made their way to the cab.

"We're all being driven in the Mercedes," Richard told them.

Nonplussed, they all traipsed over to the Mercedes and piled in, seating themselves facing each other. No one spoke. They went and had breakfast – fresh mango, pineapple, paw-paw, orange tea and cereal. Afterwards, they were taken along the Uhuru Highway to see a property recommended by Mr Mwingi. That was on the outskirts of Nairobi. By now it was obvious they weren't going to be left alone.

The road was narrow and in need of maintenance, and lined with women carrying heavy baskets on their heads. Some also had babies strapped to their backs. The Mercedes attracted a lot of attention, and as they moved into less populated districts James warned them not to talk politics. The car followed a sign marked "Industrial City". The units there were on one or two floors, and all were painted a cream colour. Many were unoccupied.

"You'll have no problem here," said James.

Dogo stopped outside Unit 4, the one practically chosen for them. There was someone waiting with a clipboard.

"That must be the agent," James observed.

Dogo parked the car and they got out. Richard approached the gentleman, who introduced himself as Mr Jumba of the Jumba Agency. He opened the front door and they all went inside. It looked much bigger once inside – about 25,000 square feet. Richard couldn't help but be impressed, but James still whispered a warning nevertheless, urging to him to look around, gather all the information he could, and negotiate later. Lucy completely accorded with him.

Dogo and Mr Jumba discussed the terms and conditions. Richard took a poor view of this, but as Lucy pointed out to him, he needed to know exactly what they were saying.

"You don't think he's negotiating the deal on your behalf?" asked James.

"Better not be."

"He is, you know! He's doing just that," Lucy said.

Dogo took them briskly over the property, as if a mere formality.

"I want to give this man a piece of my mind – what do you think?" murmured Lucy in James's ear.

"Yes, but be careful. Don't forget his boss's reputation."

Lucy ignored this advice. "Put the bastard in his place," she said to Richard. "What on earth does he think he's doing?"

"Lucy!" Lily cautioned.

A few minutes later Dogo drove the car to the front gate to leave the industrial estate, Lily and James asking to be dropped off at the Hilton.

"Won't you join us?" Lucy begged.

"Later," James replied.

"Where are you taking us?" Lucy asked Dogo pointedly.

"The Hotel Kenyatta – where do you think?"

"Richard, Lucy – maybe we'll catch you this evening," said James. He whispered to Richard: "Be firm, be wary."

The drive to the Hilton was relatively short and a hotel attendant opened the car door to let James and Lily out. Dogo then drove Lucy and Richard to see Mr Mwingi.

Mr Mwingi was at the bar and greeted them jovially. "Be my guests," he said.

The waiter was quick in attendance.

"So what do you think?" Mwingi asked.

Lucy decided to tackle the man head on. "What are you playing at, Mwingi? We told you we'd find our own premises!"

"Would you please show His Excellency Mr Mwingi some respect," Musa interjected.

"All right, but I don't care for your hospitality. We'll do what we've *come* here to do."

"We're trying to be helpful."

"We don't need your help. We can manage. If we need you I'll let you know."

"This is not England," said Musa calmly. "You need to be extremely careful, especially when you don't know the business culture."

"Oh don't I? Well, we don't do anything until I've met the manager from the Commercial Bank. As you might recall, they're no small part of our IFC backing," Richard explained.

"Don't worry, he knows you're here. He'll be coming to see you tomorrow. Everything is under control."

"Mr Mwingi, this is *our* project and it has nothing to do with you. We'll make our own decisions," Lucy told him.

"Well, if you really think you don't need me, let's cancel the whole thing. Would you care for some lemon tea?"

"Thank you, but no. We're leaving." Lucy was almost fuming.

"Mr Mwingi," Richard intervened. "We are of course grateful for everything you've done, but we do have a blueprint to work to."

"We only try to help the project along."

Lucy glared. Richard smiled. Musa thought they should take a break, and suggested the safari. Richard was happy with that, but Lucy had cooled on the idea.

"Have you booked?" Musa asked.

"Why? You can arrange that too?" Lucy snapped.

Musa laughed. "You mustn't upset yourself. We want to make your stay as comfortable as possible. This is a wonderful country."

Mr Mwingi, deciding that Lucy was too hot to handle, got up and asked the waiter to call his driver. "Musa, take care of them," he said, and he wished them all goodbye.

"We're leaving too," Lucy said.

"I'll get Dogo."

"No you won't. We're taking a taxi. Waiter, now be a good chap…"

The message on the intercom informed Richard that Mr Kawlo, the bank manager, was waiting for them.

"We'll be down," he said.

Lucy was dressed informally in a white skirt with a matching sleeveless top, and had pushed back her sunglasses over her brow. They had not discussed the meeting.

Mr Kawlo greeted them.

"What do you have for us?" Richard asked.

"Papers from the IFC. We're very happy about the project."

"You're sure you want nothing else from me?" Richard queried, looking at Lucy.

"Nothing that my good friend His Excellency Mr Mwingi cannot provide."

"You must bear in mind that we're in charge of the project. Please note that."

"These are the papers," said Kawlo, opening his briefcase.

"Can't Richard complete the formalities at your office?" Lucy asked. She wanted to cut short the meeting.

"That's fine by me. Perhaps in a couple of days…"

"We'll call you."

"In that case I'll say goodbye. I *was* hoping to see Mr Mwingi."

"*He* isn't coming, surely?"

"He wanted to join the meeting."

"You can tell him everything's fine. You can go."

Mr Kawlo got the message, collected his papers, and left. Lucy ordered coffee. As they were relaxing, Mr Mwingi appeared.

"Mr Kawlo not come yet?" he asked.

"Been and gone!" said Lucy triumphantly.

"I'm fed up, Mrs Nunn, I have three other companies interested in our venture, you might like to know."

"Why don't you just press on with them in that case?"

Richard tried to be more diplomatic, smoothing things over with Mwingi, then both he and Lucy left. Mwingi wiped the sweat from his forehead. No one had ever dared to speak to him like that.

"Give me a ring when you're back from safari," he shouted after them. "I'll be waiting."

Richard, relieved, saw all was not lost. He followed Lucy out of the room. Later, he rang Lily and James. "We'll meet you at the pool."

There, in ten minutes or so, they found James waiting, but Lily wasn't quite ready.

"What happened?" James asked.

"Mwingi got a ticking off from Lucy."

"Was that wise? He's a nasty man, and he wields a lot of power."

They finalised arrangements for the safari, with James offering to book it. They would have to fly out on the Thursday, as the following week James was due back in the UK.

Lucy, who looked forward with great excitement to the trip, nevertheless noted how Richard's thoughts were somewhere else, anxious to revive negotiations with the sinister Mr Mwingi.

"I've worked too hard on this to give up now," he thought.

That evening there was a live band entertaining, and the four of them decided to check it out together after they'd had dinner in the restaurant. They called themselves the Star of Africa. There was a drummer, a guitarist, a saxophonist, a keyboard player, two male and one female singer. The lyrics were incomprehensible, but the music was lively and the audience was clearly engaged.

Two male dancers also appeared on stage, adorned in skimpy warrior costumes made from goatskin. They wore leggings, but went bare-chested. Both carried spears, which they beat on the boards in time to the music, while wildly leaping in the air.

Two female dancers then appeared, their huge breasts naked, and clad in beaded fabric round their waists. They moved energetically, the fringes of their skirts dancing round their thighs. Their headgear was a riot of colourful beads, and they wore very large necklaces.

Richard clapped to the music. Lily got up and started to dance, just as the two female dancers jigged over to their table. Richard was quite besotted. The male dancers now came across too, and soon everyone in the hall got up and started to dance, with Lily in particular putting heart and soul into it.

Lucy, passive at first, now felt acutely embarrassed – especially when she looked at Richard. He noticed her disquiet, and immediately disengaged himself from the two women dancers, returning to his table. Lily, however, only thrust herself further into the group, gyrating with the rhythm of the music, and quite threw herself into it right to the end.

Lucy made no particular comment, but they all agreed it had been a wonderful evening.

TWENTY-TWO

They flew to Lake Nakuru, and booked into the local hotel, Lucy impressed with James's thorough organisation. Richard, however, still had work on his mind.

"When does the British Embassy close?" he asked.

"Richard," Lucy said, "leave it – let Mwingi sweat." She had no plans herself to resurrect the deal.

"That's hardly the rational thing to do. Can't help thinking he's got the upper hand."

"Only if you let him. What do *you* think, James?"

"It's a tricky one. I wouldn't presume to advise. All I will say is that humouring corrupt officials is sometimes the price you have to pay."

"That goes against my nature," Lucy said. "I feel you ought to know, Richard, that if you want to go ahead with this, it doesn't have my blessing."

"Then we're not exactly singing from the same hymn sheet." He tossed down his napkin and left the table in search of a telephone, whereby he instructed Musa to keep Mwingi sweet. "I'll be in touch next week."

"He'll be pleased to hear you've said that," Musa replied. "Enjoy your safari."

That was the easy part. Now the challenge was getting

Lucy back in line – because without her nothing could happen. He rejoined the group and pecked her on the cheek, and when she smiled he still felt he could win.

Their guide was waiting to receive them at six the next morning, with the weather already getting hotter. His name was Mazuri, and he drove a white Jeep.

"Jambo," he greeted James and Richard.

"Jambo," James responded.

"You all ready?"

"The girls are on their way. What's the plan?"

"We'll spend tonight at the lodge. The whole trip will last three days. If you want to travel to Tanzania I can arrange that too."

"There might not be time for that," said Richard, as Lucy and Lily, both looking chic, appeared. A porter carried their bags. There was excitement in the air.

Lily fretted about safety issues, asking what would happen should they break down.

"Don't worry about that. That's all covered."

They set off from the hotel car park and wended their way to the jungle.

"You're in for a treat," Mazuri said.

Everyone relaxed. They waved and tooted at other Jeeps returning from safari. The girls were doubly reassured when at least two other cars were following them.

"It's ten miles to the safari park," Mr Mazuri informed them, but even so it wasn't that long before they encountered the first of the wild animals.

"Look!" Lucy exclaimed. "A giraffe." It galloped away from the Jeep. Lily took out her binoculars, for a sweeping view of the surrounding terrain, which was largely dry and barren, dotted with tiny bits of greenery here and there. The roads were unmade, and every now and then the Jeep bumped violently from side to side.

The heat was scarcely bearable, though everyone smiled and looked content. When a herd of wildebeest crossed in front of them, they parked momentarily, and James took out his video camera. Lily glimpsed a cheetah, on the prowl to charge the herd. "God," she shouted, "that thing's going to kill them!"

The guide and the driver smiled, amused. The cheetah tried to hide in the undergrowth, with its sights on a stray detached from the herd. Low to the ground, the cat propelled itself at lightning pace. The wildebeest, having seen the danger, tried to rejoin the herd, but in an instant had the cheetah's powerful jaws clamped to a hind leg, and was toppled over. There was no escape.

James videoed everything – an awesome spectacle, everyone agreed – nature red in tooth and claw. They moved on, among zebras, ostriches, monkeys. They shaded themselves under an acacia tree, to take water from their bottles. Reassuringly, other vehicles followed their lead.

"Where are the toilets?" Richard asked.

"I'm afraid that's all there is," said the guide, pointing to the bush. Everyone laughed.

Their destination was the lodge, which Mazuri took them to in the Jeep. They refreshed themselves with fruit, and after a rest for an hour or so they resumed their drive. A lion strolled majestically across their path, a cue for the driver to stop and James to take out his camera again. There was complete silence, as they watched this particular king of the jungle slowly disappear.

"Wow!" said Lucy.

At a lake a hippo reared itself up through the surface of the water.

"Wow again!" Lily added.

"And there's another," said Lucy, pointing, birds skimming off its head and back. Then off they drove to another location.

At dusk they returned to the lodge, where they spent their first night in the jungle. Lucy swam in the indoor pool, Richard went to his room to relax as did James and Lily. The entire lodge was arranged over two levels, with its lower timber decks edging the plains. When darkness descended they heard a murmur from the security guard, and above them the sky was plugged with stars.

Lucy joined Richard in their room.

"Not showered yet, honey? Come on, I'm starving. The others are in the bar."

She towelled down while Richard dragged himself into the shower. "See you in the bar," she said.

When Richard joined them he was dressed in jeans and an open shirt.

"There you are, Richard!" said James, already slightly drunk.

"Sorry. Don't know what came over me. Tired." He ordered a cool glass of beer. "Don't know about you, but I'm for eating now and having an early night."

"Aw, come on! We're on holiday!" Lily protested.

When they retired to the veranda the mournful cries of the jungle pierced the velvety night. Eerily, they felt themselves in too close proximity to the wilds of the African landmass.

"I'd be petrified, living here," Lily said.

"I'd get bored."

"Would you really, Richard?"

James ordered four glasses of cognac. "If you're lucky," he said, "you can spot the odd animal prowling round the compound."

"Don't tell me that!"

"I wouldn't mind seeing that," said Richard.

They retired at eleven. Bright and early the following morning the Jeep was ready and waiting. They went into sites of archaeological interest, and a museum that charted the country's development over the past two hundred years, with a summary of Kenya's different tribes, and the impact of European colonisation. None of the group was keen on this part, though of course didn't wish to offend the guide, whose claim was that the museum was the best in the whole of East Africa. To them, it was no more than a publicity opportunity for the government.

They spent an hour or so there and then drove back to Tororo, where they caught a local flight to Nairobi. Richard was praying that Dogo wouldn't show up, but suspected he'd kept up-to-date with their movements, and had probably ordered his spies to keep a lookout.

"Expecting someone?" James asked.

"Not really." Richard clambered into the waiting limousine.

"I'm staying put in the hotel for a while," James said, needing to recover.

At the hotel Richard dozed off in their room reading the papers. Lucy went out, and was obliged to rouse him when she got back.

"Richard, it's after half past five – get up."

He sat up. "Where have you been?"

"Into town."

"I thought you weren't supposed to venture out alone…"

"I went to British Airways. I'm off."

"Where? New York? When did they contact you?"

"Not New York. Back to the UK."

"What on earth for?"

"Holiday time is over. And you know I can't deal with the people here – or their system."

"Just leave it with me. I'll take care of it."

"That's something you really need to think about. I don't see this as a place for our small enterprise."

"As ever, I disagree."

"Don't I know it!" She opened her suitcase, beginning to pack.

"Come on, Lucy!"

"That's final, Richard. I've got my ticket."

He let go of the dress she was trying to sling in the case. "All right, but I'm carrying on."

"Just watch yourself legally. And don't spend too much money."

"You'll just have to trust me."

"I hope I can, Richard."

"That sounds as if you think I don't give a damn about the company!"

"We both care, but we both see it differently."

"Well you'll see – my way's right."

She continued filling her case.

"Come on, Lucy. I bet you I'll earn in a month what you make in a year."

"It's not a casino, Richard. This is business."

"Wasn't it your dad's creed to gamble?"

"Dad's creed was calculated risk."

"You're just bandying words. You can call it what you like."

"You call it what *you* like. I'm off."

He grabbed his towel and went for a shower. When he'd done Lucy was sitting on the balcony, reading a book. It was 6.30 and he was in no mood to idle away the time like this.

"Oh, look," he said, "you've left your mobile on. Not expecting a call?" In flicking buttons to switch it off, he somehow brought up her last number dialled, one that he vaguely recognised, but didn't think much about. "Come on, let's go out for dinner – *not* with Lily and James."

"What shall you tell them?"

"Do I have to justify myself? That we've been invited out – by Mwingi, if you like."

"Sounds plausible I suppose."

"I'll ring James now."

Fortunately James didn't ask for explanations, which made it easier for Richard. He turned to the balcony. "Okay, that's done. Where shall we go?"

"I don't know, but my flight's in the morning. I can't be late."

"There's that Carnivore place on the Langata Road. Every visitor to Nairobi goes there."

"Yes – that would be good."

Richard wondered if that was because she now had him cornered, dancing to her tune. Worse, he could even think darkly that there was now a conspiracy to drive him out of the company, which begged the question, should he go home with her? He began to waver, but in the end decided to let her play her game to its conclusion, and see who came out the winner. Then it suddenly occurred to him that the last number dialled on her cell phone was Mwingi's.

"No," he thought, "it couldn't be."

A taxi drove them to the restaurant, where an entire antelope was being roasted on a large spit. They found a table and Richard ordered champagne.

"Cheers!" he said. Lucy raised her glass.

It was nearly eleven when they returned to the hotel, and Lucy was feeling frisky. She stroked the hair on his chest.

"You arranged transport to the airport?" he asked.

"I have, Richard."

"I'll come and see you off."

"There's really no need. Would you say goodbye to James and Lily for me?"

"Leave it with me." He flung himself down on the bed, which was covered with all that remained for Lucy to pack. He was tired, and couldn't be bothered to clear it away. Meanwhile Lucy changed into her nightdress. He got up and grabbed her from behind, and running his hands up her front started to tweak her breasts. Obligingly, she discarded the nightdress and threw herself down on the bed, spreading her legs. He dropped his trousers and launched himself at her.

In the morning when he reached for her pillow she was gone. There was a handwritten note: "Goodbye. See you in ten days' time." He felt utterly rejected, and angrily picked up the novel she'd been reading and hurled it across the room.

"Why is she doing this?"

When his anger had subsided, he sat on the bed. As he pondered what to do, the door squeaked open. It was Lily.

"We wondered where you were," she said.

"That's because Lucy's had to get back."

"That's sudden."

"Business. Urgent. You know how it is."

"Are you all right, Richard?" She sat down next to him on the bed, still sticky with his seed from the night before.

"Where's James today?"

"Working hard. Can I use your shower? Will you join me?"

"What, now that the cats are away?"

"Something like that." She removed her clothes with enticing slowness, then led him by the hand to the shower, where he slipped off his pyjamas. He took her in his arms, but after his night's exertions was flaccid and limp.

"I shall have to see what I can do about that," she said. She took him in hand, and when he was hard took him between her lips.

"Not too much," he groaned, and she gently disengaged her mouth. It excited him to think that he still had Lucy's scent on his flesh, and here was another woman, only hours later, tickling his manhood. He reached down and massaged her breasts, then bending lower parted her hair and poked in his tongue. Then, under a vigorous gush from the shower, they made love again and again.

"That was wonderful," she said, when they lay on his bed.

"You not getting enough from James?"

"James is a sweetheart, but he's developed a taste for young Indonesian girls."

"Bad luck."

"Maybe we should carry this on, in England."

"But you'll be in Yorkshire."

She put her finger firmly on his lips to stop him saying any more. "I can fly to you any time."

"Thanks," he said, more and more at a loss as to why so many women just threw themselves at him.

She returned to her room, leaving Richard with thoughts only for work. He spent much of the day planning, a process that culminated in a call he put in to the factory.

"Val, it's me."

"Richard!"

"Put me through to Samantha."

A pause. "Sam here."

"Sam, hi – any news on the new machinery from Gothenburg?"

"I expect to hear on the delivery any time. How are things?"

"That's why I'm ringing. Lucy's on her way back, determined, I think, to stir things up."

"How so?"

"She doesn't share my vision. I'm bit fed up, to be honest – she's taking it too far."

"I'll try and head her off."

"That's what I hoped. You couldn't save my marriage too!"

"Well, Richard, you know I do have ideas in that regard."

"Knew I could depend on *you*."

"What shall I do if she calls a meeting with Purcell?"

"Tell her she'll have to wait till I get back. The company's too far into this to pull out now."

"What if she *does* pull out?"

"I'll buy myself out and take the Kenyan venture with me."

"I'll stand four square with you."

"*Then* see how she gets on without us."

"Exciting times, Richard."

"I'll put pressure on Mwingi to get his end moving."

"Do we need him?"

"Yes. I'll explain why later."

"I miss you."

"Miss you too."

He next phoned Musa, requesting an urgent meeting that afternoon. Then, as he sat and looked out of the hotel window, the thought crossed his mind that Lucy might not act as he thought she would. He wondered if his pledge to Samantha might turn out to have been a little premature, and he suddenly regretted almost all he'd just said to her. The worst thing was, he might lose both of them.

He was in no mood to eat, so he got ready for his meeting with Musa, which ought to mean Mwingi too, and possibly Mr Mwanga, though he wasn't sure about him. The phone rang and it was Musa, telling him transport had been arranged.

"Ashante," Richard replied. He had picked up some few words of Swahili and was keen to use them whenever he could. He gathered his paperwork into his briefcase and made himself a cup of coffee.

Musa sent him an official car and he was driven straight into the heart of the Kenyan civil service. He was given due welcome by the officials, and was taken to Mr Mwingi's office. Mr Mwanga and the minister were waiting for him.

"Good to see you," Mwingi said. "I understand your good wife is no longer with us."

"An emergency call to England."

"So where *is* the project now?"

"On the point of moving swiftly, I hope – *as* a joint venture."

"That wasn't the understanding," Mwingi reminded him.

"Without you, I see no chance of success."

"We will participate, but unofficially of course. In exchange we want one third of the profits, and expenses naturally."

"We take all the risks – is that what you're saying?"

"We will bring our influence to bear – and very considerable that is too. We will assist in marketing the product, and we will help you export from here. It must look rather good that Kenya is instrumental in developing Africa's infrastructure, don't you think?" Mr Mwingi turned to Mwanga.

"You're not risking capital – the project's IFC backed," Musa added.

"And I'm sure the Ministry of Public Development will be happy to sign a contract to buy a great deal of equipment, at least initially, from your company," Mr Mwingi assured.

"Of course – we require a few road-paving plants," Musa went on.

"Musa's nephew is a worthy administrator, who'll oversee the entire project, which once it's successfully implemented will absorb him as co-director," Mwingi added.

"A fine choice," Musa agreed.

"Give me a few days to consult my people," said Richard.

"Delay costs."

"I have to consult the board. As you know, I don't own the company. There are procedures I have to follow."

"Two days max," Mwingi warned. "In the meantime we'll continue to look around for factory premises."

"I cannot permit you to enter into an agreement on my behalf, or on behalf of the company."

"We've covered everything, I think – don't you, Mwanga?"

"Everything."

"You know where to find me," Richard said, standing abruptly to leave the room.

TWENTY-THREE

Lucy felt well rested after her long flight back, but was suddenly feeling lonely and wishing Richard was by her side. His personal ambition was driving him on and if he could succeed, he might no longer need Lucy, and that's what worried her. She picked up the phone and rang Bertram.

"Lucy, good to hear from you. Back long?"

"Got in last night. Richard's still out there. I'd like to meet this afternoon. Can you make it?"

"Two o'clock suit?"

"Two sounds good. I'm not inviting Sam."

He didn't flinch. "See you later," he said.

On that happy note she put the receiver down, and was in two minds even as to whether to let Sam know she was back. "She'll only work things out if she knows I'm here." She went for her shower.

She rang the County Hotel and booked for lunch, and told Bertram to meet her there. He did better than that and picked her up, in his BMW. By the time they'd settled at their table, there was something obviously wrong.

"You all right?" Bertram asked.

"A little weary. Just for the moment, I don't want anyone back at the factory knowing I'm back."

"Why ever not?"

"I have reached the point with Richard where we don't see eye to eye. He'll prime his allies against me."

"You make it sound like war."

"Sometimes I think it is."

The waiter brought the menu, but Lucy ordered steak almost without glancing at it. Bertram had the salmon.

"What's this all about?" Bertram asked, bewildered.

"I don't like this Kenya project. We're just a stooge for these Nairobi guys."

"Do you really think so?"

"They cut us out of all the major decisions."

"*All* of them?"

"Practically."

The waiter brought and served the wine. Bertram split a bread roll.

"That doesn't sound very healthy," he said.

"The whole thing's riddled with corruption. I dread to think what nasty things they're capable of. It worries me."

"Does Richard understand your fears?"

"I think so, but he won't let it go."

"That's understandable, I suppose. After all, the board *has* empowered him. You should bring all this up at the next meeting. You never know, Samantha might support you."

"Whether she does or not, only time will tell. But to be honest I don't think it's likely. I mean, what's she got against me?"

"She works with Richard."

"Point taken. You will help me, Bertram, won't you? I've an awful premonition."

"I'll do all I can, but I would like to talk to Richard."

"I wouldn't have expected you to say anything else."

"I'll try to get him to see the financial side, though I'm sure he'd have weighed that risk."

"Don't let me down, Bertram."

"I promise I won't."

"And please, let everyone know I've been recalled to New York."

"That's for the best, I'm sure."

"In fact I'm going to drive to the factory to tell everyone that myself."

Bertram dropped her back at the cottage, to pick up the Discovery. It was late afternoon when she drew up in the car park. Val, initially excited, on seeing it was Lucy, not Richard, now gazed a little dejectedly out of the office window.

"Lucy, how are you?" she said.

"In a rush. It's a flying visit I'm afraid. New York beckons."

"I see. Come on in."

They were joined by Sam. "Good holiday?" she asked.

"Damned hot, I can tell you."

"What about business?"

"Richard's handling that. That's why I dropped in – to update you."

"Thanks. That's really helpful."

"You know how to reach him, don't you?"

"We do. Only thing is, Gothenburg's going to give us the delivery date any time soon—what shall we do?"

"Stall them. I'll tell Richard," Lucy lied. "Last month's accounts all done and dusted?" she continued

"Not quite. We're promised draft figures next week."

"That's not good enough. They're always overdue."

"We haven't found a suitable replacement for John."

Lucy knew that, and therein lay her approval at his departure. "Work on it," she said.

"We'll somehow muddle through."

"Glad to hear it."

Samantha left in a hurry, which Lucy hardly failed to note. Shortly after that, Lucy left, having rummaged through Richard's post. "Any problems, give me a ring," she said.

Val and Samantha now conferred in the corridor.

"You seem disgruntled," said Val.

"Why did *she* have to come?"

"She's a director. It's her company."

"But she isn't running it, is she?"

"Somehow I think she is."

"Yes, you could be right there."

"What's wrong with that?"

"Just ignore me. Nothing's going right today. The new code isn't right, and nor is the machinery – the one we're shipping to Nairobi."

"It'll all come right, I'm sure."

"It'll have to. *She* doesn't help."

"That's saying something."

"I think I'm in for an early night."

"Good idea," Val said.

Samantha identified the wrong command, and on her printout circled it in red. She corrected all other errors that emanated from it, but decided not to test it that night.

She switched off the computer, assembled all her papers and tidied her desk. She had this eerie feeling about Richard, and wanted nothing more than to talk to him. Lucy, she felt, had the upper hand over him, and she hardly dared imagine how it would all turn out. On her way home she toyed with the idea of ringing him, but in the end thought better of it. Anyway her mum had *her* demands.

In the morning, Samantha was cheery and happy. She prepared breakfast for her mother as usual, and had a spring in her step. Her mother was sitting in an armchair, watching the TV news. She suffered from arthritis as well as MS, which was a further restriction. Sam brought her some cereal, a slice of lightly buttered toast and a mug of coffee. The chair had a support for the tray.

"I've got to leave early this morning," Sam said. "I'm hoping to catch Richard in his hotel."

"That's all right, love. I'll do whatever I can to help."

She drove to the office, convinced that Lucy was planning something unspeakable for Richard. The traffic was light, and she got in early. Mr Hill was already there. The front door wasn't open, though, so she went to her office through the delivery gate.

"Morning, Sam." Hill was drinking tea and had an open newspaper before him.

She waved and trotted to her office, where she shut the door and immediately picked up the phone.

"Sam, it's you," Richard said. "I was going to ring. How is everything?"

"She didn't call a board meeting."

"Oh?"

"But she did have a meeting with Bertram."

"Are you sure?"

"I have my spies – not least the staff at the County Hotel."

"Clever you."

"She looked remarkably jovial when she visited, which must have been after. Said she's been recalled to New York."

"That's not true."

"So what do you think – they're hatching a plot?"

"I don't know, but they won't succeed, whatever it is."

"How can you be so sure?"

"Trust me. You and Hill will have to fly in and install the plant. That'll take the wind out of their sails."

"I hope you're right."

"I am, don't worry."

"And what about us?"

"We'll be together," he said, if only because that was what she wanted to hear.

He put the receiver down. His appointment with Musa and Mwingi was set for five p.m., and he looked at his watch. Still plenty of time to go.

He was now more convinced than ever that Lucy was trying to stop him as a matter of personal spite, as a man she couldn't love, but also couldn't quite possess. He was single-minded in his determination, whatever the difficulties, but at the same time saw the absurdity of it all and suddenly felt as despondent now as he was confident a moment ago. He dragged his feet.

"I mustn't give up."

At the government offices he took the lift to the fifth floor, where Mwingi had his office. He was greeted by

Miss Kyombe, and in a way was glad to see a familiar face. She shook his hand and took him to the meeting room, where Musa, Mwingi, and Mr Mwanga were waiting, with two other officials, one a civil servant from the Ministry of Finance, the other from the Ministry of Employment.

After the initial introductions, Mr Mwingi spoke:

"We're greatly looking forward to working with your company, and these gentlemen are here to smooth our negotiations."

Musa referred to the minutes. "Let me remind the meeting of what has already been agreed."

The official from the Ministry of Finance said he'd been told that Ashgrow would establish the assembly plant to manufacture road-building equipment. Richard looked at Mwingi in amazement. As far as he knew, the negotiations on that hadn't quite reached its conclusion. Mwingi nodded, looking at Richard, from whom he sought agreement. Musa saw Richard hesitate.

"Of course, the Department of Trade will help you export the equipment, and subsidies will be made available to help you create jobs."

"In principle, my company *is* in agreement, but the board will have to ratify its go-ahead. Also, I'll have to present the final package to the IFC, of course, for *their* approval." Richard tried to get himself off the hook and save himself. "Admittedly," he continued, "that *should* be a formality."

"We all hope so," Mr Mwingi said. He briefly glanced at the two gentlemen present so as to include them. Richard could see their discomfort, and imagined they must be here in the mistaken belief that, as far as his company was concerned, the project had been approved.

He considered his best option was to avoid digging himself deeper into a hole. To this end, he suggested he ought not be present for deliberations by the government officials because of a conflict of interest.

Musa supported Richard in that view, and he was excused. As he was leaving, Musa handed him a note. Outside, Dogo was waiting.

"I'm here to take you back to your hotel."

"I'd prefer to walk."

"That might be dangerous. At least let me walk with you."

"That's up to you."

Richard started walking. Dogo followed.

"Nairobi has a number of UN bureaux," Dogo said.

"I realised that."

"That's the Kenyatta International Conference Centre," he pointed out.

"We've already had the guided tour."

"Yes, I remember. My uncle has instructed me to pick you up at eight o'clock this evening. Is that okay?"

"It'll have to be."

They parted company, Dogo crossing the road before he disappeared. Richard hurried back to the hotel and rang the British Embassy. He asked for Mr Gregory, the contact name he'd been given on leaving London.

"Ah, yes, Mr Nunn. I was told you would call. What can we do for you?"

"I wonder if you have any embassy personnel available to accompany me to a supper with some officials from the government of Kenya?"

"We don't normally take part in private business arrangements."

"I'm alone and would like some moral support."

"Are you in some kind of danger?"

"No, I don't think so. But it *would* give me peace of mind."

"I'm afraid we can't get involved. There's a British Business Bureau. You can talk to them – ask for Jane Marsh. She's well used to business practice here."

Richard hung up and dialled the number to contact Jane Marsh. "Hi!" he began. "My name is Richard Nunn, the embassy has given me this number, I wonder would it be possible for you to accompany me on a business dinner tonight? I'm involved in a very complex negotiation with the government officials here."

"I'm sorry, Mr Nunn, but this is too short a notice, it won't be possible."

"That's a pity, but I do understand. Anyway a couple of my employees will be arriving here shortly. Do you mind taking care of them?"

"Delighted. Let me know their travelling plans"

Richard thanked her and now realised how alone he felt.

Dogo drove him as planned to the dinner meeting with Mwingi and his cronies. At the meeting he made several compromises, one of which was to confirm Dogo as manager. He also compromised on the profit-sharing arrangement as put forward by Mwingi. Thus a large amount of profit would be siphoned off his way, all for very little effort and absolutely no risk at all.

"That's the price I have to pay in the short term." He sighed and gave the go-ahead to his Kenya project.

TWENTY-FOUR

Richard returned to the UK on Tuesday, ten days after Lucy had left, and arranged to be picked up by Samantha from Bristol railway station. When his train pulled in he found her already waiting on the platform.

"Wonderful to see you," he said, kissing both cheeks. "How are you? How's your mother?"

"I'm fine. Mother's at my aunt's. I'm picking her up this evening." Sam was sparkling, but very self-conscious. "You must be tired," she said.

"I'm dealing with difficult people, all with fingers in the pie. That's what's so tiring. Anyway, all done now. All we need is you and Hill to set up the processing."

"We'll talk about that tomorrow."

Samantha drove a company car, a Renault Megane, which Richard spotted immediately out on the station car park. He tossed his luggage in the boot.

"Nice of you to take the time."

"It's no trouble."

He turned, and spontaneously the pair embraced, with Richard planting a long lingering kiss.

"What time do you have to pick your mother up?"

"I told her ten."

It was about half past seven when they arrived at the cottage. Richard unloaded the boot while Samantha killed the engine. He was partly surprised and partly not when she followed him to the porch. He opened the door.

"Come in," he said.

He dumped his cases and flung himself on the settee. Samantha drew the curtains.

"I missed you a lot," she said.

"Missed you too. It was hard out there, without a friendly face." He pulled her towards him on the settee and kissed her.

"Why can't we always be together?"

"That's probably only a matter of time. I *am* fed up with you know who."

He started to remove her clothes, and they both rolled over onto the floor.

He caught up on lost sleep and didn't put in an appearance at the office until the afternoon, where he was confronted with a mound of post, some of which had been clumsily opened.

"Sorry, Richard," said Val, "Lucy went through it like a dervish. I couldn't stop her."

"What was she looking for?" He pushed it aside in disgust. "Oh well, never mind – I don't suppose there's anything to hide."

"I've missed you," she said, and motioned for a kiss. "Shall I come over tonight?"

"I'll let you know. I do need to recover."

"Understood. You know you only have to ask." She went and made some coffee.

Richard in the meanwhile began going through the pile of posts that awaited him, and immediately dialled Sam to pass her the news in the letter he had just opened.

"We've got IFC approval," he said. "It's here in the mail."

She marched into his office excitedly, with a clutch of computer printouts. "Check this out," she said. "Results from the test run." She put a bound copy of the report in his hand.

"That's what I want to discuss with you."

"Program works perfectly. God, Rich, it's going to *transform* this company!"

"It means that once the Ministry of Defence buys our transportation unit, the sky's the limit!"

"Okay, let's not get carried away. Let's think what to do."

"What we do is zoom off to Kenya, set up the factory, install the machinery. You'll have to take Hill and any other mechanics."

"How long will that take?"

"Spend about a week."

"It'll give me chance to see the wildlife," she smiled.

"Absolutely. But I wouldn't recommend a hotel. Best to rent a place."

"Why do you say that?"

"It's the boredom factor."

"Have we got factory premises sorted out?"

"Mwingi's seeing to that. Now – if the new plant is due in a month, I suggest we close this production facility and remove the machinery for transfer to Nairobi. We can send a few technicians to Gothenburg for training. Tell the rest to take annual leave."

"I can't see everyone going for that," said Sam.

"We'll see. Anyway, we don't have much option. I'll deal with that – you'd better get ready for a week or so in Nairobi."

"I'll warn my aunt."

Richard picked up the telephone. "I'm going to ring Stewart Hill – prepare him for the trip. I think *you* should fly out in six weeks' time. Hopefully by then the carrier will have shipped the plant." Pause. "Ah, Stewart – come and join us, please." He put down the phone. "He's so reserved," he laughed.

"That's true. He never gets excited – about anything."

Stewart came in. He sat down, clasping his hands loosely in front of him.

"Any problems?" he asked.

"Stewart – you remember I warned you that you may have to go to Kenya for some engineering tasks? Well, you're off with Sam for a week, six weeks hence."

"I'll have to talk to my wife."

"Of course, Stewart, that you must do. We have to keep our women happy. Thanks for your time."

Stewart left. Sam followed him out, returning to her office and her reports.

Richard re-launched himself into his pile of mail, weeding out all the circulars. He lit on another letter from the IFC, which had been opened, which angered him. It outlined details of the organisation monitoring procedure and support system.

He went home at 5.30, but arranged a lunchtime meeting with Bertram for the following day, at the County Hotel. As he was jetlagged, Richard decided on an early night.

199

The alarm went off at seven, but Richard switched it off and went on sleeping, until well after nine. The answerphone told him that there were three messages – from Lucy, Val, and Lily. He smiled at the latter, having not expected to hear from her again. He reset the tape and went to work.

"Where *were* you last night?" Val quizzed, almost as soon as he crossed the threshold.

"Making up for lost sleep."

"Pity," she said. "I could have kept you warm and snug."

He decided to talk to Dogo, to find out what was happening, and that was his first phone call of the day.

"I need the address of the factory," he said. "We need it to ship the machinery."

"We're still looking," came the reply.

"Time's running short. What's the hold up? I thought you were on top of this."

"Everything so far's been unsuitable. Main problem is size."

"Well, just get a move on. It won't be long before we ship."

He didn't trust Dogo's explanation, so he rang Jane Marsh at the Business Bureau and asked her to send him details of any units she could find, giving her the specifications. "But don't commit to anything until you've got back to me."

He examined the cash-flow projection for the new project. If the targets were met, the result showed a positive outcome almost immediately. He was pleased with that, and, feeling buoyant, left for his meeting with Bertram, taking a copy with him, believing it would impress.

Bertram shook hands warmly. Richard removed his jacket

and sat at the table, where Bertram had already started eating sandwiches. He shoved a plate into Richard's place.

"How was Kenya?"

"Didn't Lucy brief you?"

"We didn't discuss it. In any case you were there longer."

Richard wondered how Bertram had known this, and Bertram noted his puzzled look.

"Oh, I'm sorry," he said, "I thought Lucy would have told you."

"No."

Richard had now convinced himself that they'd cooked up a scheme against him. "Bertram," he said, "Lucy came home early because she didn't like the set-up."

Bertram, having finished his sandwich, was now biting into an apple. "Well, if she has doubts, it's for you to put her mind at rest."

"Does she have doubts?"

"I've no idea. Presumably she does, otherwise why return home early?"

"Never mind that. Do I still enjoy your support?"

"As ever, I'm a man who likes to see both sides."

"That, if I may say so, is a bit indecisive. If I'm empowered by the board, then I'd have thought if there's no financial impediment I *can* carry on with what's best for the company."

"Yes – but we're talking *full* support of the board."

"If, Bertram, I've got seventy-five per cent of the vote, Lucy alone can't stall me."

"It's a delicate matter. You need to thrash things out with her. If it's a personal rift, that shouldn't be allowed to damage the company."

Richard was amazed at this. Where was the unequivocal support he'd been promised before he left? Bertram just wasn't telling the whole truth. Both were uncomfortable, and it ended with Bertram glancing at his watch.

"Look at the time! Richard, I've got to fly!"

Back at the office, Richard phoned Musa.

"I need you to acquire the factory premises pretty quickly. My people will be there in a few weeks' time, to install the machinery. In the meantime, I trust you'll place an order for the plant?"

"Yes – once we've completed the lease."

Richard didn't like the tone of that. "I'd prefer you to place an order now – at this stage a pro forma will do."

"I wouldn't recommend it, and please don't insist on it."

Richard was fuming: "Well, at least let Dogo find the premises as soon as possible, and send us the details." He went on to insist that if no premises were found soon he would export the machinery marked for the attention of the Ministry of Development. This he thought would make the guys in Kenya move swiftly.

"We'll be in touch."

Having secured the financial arrangements, and seen them backed up by the IFC – $5 million for Kenya – Richard had to negotiate a loan for $1.5 million to pay for the plant on order from Gothenburg. This would be repaid once the $5,000,000 dollar package was at his disposal. Accordingly, he asked his accountant to prepare a cash-flow projection for the bank manager.

"I must hold my nerve," he said to himself.

He began to wonder why Lucy wasn't ringing him as frequently as before, and why any conversation they did have was as if between strangers. He depended on Samantha for any moral support, but he didn't like this situation, especially as Lucy's financial clout was still essential. He didn't want to mislead Samantha any more than he had to, but in such an impasse it was impossible to cope on his own.

Over the coming weeks he began drinking more heavily. Val was available – as ever – but he kept her at arm's length, not wishing to complicate his dealings with Sam. Gradually, he began to spend his weekends in London to avoid contact with either.

One Monday he drove back to the factory for one p.m. The shop floor was comparatively naked, Sam having got all the manufacturing plant ready for export, while the replacement machinery was yet to arrive from Gothenburg. She was busy with instructions for her assistant.

"You okay today?" she asked. "You're looking very glum."

"It's that bloody woman – a nightmare." It was convenient to blame Lucy for everything.

"What can I say? I'm always here."

"Thanks, I know."

"It's not long to go before I leave for Kenya."

"Let's hope it all goes well."

Richard offered to meet Samantha's mother on the day he drove her to the airport.

"Mrs Bishop, we're very proud of Samantha," he said to Dorothy.

"I'm so pleased for her. She needs to get away."

"We're hoping she'll be back in two weeks at the most. Don't worry, we'll take good care of her."

"I'm sure you will," Dorothy said, despite having heard dreadful things about Kenya, mainly from David Tolchard.

"All you must observe is one or two sensible precautions. In any case, I can easily fly out, if needs be."

Momentarily, Dorothy's eyes filled with tears, but she controlled herself.

"Mrs Bishop – everything's going to be fine." He put his arm round her shoulder, a gesture Samantha was both surprised and touched by.

"Mum! Just don't worry!"

"I know, love, I know. Send me a postcard, eh?"

"Of course I will!"

Sam's aunt was there too, to add her bit of solace. Glad of her intervention, Richard picked up Sam's luggage and headed out to the car.

Samantha hugged her mother, and her aunt, then followed Richard out, who was waiting in the car. They drove to the factory, where Stewart was waiting, dressed plainly as ever but sporting a brand-new suitcase. He transferred his luggage from his car to Richard's and handed the keys to Val.

"My wife will call for the car," he said.

Richard went inside to check his messages, and Val followed him.

"I'm missing our nights together," she said. "What about tonight?"

"I shan't be back till tomorrow. After that – promise. Anyway it's safer now that Samantha's not around."

They strolled back to the car park and found the others waiting patiently.

In London, Richard dropped Stewart at his sister's, agreeing to meet them at the airport in the evening. He then took Samantha to meet his mother. During the five hours they spent together at his parents' house, they worked out their action plan. Production was to commence within a few days of installation. Samantha would return as soon as the plan was implemented, and Stewart would replace her and supervise initial production, training a couple of local operatives. It looked as if any conceivable difficulties had been anticipated, with very little left to chance.

In the evening, Richard drove Sam to the airport, then spent the night with his parents, returning to Akeminster the next day.

At Kenyatta Airport, Samantha and Stewart were met by Jane Marsh, who took them to the hotel, and advised them against driving in Nairobi.

"Tomorrow afternoon I'll take you to meet your contacts. I warn you, keep alert and be very careful. I know who you're dealing with. Don't argue with them, and stay in close contact with the UK."

After settling in their rooms they went for a late breakfast in the huge restaurant downstairs.

"I think I'm going to like it here," said Stewart, his feet tapping to the background music.

"I've never seen you so relaxed," said Sam, suddenly feeling shy.

"It's like a holiday, isn't it?"

"That's not how I see it. I hope you wouldn't mind if I leave you on your own, I'd like to meet Jane if she's free this afternoon. Gosh! I've forgotten the name of the guy we're meeting tomorrow," she continued.

"You go on. I think Richard said his name was Dogo. I might get in touch with him myself this evening."

Sam went back to her room, from where she rang Jane, who, having nothing planned, invited her over. When Sam called at her house, a maid opened the door and ushered her into the lobby.

"Come on in."

They were joined by Jane's husband, Paul, who also worked at the embassy. It struck Sam it was a large house for just the two of them, but discovered they were here for a three-year stint from Stourbridge. Paul asked her about her visit.

"People have no respect for women here, so be prepared to be patronised," he warned. "Also, remember backhanders are commonplace. And things happen slowly. And never go anywhere alone. We have a spare room, if you'd prefer to stay here."

"Thanks – but it's pretty comfortable at the hotel."

"It's an open offer," said Jane.

"You must make time to go on a safari," Paul enthused.

"I'll think about that."

"It's the chance of a lifetime."

"Yes – Richard's told me all about it."

Paul went to work that afternoon, and Jane and Sam walked through the city centre, where they visited the

Kenyatta International Conference Centre, and the traditional courthouse building alongside it. When Jane finally looked at her watch it was 4.30.

"Well, we don't have time to see much else. Perhaps we can just fit in the Parliament Building and All Saints' Cathedral."

"I doubt if there *is* time," Samantha replied, feeling hot and tired.

"Okay! Let's have some tea," Jane suggested.

She drove Sam to the Norfolk Hotel for early evening tea, where she must have been a frequent visitor, judging by the size of the doorman's smile.

"Jambo," he said.

"Jambo," she smiled back.

The two women were shown to a table, and having sat down, Samgasped a deep sigh of relief.

"You'll soon get used to it," said Jane. "It *is* really lovely here, but a bit daunting at first if you're on your own." She ordered two jugs of tea with cake. "How do you fancy eating tonight at the Horseman? It's just like an English hunting lodge."

"Isn't there a theatre?"

"Not really. There are cinemas, but on the whole the city shuts down early – even the restaurants."

"Shame." Sam added a small amount of milk to her tea. "How did you get involved in business over here?"

"I used to be PA to the MD of a large multi-national. I liked to organise people, *and* all the meetings. I took a course in Swahili…"

"Swahili?"

"The local language. It gave me a lot of work interpreting, which business people can't do without. Your boss got in touch with me on some business dealing and that's how I came in contact with Richard Nunn."

"Oh, I see."

Samantha looked across at some of the people down in the café area, and Jane whispered that the woman in the corner was married to the Foreign Minister.

"I've met her – why on earth's she ignoring me?"

Samantha laughed.

"I think we'll need to book for the Horseman. Let me ring Paul." She took out her mobile. They settled for a 7.30 booking.

"I ought to ring Stewart – see if he'd like to join us."

"Okay. And let's pick up your things from the hotel, as I insist you stay with us. I can see you're going to be lonely on your own."

"You sure it's no trouble?"

"No trouble at all."

The city centre was getting busier, with people leaving work. Jane was a confident driver, threading her way through the chaos of traffic, though it still took nearly half an hour to reach the hotel. At the concierge's desk, Samantha buzzed Stewart on the intercom, but without reply. She asked if there were any messages, and one from Stewart told her he'd be eating out with Dogo, and that she didn't need to wait for him. He'd left her Dogo's cell phone number.

They went up to Samantha's room and collected her things. Then she rang Dogo and asked to be put in touch with Stewart. Noise in the background suggested they'd gone to a club.

"Stewart," she said, "I've decided to stay with Jane. I've left her number with the concierge."

"Okay," he replied. "Have fun, take care."

At their evening meal, Samantha was telling Paul how Richard and the Foreign Secretary knew each other.

"How very interesting!"

"They known each other long?" Jane asked.

"He happens to be our local MP, and has connections with our chairman."

Paul suggested the ostrich meat, which Samantha agreed to reluctantly. In her honour, Paul ordered champagne. It turned out to be one of her most enjoyable evenings ever.

"These people are genuine," she said to herself. She wanted to find out more about them, especially Paul, though she didn't like to seem nosy.

Jane leaned forward and spoke very softly. "Did you know her company's dealing with Mr M?"

"Really?" Paul's face took on a serious look. "He has quite a reputation – you'll have to tread carefully. Why isn't your boss here?"

"Because I'm in charge of quality control, and the manufacturing process."

"Well, if you have any problems, don't be afraid to say so."

"But don't worry," said Jane, which only had the effect of making Sam worry.

The following morning Samantha was browsing through the newspaper, feeling bored, and mightily relieved when, finally, Stewart rang.

"What kept you?" she asked.

"Better not to ask. We didn't finish until after one a.m. I tell you, Dogo can drink some. Anyway, I'm fine. We're coming to pick you up, then Dogo's driving us to a prospective factory."

"I've been ready for hours."

Jane came downstairs and decided to wait until Samantha had gone. She was concerned for her safety and just wanted to be sure of seeing her off with Stewart. A black Peugeot estate appeared at the front door, and a tall thin gentleman got out. He was smartly dressed.

"I'm Dogo," he said, introducing himself. "I'm here for Mrs Bishop."

Jane looked at Samantha. "Mrs?"

"That's for extra protection," Samantha whispered back.

Jane was impressed. "If you need anything, just ring the embassy."

Dogo understood. Samantha nodded, and they joined Stewart in the car. On they drove to the factory, a large complex on the outskirts of the city. There were some workers awaiting them.

"Why are *they* here?" Sam asked.

"That's the workforce."

"But the machines – they aren't yet installed."

"We can train them."

"How?"

"Madam workers aren't easy to find."

"That's as maybe, but it's a cost we can't incur. I'm afraid they'll have to leave."

"But the machines are expected next week," said Stewart. "I'm sure if they're handpicked..."

"No," she said firmly. "Dogo, tell your men they can come next week, but there's nothing for them now."

Dogo murmured something in Swahili, with a dirty look on his face, and stamped his foot. Samantha and Stewart looked at each other.

"Don't interfere!" Samantha scolded. "You have no authority to negotiate, so please remember that."

By now they were upstairs in the building.

"Sorry!" Stewart replied offhandedly, looking down through a window where Dogo and his men were engaged in a heated argument.

Dogo was pointing his finger, telling the men to get out, but they didn't want to leave. He pushed the first one out, and the rest followed, but Dogo was jostled in the process and only extricated himself with difficulty. He shook the dust from his jacket and came upstairs, his feet thumping up the steps.

"You slapped me in the face in front of my men. Now I've lost their respect," he said angrily.

"I'm sorry, but we didn't ask you to engage *anyone*. You can't blame us."

"My uncle say I can do anything I like."

"I'm afraid I have no such instruction. Can we look at the papers? Check that everything's in order?"

"Take my word for it," Dogo replied.

"Sorry, but I need to examine the title documents."

"Don't you trust His Excellency the Minister, Mr Mwingi?"

"I'm afraid I don't."

Dogo was furious. "You're stupid!" he spat.

"How dare you!" spluttered Samantha.

Stewart decided to intervene. "There seems to be some

misunderstanding. How about we meet tomorrow, after we've talked to all our respective people?"

They agreed, and without further conversation clattered back downstairs. Once outside Samantha asked to be taken to the embassy, and, after dropping her off, Stewart and Dogo went on to see Musa, without her knowledge. Nor did Stewart mention that he was dining with them afterwards, and that also to be present were high officials of the Kenyan government.

Stewart and Dogo were accompanied that evening by Becky, who was introduced as Dogo's sister. After dinner, Dogo and Becky escorted Stewart back to his room.

"Will you please excuse me," said Dogo, "I need to make an urgent call. Becky, you wait here – I shan't be long."

After Dogo had left the room Becky got up and started looking at magazines and books – one of which she dropped on the floor. She bent down to pick it up, and looking oddly triumphant over this eased herself into his lap. His cock sprang up immediately, so she wiggled her buttocks. She adjusted herself, then, very slowly, started to unzip his fly. He knew he ought to resist, but couldn't. Ferociously, he pulled off his trousers.

"My," she said, "I've never seen one that pink!"

She took it full in her mouth and sucked till he nearly squealed.

"Come on," he said, "down on the bed!"

He clawed at her blouse, until out popped two enormous brown bosoms, nipples black and erect. He returned the compliment and sucked, pulling up her skirt, and pulling down her panties. She spread her legs, and

212

about to ejaculate he thrust in his cock. He just wasn't used to so much fun.

Suddenly appalled at what he'd done, he crept off somewhat sheepishly into the shower. When he came out, Becky had put on her clothes and gone.

The following morning Stewart was waiting for Dogo after breakfast. He didn't think to contact Sam, assuming she'd have made arrangements with Dogo direct. When Dogo finally turned up, they drove to Musa's office.

Miss Kyombe greeted the pair and asked them to wait. Stewart vaguely wondered where Sam might be, but didn't say a thing. He browsed through the newspapers. Dogo asked him if he'd enjoyed last night.

"Hmm," Stewart replied.

"You want her again tonight?"

Stewart ruffled his newspaper. "I'm sure I don't know what you mean!"

Dogo laughed.

Their chat was interrupted by Miss Kyombe, who came in to tell them that Musa had arrived. They all went into Musa's office, with still no sign of Sam. Stewart thought about trying to get in touch, but Musa immediately opened business.

"How are things progressing?" he asked.

"Not much we can do until the machinery arrives," Stewart replied.

Dogo looked at Musa and reminded him that they would need £20,000 before they could continue.

"I've no authority to deal with the financial side of things," said Stewart firmly.

"I see – so how do you expect us to do our jobs?"

"I'm sure if you explain it to Samantha she'll do everything possible."

"As the man, surely authority rests with you?" Musa sounded surprised.

"No. There's no way I'm getting into that sort of argument."

"We did you a favour."

"I don't know what you mean."

"Becky," reminded Dogo. "She didn't come cheap."

"Now I get it!"

"You're the guest. It's our duty to entertain you."

The normally softly spoken Stewart, who seldom raised his voice, was suddenly overwhelmed with embarrassment and anger. "You're blackmailing me!"

Dogo smirked.

"I can tell you, you won't succeed – I'm leaving right now."

He got up, but Dogo calmed him down. "Sorry. You're offended. But without you we can't do a thing, so please do try to see it our way. Blackmail's not our game. Please sit down and we'll try to forget that last night ever happened."

Stewart had no option but to accept the situation. If he did storm out, these swine would twist the story and try to destroy him.

"I'll think of a way out," he told himself and sat down.

Musa explained how he had managed to secure the support of the Ministry of Finance to help with the export process during the first year's production. He was trying hard to shift Stewart's thoughts away from his misdemeanour. Stewart showed signs of being receptive, but in fact wasn't at all interested and wanted to leave. He couldn't understand their ways, and he found himself wondering if they were part of a larger conspiracy against everything to do with Ashgrow.

"I'm afraid I can only give technical input," he said. "Marketing isn't my domain. I see there's nothing I can do to help, so you'll have to excuse me – you'll find me back at my hotel."

It was obvious to him that Samantha had been intentionally excluded.

"We need you to start work installing the machinery as soon as possible, but obviously no one can do anything until the money has been paid," Musa said.

This was not what Stewart had understood, and he got up to walk away. Dogo wanted to go after him, but Musa held him back as an angry Stewart marched from the room.

He hired a taxi and went straight to his hotel. He rang Samantha but there was no reply. He wanted to confess what had happened, and warn her about the depths these people sank to, but she was nowhere to be found. He thought of ringing Richard, but as *he* was seconded to Samantha he thought that might not be appreciated. He put on his trunks for a splash in the pool, to take his mind off things.

After lunch, Stewart finally got hold of Samantha, and asked her to meet him at the factory immediately. He arrived there himself at 2.30, and a few minutes later a car drew up with Jane driving and Sam as her passenger. Sam wound down her window and asked him what on earth was going on.

"They say they want £20,000 right now – or else."

"Sounds a bit of a mess," Jane said.

"What's happened?" Samantha demanded, looking suddenly pale. "I mean – where are we going to find that sort of money?"

"God knows!"

"There's something going on. They don't want us involved." Samantha was trying to find a rational explanation.

"What's Richard been playing at?"

"Have you phoned him?"

"I suppose I'll have to."

"Let's leave it till the morning. Jane, could you drop Stewart back at his hotel?"

"I'd be glad to."

Samantha looked at him sharply, but said nothing more. As they drove away, they saw Musa's ministry car driving towards the factory. Dogo and Musa were deep in conversation.

Jane could see some nasty plan was being hatched, and didn't like it, but she kept her counsel. She stepped on the gas and, disgusted, accelerated away.

TWENTY-FIVE

Richard had tossed and turned all night, and the alarm failed to wake him. He was unsettled. Something was bugging him and he expected bad news. A couple of times he'd started out of bed and made a drink to calm himself down. He'd never experienced such restlessness before. He'd turned on some music and finally drifted off, but now he hadn't woken till he heard the postman.

He sat up abruptly. The CD player was still on and sunlight streamed in the window. He looked around the room and gathered himself. He pushed aside the quilt, got out of bed and went straight to the shower.

He'd spoken to Musa and Dogo on the phone and was assured that everything was going well.

"I'll ring Samantha this afternoon," he decided, but this strange feeling wouldn't leave him. "I'll ring Lucy," he thought, desperate for reassurance. He went to the factory without any breakfast.

At one p.m. he felt calmer, and so rang New York. There was no reply from Lucy's apartment. He dialled again without success. It was too early to ring her office, so instead he rang Val on her internal line. Was she aware of Lucy's whereabouts?

"She hasn't been in touch for nearly a week. I hope everything's all right."

"It's nothing," he said.

He put the phone down and went to the canteen to get a cup of coffee.

"Shall I eat?" he said. "No, not hungry."

In his office, the phone rang. Could it be Samantha? He looked at the time, and saw that that was possible. Instead, it was Lucy.

"I've been trying to ring you," he said.

"Look outside the window, Richard!"

He made a dash to the plate glass and saw her paying off a cab. He rushed outside and hugged her.

"What are you doing here?" he raved.

"I'll explain all. Let's just get inside. On second thoughts, why don't you take me home?"

"I'm really glad to see you, I'm feeling so down. Let me grab a key." He ran inside for the car keys and passed a message to Val that Lucy was back.

Both were hungry, so he put something in the microwave – two packets of stir-fry.

"You should have let me know you were coming."

"Then there'd have been no surprise!" She had her foot over the arm of her chair and was reading a newspaper. Richard set the table.

"I'll have a quick shower," she said.

"Not too long. Food's nearly ready."

She went to her case for clothes and a towel.

"I'll bring it up to you," he said.

He found her the towel and took it up, but so soon as he saw her in the shower he wanted to join her.

"That's all right, come in," she said.

He ripped off his clothes and stepped inside the cubicle. After soap and sex he felt distinctly better. He returned to the kitchen and resurrected their lunch, but even after twenty minutes or so there was no sign of Lucy.

He shouted up the stairs: "How long are you going to be?"

She didn't hear his call. The hot water was still cascading over her flesh, and she was in no mood to step out. Richard began to wonder. Why had she returned unannounced? Something wasn't right.

In due course she joined him for lunch, wrapped in a towel, and her hair still wet. Richard was clutching the phone directory.

"Who are you calling?"

"Thought we'd go out this evening."

"I'd rather not. Can't we stay in? I've a few problems I need to think about."

"Is it business? Bertram could join us."

"Let's leave him out. It's partly business, partly not."

"Sounds serious, Luce."

"Pour me a whisky, will you – large, with ice."

He trotted to the drinks cabinet. "You return unannounced. It's not like you."

"I've left my job," she calmly explained.

"You've done what?"

"I've resigned."

"But why?"

She didn't reply. Richard waited, clutching his beer. "I can't see you as a lady of leisure," he said. "What's cooking?"

"I've got my family business to think about."

"I wasn't aware there was a vacancy you wanted to fill."

"Oh but there is. I'm taking over *your* position."

"And what about me?"

"You have a project pending in Kenya – or had you forgotten?" she said sarcastically.

"That's all in the hands of the technical people now – Stewart mainly."

"Then you'll have to find something else to do."

"You've squared this with Bertram?"

"What difference does Bertram make?"

"The board appointed me – not you."

"All right, if you want to be like that, we'll call a meeting tomorrow."

"With me as MD."

"Don't bank on it. The company won't keep paying your emolument indefinitely."

Richard was seething. She'd out-manoeuvred him, and in one fell swoop everything he stood to gain was jeopardised – his plan to buy out the Kenyan company and generate wealth of his own.

"She always does me in," he thought.

Richard slept downstairs on the sofa that night, and was woken by Lucy moving around in the kitchen the following morning. He picked up his watch from the floor, and on account of the meeting with Bertram that morning he immediately got up for his shower.

"Coffee?" Lucy asked.

"No thanks."

"Suit yourself."

He ignored her and dashed up the stairs to get ready.

He was lonely and vulnerable, and Lucy was far more ruthless than he'd ever imagined.

"I need to salvage the Kenyan venture or I'm finished," he thought. Fighting Lucy was of no benefit. He must buy out the Kenyan project as soon as he could. His pride had been hurt, but perhaps Bertram would come to his rescue, or at least offer support. After all, he'd agreed with the strategy.

His mind was in overdrive as he changed, but on coming back downstairs he decided to be nice.

"Sorry, Lucy, there's so much on my mind."

"That's okay. Please understand, you're my husband, but whatever I do for the business – well, that's business. Remember that."

Bertram's BMW rolled up on the driveway and Richard went to let him in. He kissed Lucy on both cheeks and put his briefcase on the table. She made coffee and without further ado they opened the meeting.

Bertram asked Lucy to begin. She addressed her anxiety as to the way she saw the company now being run. She was convinced that the Kenyan project would flop, at a cost of $5,000,000. She felt that Richard was so immersed in the project that it had become hard for him to see it objectively.

"I don't accept that," Richard said.

"Get real, Richard. These Kenyans – they're running rings round you. The money's for themselves, and they don't care about anything or anyone."

"How can you know that? You've refused to deal with them!"

"I refuse because I can see what's what. Mr Chairman, I want to remove Richard as MD."

Richard smiled, confident that Bertram supported his approach.

"Richard, as a trustee of the Moore family settlement I had a long discussion over the telephone with Lucy some ten days ago."

That statement opened Richard's eyes. He realised it was a checkmate situation, and to salvage his position he would have to resign. However, he wanted that to be on his own terms. He stood up.

"To keep Lucy happy, I'll step down, certainly, on the condition I'm allowed to manage the Kenyan project without interference – for twelve months say. If I fail, *then* I'll leave the company."

Lucy was stunned. She'd been looking for a fight, and the last thing she wanted was his overall charge of the Kenyan project.

"All right," she said, "it's a deal, but all key decisions will be made by me and me alone, and that applies to the Kenya project too."

"Agreed."

"Well, it seems we have concluded our business, so if there's nothing else to discuss I close the meeting."

Richard stood up. "Excuse me, Bertram, I've another engagement. Thanks, by the way." He took the car keys and without glancing at Lucy left the room.

He took the road to the factory that he had taken so very often, yet somehow managed to take a wrong turning, ending up in some god-forsaken village. His thoughts had now turned to Samantha, and how to handle his affair with her. With Lucy it was obvious they were finished, but he needed her back-up for another twelve months at least. By then the Kenyan project would be up and running. He found a pub in Fordham, but it was shut – a bit early for the pub anyway, so he headed for the factory.

A pile of post had been left for him. He took out a letter addressed to the MD and pushed the rest aside. The intercom rang and Val's voice came through.

"You're in!"

"Here for the rest of the day."

"By the way Sam rang half an hour ago. Wants you to ring her back. Sounds urgent. She has left the telephone number of people she is staying with." Val handed over a note of Jane Marsh's telephone number.

"Thanks. I'll get on to that." He slammed the receiver back in its cradle.

He put down the letter he was still holding and decided that in case Lucy made an unexpected appearance he'd better ring Sam on his cell phone. It rang for a while and he'd almost given up hope when someone answered it.

"Yes, hello?"

"Is Samantha around?"

"I'll call her." It was Jane Marsh.

"Jane, it's Richard here – thanks for looking after her."

"Hold on, Richard, she's coming."

A few moments later they were talking.

"I want to come home. I'm lonely."

"Only a week to go. Patience."

"But we can't install the machinery."

"What's the delay?"

"The bastards want more money."

"How much?"

"Some colossal figure. Obviously a backhander."

"That's all we need!"

"Can you get a flight over?"

"Gosh, I don't know. I've got some terrible news."

"What is it?"

"Lucy's resigned from her job and taken over as MD."

"Isn't that good in one way? At least you're free to leave – or *we're* free to leave."

"Well, not exactly. She *has* given me the Kenyan project."

"And you believe her?"

"I have hopes. Anyway, I've worked so hard, I can't just walk away – not without my reward."

"What are you going to do then?"

"Hang on in there, until she signs the project over."

"I doubt it'll be that easy. In any case, there are so many difficulties."

"But I can't just walk away. Look, you just sit tight."

"What sort of timescale are we talking?"

"I don't know."

"Richard, you've got to choose. It's her or me."

"This is not the right moment."

"When *is* the right moment?"

"You need to give me time to sort things out."

"It's her money – is that it?"

"That's a terrible thing to say."

"Look, Richard, I'm pissed off with this – and with you."

"Please, Samantha, try to understand. I beg you not to be hasty. It'll all work out, I promise."

She disconnected her phone, and sobbed.

Jane, hardly a model of diplomacy, said, "That's what you get when you get involved with a married man."

"But his marriage is over."

The phone rang again.

"If it's him, tell him to go away!"

"No, it's not, it's a woman."

Sam took the phone.

"Sam, it's Lucy here. How are you keeping?"

"It's stifling over here."

"But a beautiful country. I just wanted to let you know that Richard's no longer in charge. How soon can you return?"

"There's a meeting on today – depending on what happens there, I'm sure I'll be able to leave in four to five days at the most."

"Wonderful. Do take care."

"What was that all about?" Jane asked.

"Lucy – the boss – she wants me back. Bitch!"

"What's Richard say about that?"

"I really don't care."

The phone rang again and this time it was Richard. Jane answered it.

"She doesn't want to talk to you."

"I accept that. Please tell her I love her, and whatever she decides I'll accept that too. I need some space. I've finished with Lucy and I'm moving out of her house."

"I'll tell her." She cut off the call. "Lover boy is missing you. What's more he's moving out of the marital home."

"He can go to hell!"

Jane smiled. "You'd better get ready. Dogo will be here shortly."

Samantha thanked her and went into the bathroom to wash her face. "Can I borrow your car? I don't feel like going with that swine Dogo."

"If you think you can handle it. Driving here isn't that easy."

"I'll manage."

Samantha's eyes began welling with tears and Jane reluctantly agreed to lend her the car. "Please ring me when you finish your work so that I can come over there and drive back with you. And on the way there please follow Dogo, if only to put my mind at rest."

"I'll do that," Samantha said, and turned away from Jane to walk upstairs to her room. There in the mirror she looked at her swollen face. "God, what's happening to me?"

When she finally came down, about half an hour later, there was no sign of Dogo. She took out her phone and rang him.

"I'm on my way, madam," he assured.

"These guys are clearly not interested in making a success of things," she mused. "I wonder why Richard's so convinced about it all. Someone, somewhere, is pulling strings."

Dogo hooted outside, and Samantha and Jane went to the front door.

"Here's the key. Remember, the car has manual transmission."

"Don't worry. I'll ring you as soon as I've finished and you can drive me back."

"Any idea how long that will be? When do you think you'll finish?" Jane directed the question at Dogo.

"Two to three hours, maybe. Isn't madam coming with *me*?"

"I'll follow behind. But you *must* drive slowly."

Dogo shook his head in disbelief as she climbed into Jane's car. Sam pulled out behind him and followed. Immediately she saw that the roads weren't properly marked, and was rather put off by the number of pedestrians milling about, often right in among the traffic. The women, with baskets on their heads, couldn't turn their heads from side to side, so they weren't properly aware of the vehicles around them. There were menfolk pulling carts, looking quite cheerful going about their jobs, despite their heavy labours. There was a constant hooting of horns, which Samantha was slow to react to, due to her inexperience both of the situation itself and of the manual drive. Dogo made no allowance and continued to power away, forcing her to flash her headlights in the hope that he'd slow down. The opposite happened – he only got faster, so that she had to too.

At long last the roads were clearer and she felt more comfortable, despite this higher speed. It was hot and she lowered the window to get some air. She dared not lose him.

"Slow down, you bastard," she shouted.

Dogo turned towards a village along a dusty road lined with brittle-looking bushes. There were no people about, and very few vehicles. She was nervous, and when Dogo slowed outside a large unit bearing the company name, she prayed that Stewart would be there. There was a security guard, who greeted Dogo and then came over to her car.

"Jambo, mama. Musa and Mr Mwingi are waiting inside."

She relaxed a little and switched off the engine. Dogo ordered the security guard to park her car and return the keys.

There was only a handful of people inside the building and no sign of the plant from England.

"Dogo," she asked, "where's the machinery?"

"Come inside. Musa will explain."

"Not another problem, I hope!" She climbed the stairs.

She saw Musa and Mr Mwingi sitting together. Musa got to his feet.

"Samantha, nice to see you," he said. "Please come inside."

She was hesitant. "Where's Stewart?"

"Well, he *was* here, but because Dogo got delayed he's gone to Nairobi. Don't worry, he'll be along. Please sit down. Dogo, will you please leave us alone."

Mr Mwingi was shuffling through some papers. Samantha removed her bag from her shoulder and put it on the table where she sat.

"I'm afraid we've hit yet another problem. Customs will not release the machinery unless duty is paid, which means we now require $35,000 from your company."

""I don't understand: you're part of the project. I'm sure you can bring your influence to bear," she said.

"Well, it isn't that simple," Musa said cryptically. Mr Mwingi glanced at him briefly. "Your company is going to install and set in motion the manufacturing process, and that's the point where we and the government gets involved."

"That's not my understanding."

"What can I say? If Ashgrow isn't prepared, you can hardly blame us."

"You choose to inform me of this today, and I've been here for about a *week* now?"

"Madam, we're absolutely fed up of running after you

– it's nothing but trouble," Mr Mwingi suddenly said. "We'd be happy to cancel the whole thing."

"That's between you and Richard. Frankly, I don't care."

Mr Mwingi stood up. "Is this how you conduct business?" He was wagging his finger.

"I'm sorry, but clearly I cannot solve a financial issue without due notice."

"Give us the cash and we'll shortcut the process. *We* can get the machinery *now*," said Musa.

Mr Mwingi slowly sat back down again.

"Certainly not."

"All right – we cancel." Mwingi thumped his fist on the table.

Samantha jumped in nervously: "Have you got in touch with Ashgrow?"

"No, and why should we? You're their representative, aren't you?"

"I have limits on my authority. Even you, a minister, should accept that there's a limit to your power."

"Stupid! Why come here if you have no power!"

Musa tried to calm things down. "Madam, you ought to apologise to the minister."

"Afraid not. He needs to learn some manners."

"If you were a Kenyan you'd be taught a lesson you'd never forget." Mwingi was fuming.

"You do what you like. I'm not apologising, and if you want to call the whole thing off, go ahead." She got up and started to leave.

"Get out! *Now!*" Mwingi screamed.

Musa begged the minister to calm down but Mwingi picked up an ashtray and hurled it at the wall. He kicked a chair against the door, then suddenly stood up and shoved Samantha against the wall.

Dogo came into the room to find out what the commotion was about.

"You watch your step. You don't know what powers I've got."

"Why are you trying to hurt me?" she screamed at Mwingi and began sobbing.

"Mr Mwingi, please calm down. She is our guest, after all."

"Some guest!"

"You'd better get ready to leave Kenya. Your boss Miss Lucy will understand. The whole situation, the project here is doomed." Musa hoped this would calm things.

Sam was fearful. She didn't know her way out, but her anger got the better of her prudence, and she strutted out. "Wait, I'll take you home," Dogo said.

"You," Mwingi shouted at Dogo, "shut up and let her find her own way home."

Richard had let her down personally, and now in his business dealings he was turning out to be incompetent. No wonder Lucy had thrown him out.

As she was leaving she wondered how Musa knew the project was doomed. However, she was in no state of mind to analyse his comments further.

TWENTY-SIX

The weather was warm and sticky. A doorman sat outside smoking a hand-rolled cigarette. It was a normal day – tedious, with nothing to do. All he had to do was stand up and allow guests in and out. A fly hovered near his face and he swatted at it, this being the most energetic activity he'd engaged in for some time.

Suddenly, he heard raised voices coming from inside the room where Samantha was meeting Mwingi and the others.

He dared not look inside to see what was happening. Then he heard the sound of a heavy object – such as an ashtray or vase – being smashed behind the door. The man was standing by the time Sam flung that door open and ran out. She was tearful. He tried to offer help, but she stormed to her car, which the doorman had parked nearby, and set off at speed.

"Mama!" he shouted. "Be careful!" He waved his arms, but she hooted the horn and swerved. He dusted down his clothes and gingerly went back to his seat. He was an old man, and if he'd had a daughter it wasn't inconceivable she'd have been Sam's age.

Dogo came rushing out and stopped to question him.

"Which way did she go?"

"That way, very fast."

"Tell no one what you've seen, understand?"

"I saw nothing, sir," said the old man, saluting.

"Good."

Dogo went back inside and came out with the keys to a battered white van, which he drove away in haste. The doorman remembered he'd arrived in a Mercedes, but as far as he was concerned that was none of his business.

Samantha drove hard, and the car jerked the gears.

"Bloody thing!" She braked accidentally, hitting the wrong pedal. "I'm resigning, Richard, you bastard!"

The roads were unmarked and in poor repair, and the car bumped along in a cloud of dust. Suddenly she saw a car looming from the opposite direction, hooting frantically. She was in the middle of the road, and swerved to avoid it. The surroundings were lost on her, but she kept on going – at fifty, sixty, seventy mph – desperately looking for a landmark she recognised. Then came a road she thought looked familiar. She turned into it, but found herself in the midst of a plantation of some sort. She turned back.

At the junction there was a battered white van ahead of her, and she decided to follow it. It must be going *somewhere* populated. She tailed it from a distance, but then abruptly it accelerated way out of her sight.

She saw a sign and strained to read it, then, in her rear-view, she saw to her horror that the battered white van was behind her, and picking up speed. She panicked and stabbed at the accelerator, trying to get away, the van now flashing its lights. It drew up right behind her, and she thought she recognised Dogo at the wheel. He tried to overtake, but she blocked him. She spotted smoke rising from a hut not too far ahead of her, and made towards it, hoping to get help. She swerved sharply down a track towards the hut, the van so close on her tail that it had to brake suddenly as she turned. When she looked in her mirror she saw it had left the road and slid into a ditch.

"Hooray!" she said, but prematurely, because now she lost control of the car. She slewed the wheel to the left, but the offside wheels had left the ground. The car rolled – once, twice, three times.

The villagers who got there first saw the driver of a battered white van trying to reverse his vehicle, then driving away very fast from the scene of a car billowing out flames.

Jane was waiting anxiously for news. She decided to contact Dogo again, her previous three attempts having been met by his voicemail. This time, however, she was successful.

"Dogo," she said anxiously, "where is Samantha?"

"Isn't she there? She left the meeting two hours ago."

"Why did you let her go on her own?"

"She was determined to drive off by herself, so we left her."

"How could you do that? At least you should have informed me."

"I'm sorry," he said, and cut the call off.

She rang Paul at the embassy.

"No news of Samantha," she said. "Her cell phone is off, and she's on her own. I'm really worried."

"You let her take your car?"

"Dogo said he'd take care of her."

"Was that advisable?"

"As it turns out, no."

"I'll ring the police. Don't worry. I'm sure she'll be fine."

By seven o'clock there was still no news. Jane was pacing round restlessly, and Paul was making phone calls. In the end, he decided to ring the ambassador.

"Sir Timothy, it's Paul Marsh here. We've got a guest, but she's missing. I wonder could you help?"

Sir Timothy took it on, and at about 8.30 the phone rang. It was the First Secretary to the Ambassador.

"They think they've located the car," came the news.

"Where *is* the car?" asked Paul.

"Near Magamoga."

"Magamoga?" repeated Paul.

Jane looked up.

"That's miles from where she had her meeting."

"Can we get there now?" Paul asked.

"It's not safe to go alone, but I'll see if I can arrange a police escort."

Half an hour later, the First Secretary rang back again.

"The interior police say there's no point in your going there tonight. I'll drive you over there myself first thing tomorrow."

"Okay, that will have to do. We'll see you in the morning."

The doorbell rang and it was Stewart. Jane confronted him immediately.

"Weren't you supposed to be at that meeting with her?"

"They delayed the meeting, so I decided to go to Nairobi for some sightseeing. When I got back they told me Samantha had already left. Isn't she back?"

"No, she isn't. Couldn't you have done your bloody sightseeing some other time? And where was Dogo?" Jane asked tearfully.

"I don't know – he wasn't there."

"Give him a break," Paul interrupted.

Stewart sat quietly, full of remorse. If only he'd waited for her.

The lounge clock struck midnight, and now Paul was really worried, but tried not to show it. "You can sleep in one of our spare rooms," he said to Stewart.

The phone rang, and it was the interior police.

"Is that Mr Marsh?"

"Yes. Any news?"

"Well, it appears the car was involved in an accident – virtually destroyed by fire. We believe they've found the remains of a body also, but it's very badly burned."

"My God!" exclaimed Paul. He gently told Jane and Stewart the news.

"Oh, Samantha!" Jane cried, bursting into tears.

Stewart still sat in silence, twisting the tassels of a cushion round his fingers.

"Why did I let her take the car? Oh, what a disaster!" Jane moaned. "Paul, I want to go there straightaway."

"Was she okay when you lent her the car?" Paul asked.

"She was upset with Richard. I think there was something going on between them."

Stewart looked at Jane when he heard that comment, and realised what it meant.

Paul rang the embassy and arranged for a police escort to take them there that night. When they arrived, there were four policemen guarding the wreckage, with gaslights burning. The blackened roof of the car was laid on the grass, but for the rest there was not much more than ashes. A charred human arm was just about visible. Jane looked away, clinging onto Paul for comfort.

Stewart saw something shining on the ground. "Has anyone got a torch?" he asked.

One of the security officers produced one.

"What is it?" Paul asked.

"Looks like a ring or something," Stewart replied. "It *is* a ring!"

"Don't touch it," the guard warned.

Stewart bent down as close as he could to the object without touching it. "It's inscribed 'Samantha'," he said, his voice cracked with emotion.

Back in England, the Right Honourable Alex Millard was ringing Bertram's office.

"Bertram? There's some terribly shocking news from Nairobi. Samantha Bishop died in a car accident yesterday."

"Say that again," said Bertram. "You're absolutely certain?"

"I haven't got the full details, but I understand there's not much left of the body. Identification has so far been made from a ring and a pendant."

"God! There's only her disabled mother – and there are no brothers or sisters."

"It's tragic. I think it best if *you* could break the news."

"I'll do my best, of course."

"She was staying with Paul Marsh from the embassy. Why don't you give him a ring first – he may be able to tell you more – and please pass on my deepest sympathies to Mrs Bishop and to Richard and Lucy."

Bertram was aghast. He rang his secretary to cancel all his engagements for the day, then rang the factory and asked Lucy and Richard to wait for him there. Ten minutes later, he pulled up outside, and found them waiting at the main entrance.

"What's wrong?" Lucy asked.

"It's Samantha. I'm sorry to have to tell you she's dead. It was a car crash."

Richard and Lucy were stunned.

"Let's go inside," Lucy said.

"Not now, I have to inform Mrs Bishop."

"It's all my fault," said Richard wretchedly. "I'm coming with you."

At Mrs Bishop's, Richard wrung his hands and said how deeply responsible he felt.

"It's so unlike Samantha," Dorothy sobbed, clinging to her sister's hand. "There has to be some mistake." She turned to Bertram, desperately seeking assurance.

"Dorothy, I think you have to prepare yourself for the worst," Barbara said.

"What, with all my life and hope gone!"

Barbara wrapped her arm round her sister's shoulder, as the tears began to flow.

"God! Let me be with my Sam!" Dorothy wailed.

Richard was desperate to do something, but there was nothing – he couldn't bring Samantha back.

Bertram stood up. "We'll keep you in touch with all the developments. Should you both wish to travel to Kenya, that will be arranged," he said.

"I can't fly," Dorothy sobbed.

"Our prayers are with you."

Richard bowed his head, and Barbara saw them out.

Back at the factory, Lucy and Val were waiting for them. Val was dazed.

"How could such a thing happen?"

"I don't know. My heart goes out to the mother. She's devastated."

"We ought to release a press statement," said Bertram to Lucy.

"Whatever for? It's not as if she was a public figure."

"We've had quite a few phone calls for further information and condolences too. *I* think we should," said Val, shocked at how callous Lucy could be.

"I'll draft something out," said Bertram.

Val fetched her pad and pen and they sat down and tried to work something out, though this wasn't the time to find the right words.

Val was full of tears. Richard got on to the *Gazette*, with Lucy taking the phone from him as he choked with every word. It was Tolchard she spoke to, who was shocked and angered at the news.

"Are you still there?" Lucy had to ask.

"Still here, yes. It's hard to take in."

"It's tragic, I know."

"If it's all the same to you could you fax us on this. I can hardly hold my pen."

When Tolchard finally had his copy, he ran it past his editor, Graham. "What do we do with this? It's a big story, isn't it?" he asked.

Graham picked it up and glanced at it. "What's the big deal?"

"It *is* someone we've worked with."

"Okay – make of it what you can. Deadline's forty-eight hours."

Why *did* Tolchard think it such an important story? For the time being, he followed orders, treating it as just another local item. He moved on to other papers in his in-tray – a piano hoisted into a pub window by an enormous yellow crane, a funny cricket match, a charity ball, late-night hooligans puking into the post office letterbox.

He flung these aside and returned to Samantha's death. The message he had was lacking emotion, he thought, and was dry and too impersonal. He tried to consider how Dorothy must feel, someone he'd met only two days before the tragedy had struck. And what was the *cause* of it – had it really been an accident? If not, was it not his duty – if only for the mother's sake – to find out?

He dialled the factory number and asked to be put through to Richard. The phone was answered by Val, who put him onto Lucy instead.

"We're going to run the story," he said. "You've surely a few more details now as to *how* she died…"

"We've told you everything we know."

"What about Millard? He been in touch with the embassy in Nairobi?"

"You'd have to ask him that yourself."

239

"If I might say so, Mrs Nunn, you don't seem at all perturbed at the loss of one of your employees."

"You have absolutely no right to make any such comment. How can you possibly know how I'm feeling?"

Tolchard hung up.

"That man's trouble," she said. "I don't want anyone to have any contact with that bloody Tolchard. Val, please make sure everyone here is perfectly clear about that. Now, where's Richard? Somebody get him in – we've a business to run."

TWENTY-SEVEN

David, Tolchard, on publication day, usually reported to work early. On this occasion the tribute to Samantha had been left on his desk for him to peruse. To him it looked pretty thin.

"The bastards are hiding something," he said.

Peter, his colleague, quizzed: "You all right?"

"Not really. Look at this."

"Looks like just another story to me."

"To you, yes. *I* happen to know *her* and the mother."

"If I were you, I wouldn't get too personally involved."

"Sometimes you can't help it."

"What's your problem with it?"

"I don't really believe what the company's saying. The statement they've put out looks far too crafted for my liking. I've got a nose for these things."

"Like that story on the vicar?"

"That was different. This is people I know."

"But you haven't got anything concrete to go on."

David was forced to turn his attention to some other assignment, but typed only a few words before his thoughts returned to Samantha.

"I can't let this go," he thought. He stared blankly into

his computer screen. "No! I'm going to get to the bottom of this!"

"How?" Peter asked.

"I don't know."

"Well don't get carried away."

"I won't. I must talk to Graham."

That afternoon he rang the Kenyan High Commission and asked them about their newspapers over the previous weeks.

"I'm interested in one particular incident. A motor accident, involving a UK citizen."

"Sir, the newspapers don't report on *all* accidents," came the reply.

"Not even when a foreign national is involved?"

"Why don't you check it out for yourself?"

"I'm miles away. I'm in the West Country."

"I'm sorry. There isn't much we can do."

David rang the factory and asked to speak to Richard.

"He isn't here at present," said Val.

"Is he at lunch or something?"

"Yes, he is – are you David Tolchard?

"Yes. The *Gazette*."

"I thought so." She put the receiver down.

David made a dash for the pub he knew Richard habitually visited – the Fox and Hounds. Richard was alone in a corner, with a pint and a sandwich.

"Mr Nunn," he said.

"David. How are you?"

"This seat taken?"

"Help yourself. What do you want?"

"It's the report in the *Gazette*. I'm curious as to how the accident happened."

"We've told you all we know."

"But *do* you know everything?"

"Why are you so interested?"

"You know my connection with her mother. She's in a state, I can tell you."

"Let me get you a drink."

"No – I'm on duty – thanks. How did the accident actually happen?"

"We're still waiting for the report."

"You will share it with us?"

"I don't know. I'd have to discuss that with the new management."

David was surprised to learn of the changes in management and was about to ask who the new MD was when Lucy stepped into the pub.

"Mrs Nunn." David got up.

"Richard, something very urgent's come up."

"You could have rung – I have got my mobile."

"It helps to turn it on."

"Oh, yes. Sorry."

"Give me a ring," David said, and left his business card.

When he'd gone, Lucy tore it into pieces. The pieces she dropped in an ashtray.

David thought he'd begun to establish a good working relationship with Richard, and was disappointed at Lucy's intrusion. Frustrated, he drove back to his office.

"I came *this* close," he said, making a sign with his fingers.

"Close to what?"

"Finding out how Samantha died."

"I thought it was a road smash."

"I mean *really* how she died."

At the factory, there was no emergency – it was just that Lucy wanted to keep tabs on him. She and Richard didn't speak, and he went straight to his office. He knew that Stewart had returned from Nairobi, and he was eager to quiz him over the project and the accident. Disappointingly for him, Lucy had given him leave of absence, and Stewart was off for the rest of the week.

"He's distraught about Samantha," Val explained.

"I'll ring him at home," said Richard.

"Stewart, it's me, Richard."

"Richard, I feel dreadful."

"It's all terribly sad. This is hardly appropriate, but how far has the installation progressed?"

"I've told Lucy everything. Didn't you know?" Stewart immediately cut Richard off, giving him no chance to respond.

Richard gazed at the receiver in disappointment and put it down slowly. He then went to speak to Lucy. "I should have been present when Stewart was debriefed."

"You weren't in a fit state. Anyway it's your crazy ideas that have got us in the mess we're in."

"So now it's all my fault!"

"You knew very well the whole thing was steeped in corruption – didn't you?"

"I didn't engineer delays."

"You should have pulled the plug, cut our losses."

"What do *you* know about anything! You might have learned to run a department, but what about key decisions?"

"I'm the only one that *can* make key decisions! You're just a clerk from a stockbroker's office." Lucy was on her feet, outraged. Val knocked on the door but got short shrift from Lucy. "Shut up! Leave us alone." Turning to Richard: "To cap it all you talk to the papers. That's against my express permission."

"I don't need your permission."

"You need protecting from yourself, Richard."

"Is that what you really think?"

"You're untrustworthy, unreliable, and stupid."

"You think I don't know how to handle Tolchard?"

"You don't know how to handle anything."

Richard was speechless.

"That Nunn woman," he said, "is closing ranks." David had made several unsuccessful attempts to get in touch with Richard, including waiting outside the factory gate one morning, but each time he hit a brick wall in the form of Lucy. In the end he gave up.

"She knows your connection with the family."

"That doesn't stop me being objective."

"*She* doesn't know that."

"Sounds as if you doubt it too."

"You are a bit close to the coalface."

"Samantha's a local girl – or was – who died in a motor smash abroad. Why won't they tell us more than that? What are they trying to cover up?"

"It's all subject to due process, I would imagine."

"Which can't go on forever."

The telephone rang, and it was a local farmer well known to Tolchard, reporting a mysterious attack on one of his lambs, according to him by a very large cat. Normally David would look at a story like this, but not today. He asked Peter to deal with it.

Peter snatched the receiver, and tried to sound polite.

"Thanks," said David. He went to the next office to speak to his boss.

"I think we need to talk about this Bishop girl."

"I'm listening."

"I'd like to run a front-page story."

"Why?"

"Because I think there's more to it than meets the eye."

"Another of your scoops, David?"

"One day I'll surprise you."

"So what are your suspicions?"

"Look at it like this. Our MP, the Foreign Secretary, fails to take a proactive stance in the affairs of his constituents. He hasn't said a word about the Bishop girl – or her mother."

"You want to make it political?"

"Why not? It'll force him to get involved."

"I don't like it, David."

"But Graham…"

"I can't allow you to do this. If the mother or the aunt wants to consult Alex Millard, we can't stop them. The *Gazette* can't make that happen for them."

David was furious. He returned to his office, where he assembled all the papers covering the story so far, and, putting them in a folder in his briefcase, left the office early.

David didn't arrive on time the following morning. "I suppose he's still smarting from yesterday," Peter said to Graham. "Ask him to come and see me when he gets in."

When, finally, he did appear, Graham told him to close the door behind him.

"Come and sit down. I've had a phone call from your uncle. I'm surprised you felt strongly enough to talk to him about our little conversation yesterday."

"I had to do something."

"He wants me to support you. I don't like to be put in that position – but after all your uncle is the proprietor."

"I've never asked him to intervene before."

"And I hope never again."

"I feel strongly something's going on, and I want to get to the bottom of it."

"I hope it's not a wild goose chase."

"It isn't, I'm sure."

"Go on and get on with it – and remember, no more running off to your uncle!"

TWENTY-EIGHT

Lucy strutted into Richard's office and tossed down the *Gazette* on his desk.

"What do you think this is!" she said.

The headline read: "Local girl killed in Kenya – but nobody cares". The column went on to say that the girl's disabled mother had lost her only carer, and that the local MP, Sir Alex Millard, was unwilling to add his weight to calls for an investigation. It also asked why Ashgrow remained eerily silent on the matter, and called for the Foreign Office to intervene and bring back her remains.

"Well, I can't say I'm surprised," said Richard. "I for one would like to know what happened too."

"What's the point? It's not going to bring her back, is it?"

By contrast, Tolchard was really quite happy. He was making news, and now that Alex Millard was caught up in the story it could only develop. Further, he had learned the name of the people in Nairobi Samantha had been with at the time of her death – Jane Marsh and her husband, who worked for the British Embassy there. Stewart Hill, racked with grief and guilt over the whole episode, had authorised his wife to phone on his behalf and pass on information, so now a proper investigation could finally take place.

Tolchard had even booked himself onto a flight to Nairobi. Apart from Graham, no one else in the office knew about this, so his absence was marked by the time he flew to Kenya. Was he taking leave?

Eight weeks had now passed since Samantha's death, and he hoped the trail hadn't gone cold. He lost no time, and immediately phoned the Marsh residence.

"My name is David Tolchard. I was a good friend of Samantha's," he began.

The line went dead. That approach having failed, he phoned Mr Marsh at the embassy, and asked if they could meet.

"Why?"

"It's very important, that's all I can say."

Paul agreed, albeit reluctantly, and they met in the bar at the Churchill Hotel, where David got straight to the point.

"I know Samantha's mother, who wants closure on the case. I'm here to find out what *really* happened to Sam."

"Surely you've read the preliminary police reports?"

"We have not been able to obtain *any* reports. Mr Marsh, in the UK no one's doing a damn thing about this. Mrs Bishop is badly disabled, and is in no position to fight for her daughter. I'm a reporter, yes, but I'm also a friend of the family."

"I see. Well, the speculation is that it *was* a tragic accident. There is no evidence that any other vehicle was involved – hers was completely burnt out. She didn't have much chance."

"There is absolutely no possibility that it *wasn't* an accident? Sam was a responsible, sensible girl."

"Sorry – that truly is all I know."

"I see. Would it be possible to talk to your wife?"

Paul Marsh circled the top of his beer glass with an index finger. "Um," he said.

David headed back to his hotel, where he'd arranged to meet the manager, who said he may have something for him.

"Had a good day?" he asked. "No? Then I'd like you to meet my friend Mr Mazuri. He deals in giftware for tourists."

"Mr Mazuri, very pleased to meet you."

"Mr Mazuri is able to arrange transport for you to drive round Nairobi, to do your research," the manager informed David.

The following day, David received a call from Marsh advising him that Jane had agreed to meet. The three of them arrived at the Bar Déjà Vu at seven p.m., Jane feeling she'd gone against her better judgement. David asked whether in the last hours of Samantha's life she'd seemed upset or worried.

"She was okay, I thought. I didn't really want to lend her my car, but she was so confident about it. The person you really need to talk to is a chap called Dogo. He was looking after her."

"How do I get hold of him?"

"Ring the Ministry of Development. The cell phone

number I had for him is no longer in use. He worked for
Mwingi, the minister."

The next morning, David went straight to the library
seeking out the newspaper coverage of Samantha's death.
There wasn't much, but he did manage to obtain the name
of the police officer in charge of the investigation. This
was exciting – the first breakthrough he'd made on his
own. He took a photocopy of all the relevant articles and
went back to his hotel. Here he asked the hotelier if he
knew of any way he could get to speak to the Chief of
Police.

"I don't know him, but Mr Mazuri can arrange it," he
said.

Transport duly arrived, and David was surprised to note
that Mr Mazuri himself would be driving. He had been
briefed, and now knew the reason for David's visit to
Nairobi. They drove straight to the central police station.
They were shown into the chief's office, whose desk was
covered in files.

"What can I do for you?" he asked.

"This gentleman is a reporter, here to do some
research," Mr Mazuri explained. "Remember that accident
about eight weeks ago? The young white woman who died
in a crash?"

"I remember it very well."

"This gentleman knew the girl, and naturally wishes
to know everything. Can you help?"

"Our files are confidential."

David opened his wallet and slipped 5,000 shillings under one of the files on the desk, and miraculously all the papers were suddenly available.

On approaching the village of Magamoga, David saw a rusty sign and told Mazuri to slow down. "This is it!"

They drove past a few houses, little more than shacks, the rough road bordered on either side with scrub.

"I can't believe Sam came down *here* on her own."

They reached a bend described in the report, and Mazuri stopped the car. They got out. There was a deathly hush, and depressingly a gust of wind blowing the parched brown grass. Mazuri pointed out a tyre track, which petered out at the edge of the bush. A few shoots of grass had sprung up from a burnt patch of earth, which both men stood looking at in silence. This was the place where she'd died.

David shed a tear, but then pulled himself together and started to compare his observations with details in the report, which made no mention of a small ditch partially filled with water.

"Was she trying to avoid the ditch?" he wondered.

Their attention was drawn to a sound from the bush. There was an old man, walking slowly. His ears were hung with large hoops, all decorated with tiny beads. He had high cheekbones, and all his upper teeth were missing. He was wearing sandals moulded from car tyres.

"Salamu mkuu," Mazuri greeted him.

"Salamu," the old man replied. He transferred his stick from hand to hand, in an action arresting his blanket as it slipped down his shoulder.

"Wewe na take nini hapa?" the old man asked Mazuri.

"He wants to know what we're looking for here," Mazuri explained.

"Ask him if any of the villagers saw an accident some weeks ago."

"Muulize kama kuna mwana kijiji aliyeona ajali iliyotokea wiki zilizopita."

The old man moved slowly towards the road and pointed to the ditch. "Tuliona motokaa nyeupe imesimama karibu na mtaro, kulikuwa namtu anafurukuta kwenye gari, halafu badae akawasha gari moto akaondoka," he said.

"He says he saw a white van in the ditch!" Mazuri couldn't believe what he was hearing. "It struggled to get out, and then drove off."

David put a 100-shilling note in the old man's hand, which he tucked into a pouch around his neck.

"Ashante sana."

"I think this is it!" said David, looking at Mazuri.

"But what does it prove? The fact that the van drove away means nothing – people avoid getting involved with the police here even if they've nothing to hide. Especially since the driver was a white woman."

"Well it proves that there was another vehicle involved, specifically a white van. That van I think deliberately caused the accident and thereby death or even murder," David speculated confidently. "The report states that she drove the car from the direction of Baya, a town some ten miles from the site of the accident," he continued. "Can we go there, please?"

They headed off, and shortly David called out again. "There it is – it looks like some sort of industrial town."

They drove to the address in the police report and came to a building with a nameplate: Phoenix Manufacturing (Kenya) Limited. David got out of the car and pressed the doorbell. There was no sign of anyone inside.

"Is anyone there?" he shouted, banging at the door.

A smartly dressed man emerged and informed them it had been unoccupied for eight weeks or more. Nobody knew where the previous occupants had gone. He also told them that his father had been employed there as a security officer.

"Where is he now?" asked David. "I mean, can we talk to him?"

"He's been arrested. They say it was for non-payment of taxes, but I say it was to keep him quiet."

"Quiet about what?"

"I think they didn't want him to talk about what happened."

David was stunned. "What did he say?"

"My father was sorry for the white girl. He didn't like the men she was working with."

He would say nothing more, and David thanked him then made his way back to the car with Mazuri. They returned to the hotel and David resolved to get to see the old man somehow, even if it meant bribing the police.

"What are we doing today?" Mazuri asked.

"We're going to the police station to see Mzee, the old security officer."

"I'd advise you to be very careful – don't offer them any money unless they ask for it."

They drove to the police station and David asked to see Mzee. After considerable delay and the expenditure of several bribes, they were shown into a small room full of litter. The walls were riven and the floor uneven. There were insects buzzing in the air, and it was very hot. A fan that didn't work sat in a corner. The door was suddenly flung open and a police officer entered, with his prisoner.

"Mr Mzee?" David asked.

"Yes, I am Mzee."

David was horrified to see such a fragile old man being mishandled in this way. Through Mazuri's translation, David learned that he'd lost his job and was unable to pay his taxes, as a result of which he'd been put in jail.

"I'll leave the money with your son to bail you, but please, I need your help," said David. "When did you last see the white woman at the business unit where you worked?" He showed him the photo of Sam. "Did you see her there?"

"There was a lot of screaming and shouting from the room," said the old man hesitantly. "I heard her screaming 'Why are you hurting me?' Then she ran out and drove away very fast. I ran after her but she was too upset."

"And then?"

"I saw Dogo dash out of the building and jump in his van."

"How did you know it was Dogo?" asked Mazuri.

"He interviewed me for work."

"What was the colour of the van?"

"A battered white."

Mazuri and David looked at one another.

"What happened then?"

"I waited, and when neither of them returned I was asked to go home and come back in the morning. When I came back, there was nobody there except Dogo. He gave me my wages and said the business had been closed and I was no longer needed."

After promising Mzee to arrange bail, they left.

David had just two days now to find Dogo before flying back to the UK.

To Mazuri's horror, David rang the Ministry of Development and asked for Mr Mwingi, posing as a journalist interested in development issues in Kenya.

"The minister is not available at present," he was told. "Miss Kyombe may be able to help you."

By employing all the charm he could muster and promising her a "payment" of 5,000 shillings, David managed to talk the receptionist into arranging an appointment with Miss Kyombe for later that afternoon. On their arrival at the ministry building, David and Mazuri handed over the cash and were promptly shown into a room. Shortly afterwards, Miss Kyombe came in.

"What can I do for you gentlemen?" she asked. "I have half an hour."

"I'm from Akeminster in the UK. I am writing about a project a company there is involved in, to do with development here in Kenya. If you recall, I interviewed Mr Mwingi about it some months ago."

"Yes, I remember, but that project is at a standstill."

"Oh, I'm sorry to hear that. What a pity. Do you know how I could get in touch with the other gentleman – Mr Dogo, I think his name is? I believe he was also involved in the project."

"I'll see if I can find his number." She left the room and David looked jubilantly at Mazuri. The receptionist came in after a few moments with a telephone number written on a piece of paper.

"Miss Kyombe says you are not to let anyone know you got it from here."

They thanked her and galloped back to the car. At long last he had the key to solving the whole mystery, or so David thought.

"I'm amazed you got that information so easily," Mazuri remarked.

"Never underestimate the power of bribery!" laughed David.

Back in David's hotel room, he dialled the number he'd been given for Dogo.

"Mr Dogo, how are you?"

"Who wants to know?"

"I am a UK businessman doing market research. I am trying to recruit someone locally to take care of my interests."

"How did you get hold of *my* number?"

"A mutual friend. Can we meet?"

"Give me your number and I'll call you back."

"I'm afraid that's not possible…"

The line went dead as Dogo hung up. David tried again.

"Mr Dogo, even if you do not have time to help me, please could you recommend someone else. I don't have much time left here."

"All right. I'll meet you at the African Heritage Café at two o'clock. I'll be at the table by the jukebox." He hung up abruptly.

David arrived half an hour early. Mazuri installed himself at a separate table and pretended to be reading the paper.

As David sat down, a tall black man approached and asked him for a light.

"Don't smoke, sorry," said David, and the man returned to his table. Two-thirty came round and there was no sign of Dogo. Suddenly, three men came in and strode up to him.

"Are you Mr David?"

"Yes. Who wants to know?"

"Who's with you?"

"No one."

The man from the nearby table who'd asked for a light stood up and walked over.

"I'm Dogo," he said.

David stood up and shook his hand.

"Thank you very much for agreeing to meet me at such short notice," he said. " I would like to invite you to work for me. I am planning to arrange the exportation of foodstuffs from Kenya to the UK and need a reliable contact over here."

"Do you have a business card?"

"Ah, no – I'm having a new batch printed. Damn fool supplier got my web address wrong. Let me write down my number for you."

"You're no businessman," said Dogo. "I would advise you not to mess around with me. I know some very important people here, and I can get you deported, put in jail, or make you disappear. Do you understand?"

David was stunned but he felt he had stumbled on something.

However, he was back to square one. He lay on his bed staring at the ceiling and thinking about what to do next, his thoughts going round in circles. His job was to report the story, and he had to find a way of doing that, no matter what the risk. In the end, he decided to contact Mr Mwingi direct. He telephoned the ministry again, and couldn't believe his luck when he was told that Mwingi would meet him that day at two p.m. in the bar in the Churchill Hotel.

Mazuri said, "Do you think that's wise?"

"Why ever not?"

"He's a very dangerous man, and you've done a lot of snooping. I'm afraid I cannot get involved in this. It's too dangerous."

David decided to go to the bar alone, and ordered a whisky and soda, mentally preparing the questions he wanted to ask Mr Mwingi. Suddenly, Jane Marsh appeared.

"What a pleasant surprise. What are you doing here?"

She looked around her guardedly. "You're in danger, and must leave immediately. My husband has information that the police are looking for you. He's asked me to tell you. You must go!"

Jane left hurriedly, having passed the message on to David and not wanting to be seen with him.

Unknown to David, Mazuri had followed him and sat reading a newspaper in the lounge. He saw Jane come and go, and, sensing something was wrong, went over to David at the bar and asked, "What's the matter? Who was that woman?"

He told him what had happened, and Mazuri immediately phoned the British Embassy and asked for Paul Marsh. It was extremely urgent.

"Mr Marsh, your wife has just left a message with my

friend David Tolchard – could you please tell me what is going on?"

"Tell David he must leave Kenya now. I have been informed by a most reliable source that he is shortly to be arrested."

"Arrested? For what?"

"That is irrelevant. You must get him out of the country – there is a flight leaving in two hours' time."

There the call ended. He turned to David. "Get ready – you're leaving now. Don't bother packing – I'll send your stuff to the embassy. Just get in the car."

"But what about my meeting with Mr Mwingi?"

"That's a trap. Get in the car, David."

David sensed the danger and did as he was told. Mazuri drove him to the airport and saw him safely onto his flight, which took off just as a couple of police cars sped up, their sirens blaring.

TWENTY-NINE

Mr Mwingi was in a huge rage. The file on the project was missing and Miss Kyombe had searched everywhere.

"Where did you put it?" His voice was gruff.

"I thought it was in my cabinet."

"Has the cabinet eaten it?"

Miss Kyombe found this comment amusing and tried to control her laughter.

"You think this is funny?" he shouted. "I need that file or someone's going to pay." He towered above her in a rage, and for a moment she thought he was going to strike her. She backed away, sobbing.

"And don't turn on the tears." He glared at her furiously. She was in fear of her life. "Who was the last one to touch it?"

Miss Kyombe wiped her eyes and took out a register of movements of all the important files.

"Well, sir, it looks like Musa – two weeks ago."

"What do you mean, 'looks like'? Aren't you sure of the records you keep?"

Musa was summoned.

"Why did you take out that file?"

"Your Excellency, we took it out after a phone call from the USA."

"And where is it now? Kyombe, get out – I'll call you in a minute." Miss Kyombe made a dash for the door. "If that file ends up in enemy hands, you'll be in trouble."

"No one, I assure you, knows about that file. I'm sure it's just been misplaced."

"I want it found immediately – if not sooner."

"I'll give the place a thorough search."

Musa left the room, and, chasing up Kyombe, found her in a state of hysteria.

"What's going to happen? I'm in trouble, aren't I?"

"Don't worry, you're not in trouble. It's just been mislaid. We'll find it."

She wiped her tears and uttered the dreadful words, to the effect that no, they wouldn't find it.

"What do you mean?" he whispered.

"The cabinet was broken in to, and someone took it. They must have known what they were looking for. Oh, Musa, save me!"

"When did this happen? I only filed papers two to three days ago."

"I found it like that this morning."

"Was the front door broken in?"

"No, they must have had keys."

"Apart from us two and Dogo, no one has a key – right?"

Kyombe confirmed this with a nod of her head. By now she'd stopped sobbing. They both agreed Dogo couldn't be the culprit, as he would not do such a thing to his uncle.

"I'll ring him later, and ask him."

Musa got ready to leave when Kyombe suggested they could make a duplicate file, of the same colour, with copies of the documents she'd kept.

"That's one solution. Let me think about it."

Musa left her, then dialled Dogo's number and spoke quietly into the receiver.

"Dogo, were you here on your own at all over the last two days?"

"Why do you want to know?"

"You have a key to your uncle's office and it seems someone has broken into the cabinet and stolen a very important file."

"You're not saying I have done it?"

"Of course not – and don't tell Mr Mwingi about this conversation."

In the meantime Mwingi went through his official papers and rang Dogo himself, telling him to come to his office later that afternoon. Almost immediately he put the phone down, it sprang into action – it was the Chief of Police briefing him on the conclusion of Samantha's accident investigation.

"I'll be glad when *her* stuff's sent to the UK. She's haunting me," Mwingi joked.

The Chief of Police laughed. "You don't believe in rubbish like that."

The conversation ended, and as he was about to leave the telephone rang again. Miss Kyombe had put Lucy through. She had been instructed to put all Lucy's calls through, and if he wasn't around then to Musa instead.

"Good morning, Mrs Nunn."

"Just call me Lucy."

"Lucy."

"The deal is we're pulling out of the project. You know what I'm on about. I'd be pleased if you'd return our machinery promptly. I'm sure we can put it to good use."

"We're sorry to hear that. We were so looking forward to working with you."

"Too bad. I need the plant back."

"You're going back on our agreement."

"There was nothing in the agreement about the plant if the project was abandoned."

"You're very forgetful, Lucy, aren't you? The 'agreement' with Mr Nunn was that we keep the machinery in exchange for our support."

"What support?"

"You've done some very nasty things to your husband, and don't forget that I know that."

"Don't try to blackmail *me*. You have a think about what I've said, and I'll ring you tomorrow."

"That'll do just fine." Mwingi was confident that Lucy would have to give up her rights to the plant.

Musa buzzed Mwingi on his internal line: "We looked everywhere but couldn't find that file. Maybe Miss Kyombe and I should look for it this evening, when it's all a little quieter?"

"Do whatever you have to, but find that file!"

Mwingi decided to look for himself, in case he'd been tricked, and on pulling the cabinet drawer found it had been tampered with. Angrily he tried to pull it out completely, but couldn't. He applied more force and located the file index, which was torn at both ends, suggesting that the file had been removed in a hurry. He remembered Musa had gone through the cabinet, so he must have seen this himself. Musa, supposedly his most trusted assistant, wasn't telling the truth. He buzzed him and told him that Miss Kyombe must search for the file alone, and that he should leave her alone to do so.

He went back to his chair and began speculating whose mischief this could be. Dogo had a spare key, and Musa was the only other person with natural free access to the office and its cabinet. Could it be one of the many enemies he had made? He felt that Miss Kyombe was too afraid of him to be the one.

He immediately contacted Dogo and got him to come and see him. At first he made excuses, but Mwingi ordered him there at once. He obliged and Dogo was there within fifteen minutes.

He focused his wide scary eyes on him, as a man who exercised control through fear. "The Chief of Police just got in touch with me. Do you know why?" said Mwingi. "I am happy about what you did for me, or rather us. Very clever. You pushed her car off the road and caused the crash. No escape for her. Excellent!" His eyes were still fixed on Dogo.

"But sir! There was no accident between *our* two motors, I promise." He tried to explain, but Mwingi interrupted him.

"Don't worry, nobody's going to find it out. Take it easy. I'm really proud of you."

"But believe me, I didn't cause the accident. She lost the control and her car overturned, true, sir! I was right behind her."

"Is the Police Commissioner lying? There were witnesses. But don't worry. That report – it'll just disappear."

"No, sir, no!"

"You are my nephew. I expect you to look after my interests. That is natural."

"I would do anything for you – but I don't kill people…"

"You don't have to convince me. By the way, where is that van you were driving?" Mwingi picked up his correspondence knife and brought it down hard on the desk – his way of intimidating people. "These things are not good quality," he said as it snapped. "Yes – now where was I? Ah yes – the van."

"I've still got it."

"Take it to the ministry parking bay. I'll get you another one."

"Why do you need to do that?" Dogo was rather reluctant to part with the van.

"There are many things that the police don't know. I don't want them sniffing round."

"Whatever you say."

Dogo gave up, and as he was leaving Mwingi told him to get his bag ready for a trip to Kampala. He'd found him a job there with the Ministry of Development, and if he turned it down there'd be serious repercussions.

"I expect you to follow my orders. Leave at once and don't even tell Musa – or Becky. Do you understand?" He thumped his hands on the desk.

"Will tomorrow be all right?"

"Tomorrow, yes! Now just leave me in peace."

Fearfully, Dogo walked out, disappearing into a long dark corridor. On his way out he came across the Chief of Police, the head of internal security, and several civil servants all dashing round on a mission. He reflected how men like Mwingi were pulling their strings. He left the building – perhaps for last time, he thought – and drove away in his battered white van.

Mwingi returned to his office late that evening, having spent hours in a meeting with the finance department. He had no further engagements so he buzzed Miss Kyombe, reminding her to carry out the final search for the missing file. He bade farewell to Musa, and left for the day.

He usually drank in a bar frequented by government high officials, and here, tonight, he met the Minister of Information. He considered mentioning the missing file, but thought better of it, and after several vodkas summoned his chauffer to drive to the Churchill Hotel.

"Ring Mrs Mwingi and tell her I'll be late with a meeting."

He tucked in voraciously to steak and boiled potatoes, and washed it all down with a bottle of wine. He then hired a taxi to take him back to the office. He knew Miss Kyombe would be there alone. He didn't have sufficient cash, so he ordered the taxi driver to return tomorrow for his money. The driver didn't argue.

Inside, Miss Kyombe was searching for the file, hoping and praying that the file might be left behind after all. She was scared not to follow Mr Mwingi's order.

She had emptied all the cabinets, and little by little was sorting their contents. She was upset and anxious, and on looking up was shocked to see Mwingi – which turned to anguish when she saw he was drunk.

"Musa not here?" he slurred.

"Sorry, sir, but I thought you told him I should look on my own."

"Oh, yah. Forgot." He dropped himself on a chair. "Exhausted!" he said.

"Would you like me to make some coffee?"

"Hah! So you think you can take advantage of me. I know your little game."

"Absolutely not! It'll make you feel better."

"Don't want a thing. You get back to work."

Mwingi dozed, and nearly fell asleep. Miss Kyombe felt herself slipping more and more into serious trouble. At way past eleven her search had still not been successful, and she was at a loss as to what to do next. She couldn't leave the office, and she was afraid of what might happen if the file ended up in the wrong hands. Mwingi could be so very vindictive, and it began to dawn on her now that her best hope was to leave her job and simply disappear. There was no future for her in government service.

She was still at the cabinet when Mwingi came to, wiping his eyes and yawning.

"What is the time?"

"Past eleven. Don't you want to go home?"

"You found that file?"

"No – it's not here."

Mwingi stood up and tottered. "Do you know what that means?"

"No, sir, I don't."

"It means I'm going to throw you out."

"It's not my fault," she pleaded, sobbing.

"Shut up, and just do what I say!"

"Anything. Please don't hurt me."

"Get me a piece of paper."

Kyombe took out a piece of A4 and a pen.

"Good. Now sit down."

Kyombe was too afraid to disobey. "Is he going to rape

me?" she thought. "Is he going to make me write a suicide note?" By now she was shaking with fear.

Mwingi's eyes were red and wide – he was a man who looked possessed. He smiled an artificial smile. "Don't worry. I'm not going to hurt you. I want you to imagine being raped."

"Hell!" she thought, so it was that.

"Imagine a man is doing you, big and hard and brutal."

She nodded her head.

"All your clothes have been torn, you're lying on the floor, he's holding a knife to your throat. He's threatening to kill you."

Her blood froze. Tears streamed down her cheeks. She looked up at him, a lamb to the slaughter.

"Imagine! The blade, your poor quivering flesh."

"I am, I am." Her voice was a husky whisper.

"He's on top of you. He's drunk. He stinks, and he's mean and he's ugly."

"God help me!" she cried.

"He's been straddling you for twenty long minutes, and now he warns that if you tell he'll kill you."

Kyombe nodded meekly.

"There! Now that didn't hurt. All over, no need to cry. I'm going now, and I want you to leave *after* me. Good night." Mwingi put on his coat and stepped outside. She stood there bewildered.

"What's he up to?" she asked herself.

He stood by the door looking back at her. "Just you imagine Musa did all that to you. Write it all down and hand it to me in the morning."

He slammed the door behind him. Kyombe broke down,

so distressed that she began beating her head on the desk. Musa was the one person who'd looked after her – how could she write something so awful about him? "Please God, take me away. I don't want to live."

She remained motionless for some moments, the tears running down her cheeks. Then her hand hovered over the telephone: "Shall I ring Musa, or not? If Mwingi finds out, I'm dead! Mother then? No, she'll *never* believe me." She was confused.

There was a knock at the door from the security man. "Everything all right in there?"

"It's me, Kyombe. I'm just about to leave."

"Mr Mwingi ordered me to lock up, so you'll have to leave now."

She had no time to think, and still had the note to write. "Just give me a couple of moments," she said, and took up her pen. Slowly, tearfully, here she was now, fabricating those incriminating words against Musa, her friend.

She signed her name and put the note away in the top drawer of her desk, and locked it. She opened Mwingi's drinks cabinet and gulped down a glass of whisky, then on second thoughts rammed the whole bottle in her bag. That calmed her nerves and, sedately, she left.

"Working late tonight, Miss Kyombe," the gatekeeper commented. He lifted the barrier to let her through.

She drove away fast, and whatever possessed her she didn't know, but now with only a glance for the road she pulled out the whisky, swigging away to the point of losing control of the car. In an instant, thud! She'd hit a tree. All in her world went blank.

Mwingi was unusually early at the office next morning, where he searched frantically through his drawers for the note from Kyombe. He went through *her* drawers, and found it at last. He put it away safely under lock and key.

Musa arrived at nine, wanting to know if the missing file had been found.

"I don't know," Mwingi said.

Then came the telephone call to tell them Kyombe had been involved in an accident, and had been taken to hospital.

"Go and find out what you can," Mwingi ordered.

"I'll send my assistant. We've got an appointment this afternoon. There's a lot to be done."

"Miss Lucy?" Mwingi asked, his usual calm disturbed. "What does *she* want?"

"She didn't tell me, apart from the fact that it's very urgent," Musa explained.

"Okay!" He pushed the button on the system to talk. "What is it?" he barked.

Lucy's voice was sharp: "What the hell are you playing at? I gave you half a million dollars to destroy the project, and now you're pushing ahead with it. Not only that, you're exposing me and my involvement. That wasn't the deal."

"I don't know what you're talking about."

"I've had a reporter snooping round, asking questions. Who else have you told?"

"Tell me his name and I'll have him sorted." Clearly that was the person who'd got the missing file.

"Can I trust you to do even that?"

"You watch your tongue. *You* approached *me*. I didn't contact you. This is your mess. Now give me the name."

"Gazetti. He told me he was a freelance reporter."

"Just you leave this with me."

"What are you going to do?"

"We have ways of dealing with things."

"Have you no shame?"

"Not when I'm dealing with people like you – you who didn't think twice about stitching up your husband."

"Don't you dare lecture me!" She slammed down the phone.

Mwingi contemplated how best to deal with Gazetti, whose long-standing crusade was directed at government corruption, yet wasn't above thieving files in pursuit of that end. He was desperately keen to salvage the file, but more important he wished to know how exactly they'd come by it. He trusted no one, and there was even a risk in getting Musa involved. Having established he'd been engaged by a campaigning weekly, *The Kenyans* there was nothing for it but to confront Gazetti himself. Not wishing to be seen in his official car, he took his wife's Peugeot, whose shade was an incorruptible white.

The newspaper office was located in an industrial park outside Nairobi. It occupied a two-storey building, with editorial on the first floor and the printshop at ground level. He rang the bell and an attendant asked for his name.

"Tell your boss he's got a VIP."

A few minutes later a slim-looking man came to receive him. He wore glasses, a white tee shirt, black trousers, and shoes that were unpolished.

"How may I help?"

Mwingi understood this man to be Gazetti. "Let's go

inside." Mwingi pushed open the door with such force that it threw Gazetti offguard. He threatened to call the police.

"Go ahead," said Mwingi. "I don't think you're quite aware of who I am."

Gazetti suddenly recognised him. "Sorry," he said. "I'd have expected an official car."

"I believe you have a file of mine. Let's not beat about the bush – I'm here to collect it."

"Now just a minute!"

"Don't give me that! Give me the file right now – unless you want your offices raided by the police..."

"So you don't mind the police finding it?"

"They're in my pocket. You'd better hand it over."

Mr Kuba, the editor-in-chief, came to see what the commotion was. He immediately recognised Mwingi.

"So what brings you here?"

Mwingi repeated the whole rigmarole concerning his file, with added threats, which both men knew him to be capable of carrying out.

"Okay, we do have the file – but we didn't burgle your office. We do follow certain rules. Step this way, please." Kuba led Mwingi to the office upstairs.

"So, how did you get it?"

"Honestly – someone pushed it through the door."

"I'm not a child. Please tell me the truth."

"That is the truth."

Mwingi saw he'd make no progress there. "All right – for the moment let's suppose it is. I don't expect to see *anything* from this file appearing *anywhere* in the press – you understand me?"

"Perfectly."

"Good." Mwingi retrieved his property, then drove off in a hurry.

Musa was left wondering where Mwingi had gone, and assumed he must have visited Kyombe in hospital. When he saw him returning, he asked him how she was.

"She needs plenty of rest. The doctor says it's not a good idea to see her, so I didn't venture to her bedside," Mwingi explained. He didn't want to mention anything about the file and where he'd been.

Late that afternoon Lucy rang him, and this time told him not to make promises he couldn't deliver.

"What do you mean?" he asked.

"I've had that reporter round my neck again. He's trying to link Alex Millard with the money I gave you. How could you be so careless?"

"Lady, I've got the file. There's no need to worry."

"File or no file, they're not giving up on this. You'd better do something, otherwise I might just cooperate with these people."

"You'd better not do that," he bellowed, but she'd hung up. "Hallo, hallo!"

Furious, Lucy was utterly disgusted with the corrupt Mr Mwingi, and rued the day she'd ever got involved with him. She wondered, what on earth would now happen if Richard found out? She'd lost control, and her fate, uncomfortably, was solely in Mwingi's hands.

In the meantime Mwingi tried to think round the problem of Gazetti – bar eliminating him, what could he do? Although he had influence with the police – and with the army, for that matter – it was playing with fire, and it wasn't an option he'd choose automatically. With his suspicions over Musa, assigning *him* to the job wasn't very practical either.

He toyed with several other ideas, but all afternoon found no way forward. He left early, fatigued and extremely grumpy, but drank himself to the point of collapse, and had to be assisted by one of the bar staff. Usually highly manipulative, and supremely confident, Mwingi was now feeling vulnerable. Dogo had been sent away, Musa was boxed in, and Kyombe was unlikely to recover. It was time to find an escape route, and salvage as much as possible before getting out.

The following morning he rang both Gazetti and Kuba, and arranged to meet them at the Churchill Hotel.

"No tricks or gimmicks," Kuba insisted.

"May I remind you you're dealing with a government official."

"That's what chiefly concerns us."

This was the cheek of a half-free press.

Mwingi's next move was to explain his plans for Musa, with whom he'd hardly spent more than a few hours in the last few days. There had been tension between them, and Musa had become uncooperative. After all, Mwingi was holding aces.

He rang the office and informed his temporary secretary that due to an engagement he would be in at the office at about three. He had four hours to work out his strategy, and he needed to be sure of himself, as he was dealing with the kind of reporters who could so easily finish him off. He borrowed his wife's car and drove to the hotel to collect the key for the room he'd booked. Once there he ordered a drink and sat on the bed to mull things over.

Climbing the greasy political pole was full of hazards. He had made many enemies by the mere fact of wanting to be Foreign Minister. There were rumours circulating as to his fingers in lots of dirty financial pies, so now was the time to capitalise on his position for the long term. He needed to be convincing and sincere, otherwise he'd lose – and that he couldn't contemplate.

He decided to ring Lucy and as it was before office hours in Akeminster, he did so at her home. She was amazed to hear from him, but was glad in a way, with urgent issues still to be resolved.

"I'm taking a great risk and I need your help. If you say no, then I'll back out and let these people savage you instead. The good news is, I think I'm able to solve the problem."

"How?" she asked, rather dubiously.

"I want you to relinquish all interest in the plant now sitting in our bonded warehouse…" He took a breather, awaiting her response.

"Go on – I'm still on the line."

"What do you say?"

"Not in a million years!"

"Okay, it's goodbye. I've nothing more to say. You're on your own."

"I'd advise you not to be too hasty."

"You either agree, or you don't. It's as simple as that."

"I'll call you back."

"You do that. I'm at the Churchill Hotel, Room 615. I'm sure you've got the number." Mwingi put down the receiver, sounding confident, but really quite unsure.

In the meantime Lucy rang Bertram for advice, who was anxious not to drag Alex's name into Lucy and Richard's business.

"Where Richard's involved, you don't have any choice but to play his game," was all he could say. He warned her starkly. He'd rather resign than see his friend Alex Millard damaged.

She got back to Mwingi immediately. "Okay, I accept, but I'll invoice you for the value of the plant you're keeping. However, we don't expect to be paid as long as you buy the raw materials you need from us."

Mwingi couldn't believe his luck, having felt sure Lucy would refuse point blank any further dealings with him.

"I wasn't keen on buying anything from you, but you're forcing my hand," he said. "One more thing: I'll need a further $100,000 loan, strictly to pay off debts I've incurred doing your dirty work."

"You're a bastard, you know that."

"I need to reimburse people for carrying out your instructions."

"You put it in writing," Lucy demanded.

"That won't be a problem."

"Goodbye – and it *hasn't* been a pleasure doing business." Calmly, she put the receiver down. She then broke down, with no one around to sympathise. Even Richard didn't answer his phone. And Bertram, she knew, would be mightily upset with her, if he found out about her underhand dealing with Mwingi.

Gazetti and Kuba rang the room on the intercom and Mwingi invited them up. He insisted on no note-taking, no recording, just plain talking.

"I am the victim," Mwingi started.

Gazetti and Kuba stared at each other in amazement.

"I was paid a certain sum by an insanely possessive wife, who wanted to stop her husband pushing a deal through here in our country."

"You took money from the Finance Ministry?" Kuba asked.

"I was asked by Ashgrow to approach the government for financial assistance, and for job creation, and that's where the Finance Ministry came in." He tried to sound as convincing as possible.

"But no jobs were created."

"They've agreed to return the subsidy money, so there's no real loss to the government."

"So why have you invited *us* here?"

"To stop you printing anything about Ashgrow and me, and to insist you drop the story."

"That's our prerogative."

"I'm going to resign as a minister, as soon as the task the President has entrusted me with has been carried out – a couple of weeks, I guess. You print that story instead."

"It may not be enough," Kuba said.

"I can give you a lot of inside information on some very corrupt officials."

Kuba and Gazetti were surprised at how easy this had been.

"Why would you do that? You're still strong politically."

"Morally it was wrong to accept the money, though it was a genuine business deal. I feel I should step down because that's the honourable thing to do when you make a mistake."

Gazetti and Kuba knew all this was rubbish, but also

knew what a backlash awaited them if they continued to hound him.

"Okay – we have a deal. We'll publish the story in two weeks' time, in case you change your mind," Kuba said.

They shook on it. As they left, Kuba suggested that Gazetti went over to the UK to corroborate Mwingi's story. If Mwingi changed his mind, they wanted to gather evidence from Ashgrow.

THIRTY

David was relaxing in his small apartment, a place so cramped he kept his computer in the bedroom. These days he couldn't get worked up over Samantha's story. His hands were tied, both here and in Kenya. Graham had reasserted his control, and the Kenyan authorities had made it clear that all his approaches were unwelcome. He remembered Graham's advice: "Don't push it."

As there was not much to occupy him nowadays he'd become quite lazy, especially on Sundays. Today was no exception. He got up late, picked up the newspapers and took them to his tiny sitting-room-cum-kitchenette. He stretched out on the sofa, flicking through the sports page while waiting for the kettle to boil.

"No quality – all quantity," he muttered. He turned to the recruitment section, searching for the right opportunity.

"Nothing," he sighed as he tossed the paper down. He made himself coffee, then returned to his reading for the political news. All incredibly boring (another Westminster scandal). He switched on the TV, but there was only a religious programme and cartoons, so he made himself some breakfast. After that, he checked his email, finding one whose sender he didn't recognise:

> Mr Tolchard, I do hope you'll excuse me. I got
> your address from Mr Mazuri in Nairobi. My
> name is Gazetti. I am a freelance journalist. I
> would like to meet you as soon as possible. Please
> can you ring me.

A London telephone number was given, but David preferred to reply to the email:

> Why do you wish to meet? I can't be more
> positive unless I know.

After visiting his usual websites he was about to disconnect, not expecting a reply from Gazetti until the next day. To his amazement he had responded immediately:

> It concerns Mr Mwingi. I cannot say any more,
> but if you're willing to give me your telephone
> number I'll explain.

He signed off with the letter G.

David immediately dialled his telephone number and a few minutes later was in conversation with Mr Gazetti.

"Mr Tolchard, I would like to see you very quickly, as I have not much time in the UK. I'm leaving on Friday."

"You said it was about Mwingi. What do you know about him?"

"Some wild rumours have been spreading about His

Excellency Mr Mwingi," Gazetti replied formally, "and I'm trying to investigate."

"What kind of rumour?"

"I'll tell you all when we meet."

"I can see you tomorrow evening. I'll pick you up from Akeminster railway station, you can catch a train from Paddington. Let me know which train. I can arrange accommodation."

"That is very kind."

Suddenly his boring Sunday had taken on a new complexion. He pulled out papers from his portable filing system and flicked through them, making occasional notes to remind himself of the salient details regarding Samantha's story.

In the early afternoon he left his flat for his usual trip to the local pub. Today there was an added reason to go, as he wanted to arrange a room for the following night for Mr Gazetti. He must be discreet, as he'd become known locally because of his reporting on Samantha's death. Some folk remained hostile because of his criticism of Sir Alex Millard. He ordered his usual drink, then secured the room – for a friend on work experience.

At long last Monday came round, and David went into work early so as to knock off in time to meet Mr Gazetti. His train was due at 17.39. His in-tray was full as usual for a Monday, and when one of his colleagues arrived he mentioned that Richard had been in town over the weekend – apparently on his own.

"Has he gone back again?"

"I don't know."

"Where did he stay?"

"I didn't talk to him. The County Hotel, I guess. What's it to you?"

"Just curious. I wonder what he was doing here?"

"Probably came to see Lucy."

"Hmm."

At lunchtime David decided to try and find out if Richard *was* still in town, so he went to the County Hotel. As he was pulling up, he saw him leaving.

"Mr Nunn! Mr Nunn!" he shouted after him.

At first Richard ignored him, but David persisted.

"What do you want? I'm waiting for a cab."

"You're leaving?"

"What do you think?"

"I'm sorry to bother you about this again, but there's a reporter from Nairobi who wants to talk to me."

"Then talk to him! What's it got to do with me?"

"He said something about Mr Mwingi."

"I'm afraid I can't help you."

"Yes, but you never know. There might be something in it to your advantage."

"Like what?"

"Well – had you considered making a claim for wrongful dismissal against the company? Or I think they call it constructive dismissal."

"The Kenyan matter has no relevance to that. Now please excuse me."

David parked his car a little way from the station, and got there ten minutes after the train. There were few people about, so it didn't take long to identify his guest.

"Mr Gazetti, so sorry I'm late."

"I was wondering if you'd got my email."

"I got delayed at work. Please follow me." He led his guest to his car, hoping to avoid being seen. "I've booked you a room," he said. "I'm afraid it's only three-star, but you'll be very comfortable. Let's get you checked in, then we'll go for supper."

David had booked a table for two in a bistro in a village thirty-five miles away, where nobody knew him or his newspaper.

"The driving here is so disciplined, it's unbelievable," Gazetti marvelled, as they wound their way through the country lanes.

"How come you know Mr Mazuri?" David quizzed.

"Through you, in a funny sort of way. Mazuri got to know one of Mr Mwingi's secretaries because of your investigation, and her boyfriend got in touch with me. He told me all about the venture with Ashgrow – I think that's what they're called."

"Ashgrow Engineering Limited," David confirmed.

"Mazuri told me about your investigation and gave me your telephone number. It seems you took a very great risk." Gazetti had become quite talkative.

"I never managed to get any information out of Dogo," said David.

"And now no one knows where he is."

"Really?"

"Yes. His girlfriend Becky told me everything."

"Like what?" David's curiosity was well and truly aroused.

"Mr Mwingi thought Dogo was talking to you…"

"No – that didn't happen."

"Becky told me that Mr Mwingi became so suspicious that she believes he had him removed."

"But Dogo was his nephew!"

"Mr Mwingi believes in total control and is prepared to put fear into everyone working around him."

"What are you going to do about it? More importantly, how can you get anywhere against a man like that?"

"There's a rumour circulating that he's taken a huge bribe from Ashgrow."

"Bad luck. The person there responsible for the Kenyan project is no longer in charge, so the present management wouldn't have a clue."

"There'd be a record of transactions."

"Maybe, but they're not likely to give it to you," said David, thinking him a bit naïve.

"Mwingi let it be known that he's friendly with your Foreign Secretary."

"Has that got anything to do with the bribery allegation?"

David was puzzled by Gazetti's attitude. He began to think less well of him, and couldn't envisage that Lucy would agree to meet him, let alone help.

"So, how do you intend to pursue your investigation?" asked David, by the time they were sitting down to food.

"I want to talk to the Ashgrow management, to confirm the bribery allegation, and then talk to the minister."

David wanted to laugh, but managed not to out of courtesy. "I've wasted my money, my time and my reputation," he thought. Having to finance his trip made him even angrier. There was *nothing* to be gained.

"In Kenya, the people are fed up with bribery. There is an election next year and the President has established a force to root out corruption. It is said he intends to begin with a high-profile sacking or maybe even an arrest."

"I'm not interested in local politics. I'm interested in proving that Samantha was murdered – can you help me on that?"

"But how?"

"I want you to locate the white van that I believe was involved in Samantha's murder."

"According to Becky, it was an accident."

"She *would* say that, wouldn't she? Dogo wasn't going to admit he'd killed her."

"I'll see what I can do, but I do think the police did a thorough job, and concluded that it *was* an accident."

"They failed to interview some vital witnesses."

"They were villagers, not very reliable – they'd tell you what you wanted to hear."

"I'm still convinced Dogo murdered her."

It was after ten o'clock when they left the bistro. They arranged that David would pick Mr Gazetti up at 9.30 the following morning, and that they would go and see Bertram Purcell together.

"Not Miss Lucy?" Gazetti asked.

"Lucy won't help, trust me. If there's anyone who might possibly help us, it's him. Bear in mind this is not a level playing field – play it rough if you want a result."

"Thanks for the advice." Gazetti did not like David's patronising attitude.

Next morning they drove to Bertram's office.

"You introduce me to Mr Purcell and then you can leave," said Gazetti. "I'm okay to get the train."

"What's the matter with him?" David thought. There was no way he was going to miss out on the action.

"Don't worry, I've taken the rest of the morning off," he said.

"It's up to you, but I'd rather you weren't with me during the interview."

David was surprised at this but had no option but to agree that he would wait until the meeting was over. Bertram's secretary was reluctant to let them see him, but eventually she relented when Gazetti handed her a business card. After a few moments, Bertram came out and invited Gazetti to follow him. David remained in the waiting room, feeling rather snubbed.

Bertram opened the door to the meeting room.

"Are you working with the gentleman downstairs?" he asked, without offering Gazetti a seat.

"He simply gave me a lift."

"What can I do for you, Mr Gazetti?"

"I am investigating the conduct of a minister in our Kenyan government."

"Yes, and –?"

"He's been talking about a connection with your Sir Alex Millard."

"Have you approached the British government?"

"There's a rumour that our minister has taken a large bribe, and what I'm investigating is how much Millard knows about this."

"I can tell you quite categorically that he knows nothing. If that's all, good day."

"I've got a sworn affidavit, which states that Millard is known to the minister. Before we publish this, perhaps we ought to inform Millard himself." This wasn't true but Gazetti made the misleading statement to make sure the conversation continued.

"You could have rung him, surely?"

"Actually, sir, it's not so much Millard I'm concerned about. It's a company known as Ashgrow Engineering. Millard has connections with it, I believe."

"I can tell you Sir Alex Millard has no connection whatsoever with the company you mention."

After a short pause, Gazetti tried another tack: "Sir, I believe you represent both these parties."

"No. I'm chairman of the company. I'm giving you this information in my capacity as such."

"In that case I'll have to contact Millard or one of his people."

"Do you really need to do that?"

"I've no alternative. At least, I imagine he'll be more cooperative than you."

"If I can arrange a meeting with the MD of Ashgrow, will you leave Millard out of it?" He was worried now in case the story got out of hand and the blame for it was hung on him.

"I *could* run to that," Gazetti said. He knew that Mwingi had no real contact with Millard, but it was convenient to use his name.

"Obviously Mr Tolchard cannot attend the interview," Bertram added.

"I understand."

David was busy reading the newspapers when Gazetti came back downstairs.

"I think I'm all right here – you can leave now. I'll ring you later."

David was visibly annoyed. He had been used, and he

had no alternative but to accept the situation. "He's smarter than I thought," he said to himself.

Gazetti waited for Bertram, who had already contacted Lucy and given her an ultimatum: he was prepared to resign to protect Alex if she refused to come. Lucy duly obliged and made her way to Bertram's, where she was shown into the meeting room.

"Allow me to introduce Mr Gazetti, Lucy," Bertram said.

"I understand you have something to ask me," she said, getting straight to the point.

Lucy was completely different from how he'd imagined, and much younger.

"There are a few details I need to resolve. Perhaps you can help me sort them out."

"I'll do my best."

He took out his business card and a notepad. Lucy picked up the card to familiarise herself with the name.

"You know Mr Mwingi?" asked Gazetti.

"No, I don't know him."

"That's interesting. Are you sure?"

"I met him once, maybe twice, with my husband. I mean my *ex*-husband."

"Are you sure?"

"Come on," Bertram intervened. "She'd remember a thing like that."

"I have evidence to confirm that you used to keep in constant touch with him – there is a log of nearly twenty calls from the USA. Are you saying that isn't true?"

"Absolutely," she insisted. Bertram folded his arms.

"How much money did you offer him? Sorry, *give* him?"

"You're crazy!" Bertram was furious.

Gazetti raised his hand, calling for quiet.

"Why should I give him money? My husband was dealing with him – ask *him*."

"No, Miss Lucy. You gave him $500,000 and offered him more."

"I don't have to listen to this. Bertram, I'm leaving." Lucy was standing up to leave when Gazetti took out a tape and put it on the table.

"It's all here," he said.

"It's a lie. You're bluffing."

"Sit down, Lucy," Bertram ordered. "Why would she need to offer him money? She was not even involved in the project."

"To help her husband?" Gazetti speculated.

"She wouldn't have assisted him in any case," Bertram said.

"Mwingi has a reputation for taking bribes," said Gazetti, "and I want to know why you gave him so much money. Normally something like this would have gone virtually unnoticed, but he's upset so many people that the knives are out and the President is determined to make an example of him."

"Is it true?" Bertram asked. Lucy didn't reply. "My God, so it *is* true. Did Richard ask you to do it?"

Lucy shook her head. "I wanted the project stopped. Richard wouldn't listen."

"Why offer him money?"

"It was his payment for killing the project off."

"Did Richard find out?"

"No – I don't think so."

"Poor Richard."

"Don't feel sorry for *him*! If he'd listened to me, none of this would have happened."

"Do you think Samantha was murdered because she found out?" Bertram asked Gazetti.

"Samantha's death was an accident, I'm sure of it. Whether she knew about Mrs Nunn's dealings with Mwingi, I cannot say."

"Would you be prepared to make an official statement that you gave Mr Mwingi $500,000?"

"Not in writing."

Gazetti leaned back, a little more relaxed. Nothing more to be written, nothing more to be recorded. Lucy had made his life a lot easier.

"Will it cause problems for Ashgrow when Mwingi is exposed?" Bertram asked.

"What do you mean?" asked Lucy sharply.

Gazetti leaned forward. "Maybe, maybe not. If he goes without a fuss, there is no real problem. If he fights, Ashgrow's name will come out."

"In that case I would have to say that the amounts paid were consultancy fees," said Lucy.

Gazetti laughed heartily. "The whole thing would have remained under wraps if Mwingi had kept a low profile, but being a politician he wanted to climb higher. He was aiming for the post of Foreign Minister. He forgot there was a long way to fall."

There was a short silence.

"If Richard did find out, we need to make sure he also understood the nature of the payments, right?" Bertram said.

"He's so stupid I don't think he'd even spot a wall in front of him," said Lucy contemptuously.

Gazetti had no interest in their personal dispute and he asked Bertram to arrange transport back to his three-star.

"Have lunch with us?" Bertram invited.

Gazetti was feeling uncomfortable in Lucy's presence. "No thanks," he said. "I might be able to catch an earlier train."

Bertram arranged a cab for Gazetti, who left the meeting room and waited outside. Lucy was getting ready to leave as well, but Bertram insisted that she stay. She knew she was in for a ticking off.

"I wouldn't have thought you capable of this," he raged. "Poor Richard stood no chance at all. You owe him an apology."

"Not a chance. He needed to be stopped. If he'd done the right thing, we wouldn't have this mess."

"If Richard finds out, he'll have solid grounds for action against you."

"And *how* is he going to find out?"

Gazetti rang David to tell him he was returning on the five o'clock train. David begged him to stay another night, but he refused. Gazetti didn't trust him, and didn't care for his agenda. Nor did he wish to divulge information accidentally – David was too capable of manipulating it.

"Let me at least drive you to the station," David insisted.

"A taxi has been arranged, please don't waste your time."

"I need to talk to you. Will you meet me at the station at four o'clock?" David persisted.

Gazetti was in a fix, but felt obliged to David for looking after him and so he agreed.

This was David's last chance to prize out of him as much information as he could. He had a good excuse to leave work early, as the local football derby had been a disaster, so he left on the pretext of interviewing the respective managers. Graham had already left. There was no time to waste – each minute he was able to spend with Gazetti was valuable. He took a seat in the station bar and Gazetti appeared a few moments later. David ordered two orange juices.

"Tell me about your interview," he asked immediately.

"You know I can't."

"I won't disclose it to anyone – no one wants this story any more."

"The meeting was very successful, and that's all I'm telling you."

"Whom did you interview?"

"I'm not going to tell you."

"Don't tell me you talked to Alex?"

Gazetti did not respond.

"I can't believe Alex agreed to talk to you. He must be in some bother."

"Sir Alex Millard has no connection with the story, so there was no need to talk to him," Gazetti conceded.

"So you must have spoken to Lucy."

"I'm not going to tell you anything."

"Okay. Now that you've had your interview, do you still believe that Samantha's death was an accident?"

"Let me put it like this. I'm now convinced more than ever that Dogo had no motive to kill her. I think Samantha got frustrated and fed up, not being fully aware of how things are done in Nairobi. It's quite possible that something made her upset and angry and so drove that car too fast and crashed it. That is what I believe happened."

"How can you be so sure?"

"Dogo followed her because they were all so worried about her. As far as I'm concerned, that's the end of the matter."

THIRTY-ONE

The train was running late and arrived at Akeminster at 11.45. Richard had spent the weekend with his mum and dad in Fulham, but now set off at a leisurely stroll from the station. His hair was slightly dishevelled, and he hadn't bothered to do much about it. He wasn't meeting anyone, and his personal appearance wasn't high on his agenda.

He wore blue denim jeans and a light check shirt, and a jacket – a casual one – to keep off the chill. He was carrying books and other personal possessions in a backpack. There were no jobs outstanding at the factory requiring his attention – urgent or otherwise.

His cheeks were drawn. "You've lost weight," he recalled his mum telling him, as he was leaving the house for Paddington.

His taxi was the same one that had ferried him to the factory each Monday over the past few weeks, and he was getting to know the driver.

"Good morning, Mr Nunn."

"Hello."

"Train running late again, I see. How do they get away with it!"

Traffic was light and they made it to the factory in

fifteen minutes or so. Richard paid him the £10 he charged and took a few small steps to the front door, where Mr Hawkes was virtually blocking the entrance. Val looked out of her window on hearing the car door slam, but contrary to habits of only a few months ago was in no rush to meet him.

"Poor bloke, he looks so tired," she thought. She would have made him a cup of coffee but these days this had been one of his duties.

He passed the stock room and trudged to his temporary office, which had once been Samantha's. The door was open as he stepped inside and a man was working at the computer.

"Good morning, sir! My name is Ravi." Ravi was Indian – a computer programmer only just hired by Lucy.

"Morning," Richard greeted him, squeezing past the desk.

Ravi returned to his work, tapping away at the keyboard. Richard could see he was working on his and Samantha's unfinished project. He checked his post, and still feeling unsettled squeezed his way out again to make a cup of coffee.

"Excuse me, Ravi – need to get through."

"Pardon me, sir!"

"My name is Richard. Please call me Richard."

Ravi nodded and let Richard through. On his way to the kitchen he bumped into Stewart Hill, who more or less ignored him. Richard flicked the kettle on and waited for it to boil. Val caught sight of him and put her head round the door.

"Richard, how are you?"

"Not too bad."

"I'll do the coffee, if you like."

"No need – I'm almost done."

Lucy heard their conversation, and she also came into the kitchen.

"Richard, hi! I didn't hear your cab."

"I see, Lucy, I'm now having to share my office."

Val thought it politic to leave the two alone.

"I thought you'd need some assistance. I'll move him out if you want."

"Thanks – that would be appreciated."

"In the meantime could you please come to my office. There are things we need to discuss."

"I'll bring in some coffee."

"That would be marvellous."

When they got to Lucy's office, Hawkes was in there, ensconced.

"Richard, how are you? Keeping well, I hope…"

"Mr Hawkes is helping me with a little technical issue," Lucy informed him.

Richard pulled up a chair and sat down. Mr Hawkes put his head down and carried on with his calculations.

"Mr Hawkes, would you please excuse us," said Lucy.

"Absolutely," and he got up to leave.

"You can use Stewart's office."

"What a mess! I end up enlisting the person who failed before us."

"Perhaps he's the answer to your prayer. A good obedient yes man."

"I've got no choice."

"That's a matter of opinion."

"I don't need your advice. What I do want is for you to work towards rejoining the board."

"No! That will never happen. I'm only around for two reasons – firstly, to complete the development work started by Samantha."

"Well of course, you *would* do anything for *her*…"

"That's no way to talk about the dead."

"Well, let's not go into that one. This whole world of work is littered with your old flames."

"If you *want* me to leave…"

"Well of course not."

"Good. Because the only other reason I'm hanging around is the Kenyan project. As soon as I've got it I'm out of here."

"I'm not interested in the Kenyan project."

"Don't I know it!"

"The Kenya thing's caused us nothing but hassle."

"Is that the only thing that's caused us hassle?"

"I don't know what you mean. You just finish what you're doing here and take that nasty project with you."

"I will. The prototype's almost ready."

Richard got up and turned his back on Lucy and made for the door, which unusually he didn't slam behind him. He went to the factory, seeking a progress report, but Hill and Hawkes were in conference and treated him dismissively.

"All I want is your report on the *carrier* performance."

"Please, Richard, this isn't a good time."

He stepped aside and left them, a naughty pupil ejected from the class. He returned to his office and mulled over Samantha's original computer design from the Gothenberg era, from which the prototype had been built. It was the test report from this that he awaited.

He had to admit to himself he was proud of his clever

idea to manufacture the carrier for military purposes. Its lightness of structure and its frictionless technology were the selling points, in a vehicle he codenamed "Hardcore" (for use in difficult terrain such as deserts). Samantha had disagreed with it strongly on account of cost and reliability.

"The major wars of the future," he argued, "are going to be fought in the world's most arid environments. This unit if developed successfully will be wanted by *all* armies."

The bodywork was identical for all three different types of equipment under development. Samantha had no similar doubts as to the success of "The donkey", which was proposed for use in transportation in urban areas. "The puller" was another one, which would be attached to a Jeep. After her death Richard took personal responsibility in finishing her work. He had gathered a little technical know-how from her, and was reluctant to acknowledge shortcomings such as Ravi might point out.

Later, he was studying Samantha's notes on the working of the lifting gear when Lucy invited him to lunch with her and Hawkes.

"Too busy," he said, almost sneeringly.

When she and Hawkes had gone, it was an ideal opportunity to get in touch with his friends in Kenya. He dialled Musa on his private line.

"Musa, it's me, Richard. How are you and Mr Mwingi?"

"Extremely busy right now. What do you want?"

"It's about our agreement. I'm ready to take charge of things in Kenya in a couple of months."

"We'll have to talk about it later."

"Is Mr Mwingi about?"

Musa put him on hold, then informed *he* was busy too. "In future we'll ring you."

After lunch he went to see Lucy, insisting that Hawkes shouldn't be present.

"Why is Stewart Hill ignoring me?" he asked. "I may have been relieved of my directorship, but that doesn't mean he no longer has to cooperate."

"I'll have a word with him."

"You've got him well trained. But I'd have thought it's in his interests that he *does* cooperate. Once I've finished the job I'm out of it."

"What makes you think the people in Kenya still want to work with you?"

"I've got a deal with them."

"Yes, but you know they can't be trusted."

"I'll take my chances."

"Don't say you haven't been warned. But anyway – about outstanding projects here. When do you think we can knock them on the head?"

"Now you're talking!"

From that moment on Richard *seemed* to have all the support he needed, from *all* personnel, and in particular Stewart Hill. Nevertheless, Stewart had no faith in Richard's technical ability. As far as he was concerned, there was no one quite like Sam (who tended to stroke his ego). Furthermore Ravi lacked the authority ever to confront Richard.

That afternoon Richard went over the report of the new computer codes Ravi had assembled.

"The end product was incoherent, sir! What you had in mind cannot be translated into computer terms," Ravi protested. Richard overruled him and persisted.

Stewart joined them. "Richard, how can I and my team help?"

Richard, faintly smiling, showed him Ravi's work. "What do you make of it?" he asked.

"Ravi's already discussed this with us. The units are unworkable. If you persist with this, I'm sorry to say we will all be wasting valuable time."

"Why? What's the problem?"

Ravi glanced up and gauged Stewart's look, the message being that Richard had no engineering background, and couldn't design anything of even the slightest sophistication.

Richard then looked to Ravi: "Why don't the two of you help me to resolve the technical issue?"

"Ravi, come to my office," suggested Stewart, "and we'll assemble the workable computer codes." The two of them left.

Richard, still confident that with sufficient technical support his plan would succeed, felt he might be getting there at last.

As soon as the door shut he picked up the phone and dialled Nairobi.

"Is that Miss Kyombe?" he asked.

"I'm sorry, sir," was the obstructive reply.

"What about Dogo – is *he* around?"

"*Who?*"

"Dogo – who works with Musa and Mr Mwingi."

"Sorry, but I do not know about him. I've just started. I haven't come across *that* name."

"If you ask Miss Kyombe she'll tell you about him. My name is Richard Nunn. Can you please put me in touch with Musa or Mr Mwingi?"

"Miss Kyombe's in hospital. She's had a bad road accident. I don't know when she's due to return. Hang on and I'll try to find Musa."

After a few seconds Musa was connected. "What's your problem this time? Didn't I tell you we're extremely busy! Please don't ring again."

"If I don't keep in touch how am I going to find out what's going on?"

"Nothing is going on." Musa slammed down the phone, and when Richard tried again on his direct line the same girl answered, but this time did not put him through to Musa. Chillingly, he recalled Lucy's advice.

He got up and stood at the window looking out over the slightly depressing landscape, a dull mizzle sweeping the trees, with dark ponderous clouds suspended overhead. He bit his fingernails and felt, suddenly, desperate.

"What's going on?" he wondered.

He sat down and gently picked up the receiver once more.

"Can I speak to Edward Turner?"

Turner was a buying director for Defence Contractor Limited, a firm based in Hounslow.

"Hello, Edward. We've finished the design work on the *carriers*, and before we go into development I want to discuss the blueprint."

"You know our specification. I don't see the point in going over all that again."

Richard argued that he didn't wish to over-shoot the budget, and the short session he had in mind would identify both the equipment's weaknesses and potential – which was in everyone's interests. Reluctantly Edward agreed to meet up with him on Wednesday the following week.

The rest of his day was more or less routine, until at six his taxi took him to the hotel. He had a quick shower and visited the bar. He hardly knew anyone here, but he didn't care to spend any more time with Lucy than necessary. Neither was his relationship with Val what it had been before. He sat alone with a glass of beer when surprisingly Lucy showed up.

"Is that what you get up to these days?"

"That's my affair."

"You've been drinking a lot lately. And when was the last time you had a proper meal? Come on, I'll take you home."

Richard looked at her quizzically, then drained his glass. He half got up, and for a moment detected warmth in her eyes.

"No! It's just another deception. Please leave me alone. All I want from you is my project. I'll pay whatever it costs and walk away."

"Not a good move, Richard. Why not see it my way? There's still a chance, you know, that we can run this firm as a team. You could start another project – even in Kenya. If it's viable, I'll support it."

"Why do I need another one? I've got one already. I'm sorry, Lucy. You might mean well, but I can't forget what's happened." He sat back down.

Lucy, looking slightly disappointed, picked up her bag and left. In no mood to be alone, she rang Val to ask her if she wanted to eat out, but couldn't get in touch. She ate solo that night and slept fitfully.

The next day Richard arrived in early. Ravi handed him his blueprint for the codes.

"I worked all night after the technical briefing with Stewart."

Richard unfolded the print-run, where Ravi had highlighted variations from the original design and report.

"You have only partially incorporated my original idea," Richard said. "And look – you've reduced the function of the lifting gear."

"No, sir! The lifting gear has gone completely. This was making the unit too heavy, affecting its manoeuvrability."

"Well to me it's not much different from what we're making now. After all mine and Samantha's hard work, we're virtually back where we were."

"Sir! I'm happy this version's an improvement, and according to Stewart we can attach the heavy-duty plastic hydraulic arms to some of the units later on – once we've improved it."

"Leave it with me. I'll talk to you both later." He thought to chase up Lucy, but she wasn't in – no light in her office, blinds still drawn. "Strange," he thought. He dialled the cottage number, but there was no reply. He then contacted Val to find out if she had appointments, who said she hadn't. He decided to visit the cottage.

There the Discovery was still in the driveway, but there was no sign of anyone at home. He knocked on the door and rang the bell repeatedly. He lifted the flap over the letterbox, and saw the morning mail still on the doormat. He shouted, but there was no response. Anxious, he took out his key and opened up. It was unlocked from inside. "Careless," he sighed.

Lucy was in bed, with an arm hanging out. He nudged her, and she twitched.

"Who is it?" An empty bottle of whisky fell to the floor.

"Gosh! Have you drunk all this!"

Lucy wrenched open her eyes, which were still a blazing red.

"Look at the state of you!"

"How did *you* get in?"

"I was worried. When you didn't open up I used my key."

"'A' for initiative." She made a grab for his hand.

"Look, I'll make you some coffee."

"Don't go."

"Lucy!" Richard was forceful, and instantly she let go of his hand.

After her coffee and a hasty shower Richard bundled her into the car, and drove. It was well past midday.

"Let's go for a late breakfast," she suggested.

He told her he was off to London to meet Edward Turner, and was taking a week off. As it turned out Richard cancelled the meeting with Turner and flew out on the Tuesday to Nairobi. No one knew.

His flight landed in the early morning, circling over the National Park – a sight he'd missed with Lucy.

The airport, elegant from above, was tatty on the ground. The queue for immigration and customs clearance bore no relation to the actual number of travellers. There were very few aircraft that had landed at that time.

The officer surveyed him thoroughly and examined his ticket carefully before stamping his passport for him to proceed.

He hired a taxi to take him to his hotel. He told the

driver this was his second visit within the past few weeks, as a message he was familiar with Nairobi in case he had other ideas. Just ahead was the misty outline of the Ngong Hills.

"Bwana, just over a mile away the lion is roaming like a king in the National Park."

Yet in a very short space of time they were passing through the industrial area. The change of scene was stark.

"Last time I came I went on safari," Richard told the driver.

The taxi caught itself up in the morning rush hour, getting frequently overtaken on both sides. Everyone hooted at everyone else. Almost colliding with another taxi at a junction ahead, his driver braked hard.

"Sorry, bwana."

They made their way through the National Sports Stadium, which was close to the main intersection of the Mombasa-Nairobi highway. Other landmarks en route were the golf club he'd partied at, and the parliament buildings, which the driver seemed excited about.

"What's your name?" Richard asked.

"Toto Samburu," he replied proudly. "I am the youngest son and since I am from the Northern Kenyan tribe my parents gave me this name."

"It suits you," Richard commented.

The taxi followed the sign to the city centre, now on a surprisingly good road. In all the busy street life, a pedestrian unexpectedly crossed right in front of them. Toto slammed on the brakes, and the pedestrian, in dodging to avoid being hit, lost his shoes, which the taxi ran over. Toto gesticulated mercilessly, at a crossing point just a few feet away. "Stupid," he said.

They turned into University Way and shortly arrived at the gate of the Norfolk Hotel. Richard handed him 300 shillings and took down his cell phone number. He checked in to a room, and there slept, trying to shrug off his jetlag.

He woke up at about three p.m. and decided to make contact with Musa. Once again his approach was rebuffed. Later that afternoon he dialled the switchboard number. A woman answered in a small, soft, African accent.

"Can I talk to Kitty Kyombe, please..." There was silence. "Hello, are you there? I want to speak to Kitty."

"What's your name?"

"Mr Nunn, I know her from London. Is she in today?"

"Didn't you know she's in hospital?"

"Hospital? Oh yes. I remember. Which hospital?"

"Nairobi."

"Thank you very much. Appreciated."

He left his hotel room and went for a walk into the city centre, not very far. He needed to buy some vital drugs. It was a pleasant day, and there were plenty of people about. A large number of the men were in short-sleeved shirts and khaki shorts, shopping for goods shipped over as good second-hands from the West. Some of their womenfolk were in traditional African attire, frocks in bright colours, though generally the young women wore modern clothes with high-heeled shoes. There was an hour or so to go before the shops closed, but there was a lot of street trade, with hand-woven baskets and African woodcarvings for sale. The tourists flocked.

He found a drugstore run by a Mr Patel and bought all his medical needs. He strolled around for more than an hour, and when the crowds began to thin he went back to his hotel. He ordered a meal and retired early, still feeling the effects of jetlag.

He no longer had oodles of money to spend, so he was forced to budget for his outgoings. Lucy had put him on a fixed salary with no expenses, so before he went to sleep he contacted Toto to hire his cab for the whole day. He haggled over the rate. It felt demeaning, but nowadays he had no choice.

He slept for twelve hours and got ready at 8.30, and on coming down found Toto already waiting for him. He talked briefly with the duty manager, and was relieved to find out that Toto had been given strict instructions to look after him.

They drove to Nairobi Hospital, which was in the private sector, boasting up-to-date equipment and techniques. Toto came with him, in case he needed a translator. More or less immediately he did.

"This gentleman has come over from London, to meet his friend Miss Kyombe."

The duty nurse went over her list, disappeared into her office, then returned after some minutes with the news that Miss Kyombe had been discharged.

"Do you know her home address?"

"We don't breach patient confidentiality."

"But the gentleman is here for only two days – you must help him."

"I'm sorry, I can't."

"Please call your senior."

"*Nobody* can help."

"Nevertheless, please call your senior." Toto raised his voice.

The senior nurse came out when she heard the

argument and Toto began his story again, rather heatedly. Richard felt uncomfortable and moved away from the reception area to the other end of the room. Toto came over after a while. "I have her mother's address. She's staying with her parents."

"How on earth did you manage that?"

"She is of the same tribe as me and when I told her that I'm your guide she gave me the details."

"Did she tell you what was wrong with her?"

"Car accident. Very bad."

"I hope she doesn't mind a visit."

Toto drove them out onto Highway A2. "We're going to Thika. It's a little town to the north of the city."

He was no different on the highway from the other drivers, swapping lanes and overtaking just anyhow – no discipline, constant hooting. In one instance his car skimmed a passer-by, too close for comfort. It took him about an hour to make the forty-kilometre drive. He parked up by the market.

"Over there, in that building, on the second floor. That's where she's staying."

"Aren't you coming with me? I'll pay for your waiting time."

Toto smiled, and led him to an alley by the building. The staircase to flat number 12 was located behind it. A middle-aged woman opened the door.

"Good afternoon. You are?"

"This gentleman is from London, wanting to see Miss Kyombe."

"Who gave you this address?"

"Why? Can't we see her?"

"She had a very nasty accident. She's lucky to be alive.

But she doesn't recognise people – even her boss, His Excellency Mr Mwingi."

"Is she working for *him*?" Toto asked, looking at Richard.

"Yes, but nobody from the office has bothered to visit her."

"This gentleman is looking for someone your daughter might know."

"She doesn't recognise anyone. Please don't disturb her."

"Just let me look at her. If it's too much, I won't bother her," Richard pleaded.

"My beautiful girl," she moaned, and very gently lowered the door handle. The door opened. The mother held it and let Richard and Toto in. Kitty was sitting in a wheelchair, staring blankly into space.

"My god! She used to be so feisty. I'm *so* sorry."

Richard moved to the wheelchair, where he rested his hands tenderly on hers.

"Just who is it you're looking for?"

"One of her colleagues."

"Why not ring the office?"

"No one is helping me. I'm deeply sorry to have bothered you. My problems are nothing compared to this. Why oh why!"

The old lady wiped the tears from her eyes.

"Hello, Kitty." Richard began stroking her hands, and when she stiffened he immediately stopped. Tears began to form in her eyes, but her face remained immobile.

"Please Kitty, don't cry. I'm looking for Dogo."

She began to sob, and Richard gently stroked her arm.

"Please leave now. Can't you see she's distressed…"

"This gentleman has travelled very far. What can he do if no one will help?"

The old lady petted Kitty's shoulder, but took out a card and gave it to Richard. "He knows quite a lot about what is going on."

Richard read the card and passed it to Toto. "Thank you. Do you mind if I call again?"

"We'll see."

They drove to a restaurant for a lunch.

"You know about this Saeed Juma?" Richard asked. That was the name on the card.

"Nothing at all."

"Let's visit his address."

Toto looked puzzled. "I don't think you know about Nairobi at all."

"I do, I promise. You'll just have to trust me."

"This address – it doesn't officially exist."

"Why doesn't it?"

"Kibera!" Toto whispered. "It's one of the biggest shanty towns in Africa. Police won't give you protection. I mean, you do want to leave here alive?"

Richard laughed.

"Then forget it. I won't take you there."

"I shall just have to make my own arrangements then."

"In that case please settle your bill now."

Richard realised that Toto was serious. "Look, I want to find Dogo. I'm sure with his help I can get my venture started. He's is the only businessman I know."

"Give me 5,000 shillings and I'll see if I can arrange security."

"Okay," said Richard, "go ahead."

"I'll ring you tomorrow."

Richard went for a stroll to kill some time. He wanted to get in touch with Jane Marsh, but he felt awkward, because of his affair with Samantha. Pondering this, he visited a bazaar near his hotel, mooching round its various stalls without making a purchase. He wasn't keen on the woodcraft, and so visited the library – that rather pointlessly too.

"I'm getting nowhere and wasting my time," he thought.

He returned to his hotel, where a message from Toto was to the effect to be ready at nine the following morning.

That evening he found out as much as he could about Kibera. It was the home of tens of thousands of AIDS orphans. It had no electricity and not a single flush toilet. Prostitution and drug-dealing were endemic. Laws and common morality didn't apply here.

Toto arrived in his Peugeot. He'd brought with him two very tall, meaty men, wearing black trousers and white tee shirts, whose design was the sign of the cobra. Richard sat at the front.

"Good morning, gentlemen."

"Sir, these are our bodyguards."

There was no acknowledgement from the two men sitting in the back. One had his arm draped over the seat and the other a hand dangling from the window. They were unshaven.

Kibera was on the south side of Nairobi, and was a sea of rusty tin roofs. Toto parked up some distance away, and all four got out and walked. The passageways were narrow and muddy, with potholes full of unsanitary water.

"The rain last night," Toto reminded Richard.

The average home here was no bigger than about ten

feet by ten, housing families of almost a dozen. There were plenty of stray dogs on the loose, and the children went about naked.

They stopped outside the house they were after. A man stepped forward when one of the bodyguards knocked.

"Yes?"

"We're looking for Saeed Juma."

"Who are *you*?"

"This gentleman knows Miss Kyombe."

They were in luck. "Come inside."

Richard and Toto went in. There were no amenities and the floor was covered with a torn rug. He asked Richard to sit down on a stool made from a cooking-oil can.

"I'm looking for Dogo, who was working with Kyombe."

"I expect you know that something happened at work, and Kitty had an accident. I know a few of her work colleagues, but that name I cannot recall." The man had good command of English and spoke with confidence.

"Do you live here?" asked Toto.

"Let's say this is temporary while the dust settles."

"Any idea how can I locate Dogo?"

"Her boss has started a factory about five miles from here. You might try there. I'll write it down, but remember – I didn't give it to you."

"Absolutely."

"Good, this is a safe place for me, so now please leave."

Toto took down the address and they left. Toto relieved the two bodyguards, and they drove to the factory unit – two floors on an industrial estate. Unlike other units of its kind it was neatly painted and had a well-made road running past its doors. A signpost displayed the name: Kenya Tool and Equipment Company Limited.

"Do you want to go inside?" asked Toto.

Richard signalled yes.

"You stay here. If I need you, I'll call."

Richard pressed the bell and was led inside by a well-dressed man who asked him the purpose of his visit.

"I am visiting from the UK. I export tools and machinery, and I thought I'd see if I could interest you."

"Have a seat here. I'll call the general manager."

Richard picked up some leaflets and was shocked to learn they were all from his company, with no attempt to change or erase the name of Ashgrow.

"Bwana, someone will be with you in a minute."

A few moments later a white gentleman entered the waiting room – Mr Bearish.

"Wow! How on earth did you get here?" Richard quizzed.

"Didn't you know? Lucy sent me over to help them install the machinery."

"When?"

"Three weeks ago."

"It's *our* machinery in the factory."

"*Their* machinery. We've nothing more to do with it – we sold it to them."

"Is someone called Dogo working here?"

Bearish thought for a while and replied no.

"*I'm* supposed to be the owner of this. It just doesn't make sense. Who's your boss here?"

"You know him. He came over to Akeminster. His name's Musa."

"Musa! Great, I want to talk to him."

"Come to my office."

Bearish dialled Musa at his ministry office.

"Musa, I have a surprise for you. Please talk to Richard Nunn."

Musa protested, but Bearish passed the receiver to Richard.

"You owe me an explanation," Richard demanded.

"You stay there. I'll be there in a minute. Put Bearish back on."

Bearish felt uncomfortable as the phone conversation went on and on. He told Richard, "You'd better not leave these premises. Please don't ask any questions."

"My taxi's waiting outside."

"Settle the fare. Please trust me – don't venture out now that they know you're here."

Richard looked worried and took Bearish with him to settle with Toto. Then they went inside. When Musa arrived, Bearish left the two alone.

"Why the hell are you here?" Musa demanded.

"This is *my* factory. I've come to take charge."

"It isn't your factory – not now."

"Lucy had no right to sell it."

"She didn't sell it. We set it up ourselves, and we're paying for Mr Bearish's services."

"The machinery's mine."

"No – we've paid for that too."

"But *Samantha* came to start it up. Ask Mr Mwingi. And where is Dogo? He was looking after her."

"Mwingi's about to resign as minister, to become Vice Chairman of the party. And anyway, don't tell me you're stuck on that Samantha story!"

"No! I simply want my factory back."

"Mr Nunn, you are not supposed to be in Kenya. If they find out you'll be in trouble. Let me drop you at the airport – please just forget about this."

"You can't steal my property. There are laws." Richard tried to stand up.

"Sit down at once, I'm ordering you. Just you listen to me."

"I'm not afraid of you."

"Shut up and listen. I warned Samantha to leave. I told her you wouldn't succeed."

"Why? We did everything by the book."

"Someone *didn't want* you to succeed."

"I know – it was that bastard Mwingi. I knew it. Have *you* seen Miss Kyombe? Do *you* know what he's done to her?"

"It wasn't him," Musa shouted.

"Who then? Some mysterious man? Don't give me that, when Mwingi's so powerful?" He dismissed his comment.

Musa looked away. Richard stood up immediately, and Musa followed him, grabbing him by the shoulders.

"It was your wife, Lucy. It was she who gave him money. She did it to stop your project going ahead. Is that clear now?"

"I don't believe it!" said Richard, and, returning to his chair, slumped into it.

"It's true."

"Did Samantha find out?"

"No – and she wasn't murdered."

"But Dogo."

"He had nothing to do with her accident, though the reporter from the *Gazette* wrongly assumed so."

"And where is he now?"

"No one knows – not even his mother. Mwingi does, but he's not saying."

"Why?"

"Let's say a family affair. Now please get ready to leave. Does your wife know you're here?"

"No."

"I thought not – otherwise she'd have tipped us off, and you'd never have made it this far. Now, let me drive you to the airport."

Richard wiped his forehead, a man plunged in the nastiest nightmare, but, after collecting his luggage, Musa drove him as he'd said. He boarded an evening flight for Heathrow.

As he left for the departure lounge he handed Musa £1,000. "Please do me a favour. Give this money to Miss Kyombe, and please look after her."

"I promise you I will."

Back in London he phoned his old stockbroker cronies a second time, insisting that this time he really did need a job.

"I can start next week," he said.

"Come over. We'll sort you out a package."

In the afternoon he slept, and was told by his mother that Lucy was looking for him, as nobody knew where he was.

"Mother, I want you to know that it's all over between me and Lucy."

He'd got a new girlfriend now, or rather reverted to his ex-girlfriend. Amanda (the one he'd had before meeting Lucy) had been showing an interest in rekindling her love with Richard over the past few weeks, having discovered what was going on in Richard's life. He had resisted in his confusion and despair, still trying to piece together all that had happened. They had been spending time in London and he found her a calm and loyal friend to turn to. On finding out the truth now he had no reason to look back and decided without hesitation to see how it went with Amanda. She was an expert in employment related matters, and she reiterated the point that he'd a very good case for constructive dismissal.

The following morning he drove to Akeminster in Amanda's convertible, a BMW. Lucy and Val were there to greet him.

"Where on earth have you been? We were worried about you." Lucy embraced him.

"I took a few days off. Sorry."

"Well, never mind."

Val left them to it.

"I've failed you, Lucy, yet you're still so very sanguine."

"It's because I want a new beginning, for the two of us. I'm taking my old job, and I want *you* to have charge of the company – and I really do mean that."

"Strange. I've also taken my old job."

"Oh, really?"

"Really."

"But I'm giving you everything you wanted."

"For you to play your dirty tricks again? Do I *look* stupid!"

"I don't know what you mean."

"You're a liar – even now! I've just got back from Nairobi. You know who I met? Bearish. How much you must have hated me…"

"I was jealous. I didn't want to lose you."

"That's pathetic."

"I'm truly sorry. Please, Richard. I don't know how to love." She began sobbing uncontrollably.

"Do you realise what I could sue you for? Millions."

"I can give you millions, if that's what you want. Please stay. Please teach me how to love." Lucy was breaking down.

Val heard what was going on and came in, finding her boss in a state of collapse with her makeup in a mess.

"My god!"

"I'm leaving for good. Would you please ask Bertram to come to the office at once."

Val rang there and then, and when Bertram arrived – exceedingly prompt – he was looking highly perplexed.

"What is it now?" he asked.

"Lucy will tell you everything. While you're at it, please initiate divorce proceedings. It's all over."

"Bertram, please tell him I'm sorry. Don't let him leave me alone."

Richard stood up. "I'll be at the cottage collecting my things. You can send someone with me if you wish."

"Surely we can salvage the situation," Bertram pleaded.

"Not a chance," said Richard. He stepped out, and with a new spring in his stride walked out into the late-afternoon sun. There in that instant Akeminster fell from his life for good.